Redemption Rising
Part Three in The Unfading Lands Series

Katharine E. Hamilton

ISBN-10: 0692700242
ISBN-13: 978-0-692-70024-2

Redemption Rising
Part Three in The Unfading Lands Series

www.katharinehamilton.com

Cover Design by Kerry Prater.

DEDICATION

Dedicated to Daddy, Momma, Jared, and Kerry.
So thankful God placed me in our family.
Love you.

ACKNOWLEDGMENTS

I have loved every second writing this series, and I want to thank everyone reading this book for following along with me on this journey. Your interest in the story has meant the world to me, and given me hours of fun as I sat and wrote line after line. Thank you.

My husband, Brad. I love you. Thank you for putting up with the piles of laundry and dirty dishes while I finished writing this book.

Everett, for crying and wanting to be held when I needed a break from the computer, for listening as I read scene after scene to you. You smiled despite the rough draft. Thanks kiddo.

Momma, Daddy, Jared, and Kerry. I love being a part of our family. I love you guys.

My Beta Readers: Megan Wellborn, Annetta Hamilton, Kerry Prater, Megan Kruckemeyer, and Erin Davis. Thank you for taking the time to read my manuscript. You guys give me so much feedback it is awesome.

My editor, Lauren Hanson. Past, passed, whom, who… that is the reason I need a great editor. Ha!

Kerry Prater. For my incredible cover design and website designs she creates for me, usually with little notice.

My puppies: Tulip and Cash: They play the part of enraptured audience well. It really boosts the ego.

My friends and fellow authors in the Indie Author Support and Discussion Group. You guys have helped strengthen my confidence and my skills as a writer, and I love being part of such a wonderful group of people.

Redemption Rising

Part Three in The Unfading Lands Series

Katharine E. Hamilton

PROLOGUE

Many years ago...

His breathing stopped. The trapped breath aching to be released in a loud exhale caused his lungs to ache and his pulse to quicken. He listened. The sound of boots against the floor echoed down the halls of his father's castle and had him hiding in fear. His father warned him of this day. The threat of King Abner moving upon his father's kingdom had lurked beyond the castle gates for weeks. Villages burned and plundered, his father's people killed or subdued, and his family's lives at risk. Lancer listened intently as silence took hold. He creaked the heavy wooden door open and peered down the long hallway. No guards rushed by and he quickly slipped out and sprinted down the hall towards his father's chambers.

He burst through the heavy-laden doors to find his father gazing out the open arched window at the ruin and destruction headed their direction.

"Father! They march upon the city markets!" His voice hitched as his father turned with sad eyes and a defeated expression.

"Lancer, come inside my son and shut the doors."

His father's voice was quiet, hollow, and full of remorse. He gestured towards the window and Lancer swallowed the distance in quick strides. His father's hand rested upon his shoulder as they both turned to look out over their kingdom.

"We cannot defeat Abner."

Lancer turned to his father in shock. "W-what do you mean? We have to. He has yet to breach the castle gates. There is still time."
His father turned to him and cupped his son's face in his large hands. "There is no more time. The gates will be breached. You must go. I

have prepared for your passage, but you must be quick. You must escape."

"I don't understand." Lancer's eyes clouded as he saw the grief in his father's gaze.

"You must go. Abner has but one goal: to annihilate us all. He wishes to overtake our kingdom and lands. I stand in his way. You, my heir, stand in the way. If you escape now, there is a chance you may one day take our lands back from him. But only if you survive. You must go."

"I cannot leave you here to die." Lancer grabbed his father's elbow and began pulling him towards the doorway, but his father jerked from his touch.

"No, son. I must stay. You must go."

"But where? Where will I run?"

"Anywhere but here."

Lancer shook his head in disbelief and ran a hand through his dark hair as he tampered down the despair in his heart. "You must come with me." His voice was low. Sad. But his father remained firm and shook his head.

"My place is here. Your place is outside this kingdom until it is your time and turn to take it back. Abner will not be strong forever; for evil acts soon corrupt to the point of destruction. You must remain strong. Cultivate kindness. Be aware of others. Everyone you come into contact with leaves a mark upon your character whether you wish it so or not. Be wise in your friendships. Pave a new destiny for yourself. But you must leave now." His father pulled him into a tight embrace and removed his signet ring and placed it in Lancer's hand. The warmth from the gold heated his palm as he took one last look into his father's kind face and ran.

It had taken him days to reach the fringes of The Realm of King Granton. To remain off the common paths had caused delay in his travels and he sighed in relief at the sight of the Eastern Kingdom's castle on the tip of the horizon. His sister. He knew she would take him in until tensions in their home kingdom subsided. She would protect him. After all, it was his idea for her to marry so young and leave the Valleylands. If he had not suggested it, she would be riding along side him or worse, preparing for death at Abner's hand. It seemed fortuitous that King Eamon of the Eastern Kingdom had been searching for a bride at the time. And if Erica had not been so lovely, he doubted the marriage would have taken place so swiftly. But as it were, his sister and the young king had meshed rather nicely and their relationship blossomed swiftly. She owed him for seeking out a suitor. She owed him.

He made his way through the market streets and up the stairs to the front of the castle. Two guards flanked the doorway and he straightened his regal purple tunic and attempted to appear at ease. He knew his appearance was road worn, but he mustered what little dignity he had left and addressed the two men. "I am Lancer, Prince of the Valleylands, brother of Queen Erica. I wish to see my sister."

The guards looked at one another and nodded, one disappearing into the castle.

The doors creaked open and there before him stood his sister alongside King Eamon, both wearing expressions of surprise at his abrupt visit.

"Sister." He greeted.

Erica's dark brows rose slightly as she surveyed his appearance. "Brother." Her voice held caution, and her hand draped around her husband's waist tensed. "To what do we owe the surprise?"

Lancer glanced over his shoulder towards the direction he had come and shook his head. "May we discuss the matter inside?"

"No." She stated quietly, suspicion evident on her face.

Lancer's temper flared but he inhaled deeply to maintain his self-control. "Please, Erica. It is important. Our father is dead."

Her brows rose once more and he saw the briefest flash of sadness in her eyes before they steeled to the sharp icy blue she inherited from their father.

"Abner has overthrown our kingdom. Father is dead. I have escaped. I need a place to hide for a bit until the current hostile circumstances die down."

"And you come here seeking refuge?" She asked with a slight edge to her voice.

"Yes. It is the only place I could think of at the time. I presumed since I helped you find your happiness you could help protect me in return so that one day I might find my own."

"No."

Lancer's chest tightened and his gaze flashed towards Eamon who seemed equally surprised at his wife's refusal.

"No?" Lancer asked.

She nodded. "You are not welcome here, Lancer. Take your troubles elsewhere." She began to turn away but Lancer reached out and grabbed her elbow. His eyes flashed with anger and Eamon quickly came to his wife's defense and withdrew Lancer's hold.

"You sentence me to death if you do not help me." His voice was low, almost a growl as he pierced his sister with the sharpest of gazes.

"You have sentenced yourself to death. Perhaps if you had been kind to me in the past I might be of more service. But you were cruel. You have always been cruel. And though I find happiness here as a result of your cruelty, I do not owe you anything." Erica looked to Eamon for support and he nodded.

"How dare you." Lancer hissed. "I was never cruel to you."

"That is not how I remember it, brother. Or do you not remember trying to sell me to the highest bidder so that I may not stand in the way of father's affections or your right to rule?"

Lancer stepped forward and stopped quickly as a small boy ran up to his sister and hugged her around her skirts. She gently placed her hand on his head and smiled down at him. The boy, hair dark like his mother's and eyes to match looked at him with curiosity, intrigue, and wonder. The sharp blue gaze in a soft face softened Lancer's resolve.

"I will leave you then. But I will remember this." He warned.

"And you," he pointed at Eamon, "I will remember your silence on the matter as well."

Eamon straightened his shoulders. "Threats will do you no favors, Lancer. Be gone. And take your troubles with you. We do not wish for Abner to set his eyes on our kingdom because of your presence. Please leave."

The two royals turned to walk away and the young boy remained. Staring. The look of childish marvel constricted Lancer's chest as the doors began to close and the blue eyes disappeared behind them.

Twenty-eight years later...

Chapter 1

"My Lord?" Prince Edward waved a hand in front of Lancer's face but the dark scowl remained and the distant shadow of memories in his eyes slowly cleared. He shook his head to clear the images of the small boy, but the eyes before him remained the same. Only now they resided in a man. His nephew. Prince Ryle still had his sister's eyes, only now they held contempt, anger, and tinges of fear as he surveyed Lancer from the chair he claimed, his bound hands tied behind him. The effects of recent torture slowly fading from his body as the Unfading Lands power healed his body.

"Again." Lancer ordered Edward.

"But my Lord, we have completed three rounds of torture already. Perhaps we should take a rest to compose ourselves and create a plan." Edward cast a pointed gaze towards Ryle in apology as Lancer turned away from them.

"I said again." His voice firmer and his shoulders straight. "I expect to hear screams from my chambers, Edward. Do not disappoint me." With that, he lightly tugged his tunic to straighten his resolve as he stormed out of his reflection chamber and made his way down the hall.

"I will allow you to catch your breath." Edward stated as he sighed in defeat and removed the gag from Ryle's mouth.

Ryle sat, chest heaving as his wounds slowly continued to heal. "Why wait?" He growled. "Lancer has made his demands."

Edward watched as a deep gash on the former prince's arm slowly closed and all that remained was the frayed fabric of his emerald tunic. "I am sorry, Ryle, for what you have had to endure."

Ryle tilted his head as he studied Edward. "You stood there and accepted the darkness. What is it? Where does it come from?"

Edward shrugged. "I do not know."

"You have to have some clue." Ryle challenged. "Why would you allow such an evil to seep into your veins without knowing its origins?"

"I confessed to you already that I consumed the darkness out of hatred for these lands and in hopes of helping the realm. I did not think beyond that at the time. Now, I must accept it each time in order to maintain Lancer's weakened state. It is my sacrifice that I am willing to bear for the sake of the realm." Edward explained.

"And me? He wishes to turn me?" Ryle asked.

"I believe so. I believe he thinks you will eventually consume the darkness as well and aid in the destruction of the Realm; for if he turned another prince, then the strength of The Land of Unfading Beauty will only continue to grow. Plus, it would bring him great pleasure to turn one of Eamon's sons. He has quite a hatred of your father."

"Apparently. Though I must say the feeling is probably mutual." Ryle added with a smirk. "Now are you going to hit me or stab me so Lancer will be pleased?"

"He will not be able to hear your screams even if he were standing outside the door. This room relays no sound. His comment was a coded way to tell me to not hold back on you." Kneeling to one knee, Edward eased to the floor to converse more comfortably on Ryle's level as he sat bound to the chair.

"So what now then? You free me?"

"I can not do that." Edward shook his head. "If I did, he would certainly know I was involved. Besides, I need you here."

"You? And why is that?" Ryle challenged.

"We must find out who betrayed the Realm. Together we can do that."

"How can I accomplish anything when I am tied to a chair?" Ryle asked.

"Point taken, but you will not always be tied to a chair. I have a feeling you will be taken to the prison chamber soon. Once there, you will be right next door to the armory. I oversee the armory and prison cells myself. We can make trips to the Uniters' camp frequently."

"You sound confident. How will you explain our trips to your fellow guards? The men loyal to Lancer?"

"I can tell them anything, and they will trust my words." Edward stated. "Do not think my time here has been wasted, Prince Ryle. I have a position of authority, and it is respected."

Ryle studied Edward a moment longer. "Fine. We play this your way. Though I must say, if I am to experience torture every day, I may need new garments soon, for these are almost shredded."

Edward nodded. "I imagine you will be dressed in some of the finest apparel the Lands has to offer if you will agree to a position of friend instead of foe."

"I will not."

"I figured as much." Sighing, Edward rose to his feet and walked over to Ryle and untied his hands.

Ryle rubbed his wrists and tried to shake out the numbness from the uncomfortable position and then stood. "Take me to my cell, Captain."

"Right." Edward motioned to the doorway. "I warn you, Prince Ryle-"

"It's Captain Ryle." He clarified.

"Yes, well in these lands you are the prince of the East." Edward led him down a long hallway to the back side of the castle. "I warn you that Lancer will not take kindly to your rejection of his offer of friendship and to be brought into the fold."

"He has not offered." Ryle stated.

"Yes, but he intends to, and when he does, if you do not accept... I cannot promise your safety."

"I understand completely."

Edward nodded as he nudged Ryle into a darkened cell that had but straw and dirt for company. He locked the door as Ryle eased slowly to the floor, his body sore and still healing from the atrocities from the reflection chamber. The Eastern prince was stubborn, and Edward prayed Ryle would see reason and allow him to help him. However, the only way to help the prince was to convince him to play along with himself as an ally to the Lands. He feared the Eastern prince would forfeit his life if he did not side with Lancer, even if it were just an act. That, Edward realized, was his new task. To convince Ryle to immerse himself in the Lands as another asset, otherwise the torture would only continue until death should take the prince.

Elizabeth stood in the gardens of her sister's castle, grief-stricken as she stared down at the small stone with Mary's name engraved upon its smooth surface. It was odd losing her attendant, but standing before what was left of her memory, Elizabeth felt even more devastated over losing such a friend. Mary had been with her since they were children, and the close camaraderie they shared was now gone leaving a hole of grief Elizabeth did not know how to fill.

"You still in the gardens, my love?" She felt Clifton's hand slowly press against the small of her back as he came to stand beside her.

"I'm finding it hard to leave her here." Elizabeth admitted.

"You can always come back out after breakfast, but you need to eat, Elizabeth. We all need our strength today if we are to face what lies ahead in the coming days."

She leaned her head against his shoulder and sighed. "I suppose you are right." She gently kissed two fingers and laid them against the cold surface of Mary's stone and turned to leave. "How is Isaac?"

"Pulling through. He survived the night, which is a good sign. Arnos is seeing to him closely and Katarina has yet to leave his side."

"I guess she is not upset about him killing her father."

"Truth be told, I think she is still in shock at the moment." Clifton replied. "I'm not sure the death of Abner has sunk in just yet."

"Do you think she will handle his death well?" Elizabeth turned her face up to Clifton as they walked awaiting his response and studied the firm set of his jaw as he contemplated his answer.

"I do not know. I hope so, but as much as I wish to say yes, there is part of me that feels she will have a harder time than we believe she will."

"I agree. I know he was an evil tyrant, but he was still her father." Elizabeth added. "Though we only knew of his wickedness,

I'm sure at some points in her life he showed kindness and love towards her. It is still a loss of a loved one, and those are hard." Her voice quieted. Clifton knew her mind had wandered to the loss of Mary again as well as the loss of her father, King Granton. He lightly clasped her hand in his. "We will just have to make sure she has support from us during this hard time."

Elizabeth nodded. "Yes, indeed. I pray Isaac pulls through as well. The Realm cannot lose him, and I believe Katarina will have an even harder time if he passes as well."

"All of us will have a hard time if Isaac does not make it. But he will. He's a fighter." Clifton waved his hand for the guards to open the castle doors so he and Elizabeth could enter the castle. As they walked through the corridor towards the conservatory, Samuel rushed by them in a sprint.

"Samuel?" Elizabeth's voice caused the young king to slide across the floor as he tried to stop his current pace. His breathing was heavy as if he had sprinted the entire way from his chambers on the upper level of the castle. "What has you in such a rush?"

"Prince Isaac. He's awake." Samuel's words had them all hurrying their speed as hope ignited in their hearts. When they reached the Western wing and Isaac's personal chambers, Melody paced outside the door. When she saw Elizabeth, relief sagged her shoulders and she accepted the comforting hug from her dear friend.

"How is he, Melody?" Clifton asked.

"He just awoke. Arnos is with him now. I am awaiting his permission to enter once he has looked over Isaac's wound once more."

"Katarina?" Elizabeth asked.

"I sent her to her chamber to rest. I have not sent anyone to alert her just yet." Melody stated. "I wish to wait until I have gotten to see my brother for myself. Though she is a new friend, I wish for only those closest to him to see him first."

Elizabeth nodded at Melody's wishes and waited with bated breath for Arnos to appear.

"My dear," King Eamon began, "you must stop your pacing and worrying. Both are not accomplishing anything but making my head spin."

Alayna stopped in her tracks and turned to the king, his eyes held worry and fatigue. "I am sorry, my Lord, it's just… we must act. We have no idea where Ryle is, Lancer is weak, and we have removed our largest obstacle, Abner. It is now or never."

"You wish to conduct a retaliating attack without your captain?"

"I know it sounds reckless, but Ryle will join us when he comes back. In the mean time, he would want us to be proactive and take advantage of this shift in our circumstances." She waved her hand over the maps before her. "We must take back the Land of Unfading Beauty while Lancer remains weakened. It is the only way."

"And what of Isaac? What of Anthony?" Eamon continued to press her. "We have a prince on his deathbed and a king who we have yet to reach. We cannot jump into another battle without everyone in place. Trust me when I speak to you, Alayna, we are not ready."

"I will have Mosiah lead the troops. He was our former captain and he will gladly serve in that capacity again until Ryle returns."

Eamon shook his head and watched as Alayna continued pacing and ranting about her unstable plan to attack the Unfading Lands. She did not wish to see the larger picture, the higher stakes that the Realm was facing.

"I do not advise such a plan." Eamon stated firmly. "It is foolish."

Alayna's head popped up at his words and her eyes narrowed in anger as she faced him. "I appreciate your counsel, King Eamon, but I believe I can take it from here. Please see yourself out."

Eamon, frustrated, bit his tongue to prevent a harsher reprimand from escaping his lips and he stood to leave. He straightened his tunic and looked at her one more time. "There needs to be a time of reflection, Alayna. For everyone. I know you are upset at the current circumstances, but I say this now, I will not risk the lives of Eastern guards for an ill-advised mission. I will not risk my son's life either. So know this, if you decide to push through on your plan of a swift attack this close to our latest defeat, you will not have support from the East." He bowed as he left her to reflect upon his words, praying the new queen saw reason.

Alayna softly growled under her breath as the doors closed and she crossed her arms in a huff. How could King Eamon not support her decision? It all made sense. Lancer was weak. He was recovering from Abner's attack just as much as they were, and yet no one wanted to take advantage of the situation. She knew Ryle would stand beside her decision. He always did. They worked harmoniously together, which was but one reason why she wished he was with her now. That and she grew more and more worried about his current whereabouts more now than ever. He had yet to make it back to the castle and the battle ended two days prior. Perhaps he was wounded and his slow progression was due to discomfort and fatigue. She could think of no other reason for his delayed arrival... well the other possibility she refused to think upon. She would not allow herself to think of losing him in battle. He survived. She would feel it if he hadn't. Wouldn't she?

She eased into a chair and sighed as she gazed out the window and watched as the foggy veil of the Unfading Lands held strong. A deep bitterness welled inside her chest and determination flooded her mind as she began mapping out strategies for war against the Lands in the coming days with or without the support from the East.

Ryle heard voices echo outside the door of the prison chamber as he sat awaiting his daily punishment. If he calculated correctly, Edward would walk through the door at any moment and lead him to the reflection chamber for the day's torture. Lancer would stand cowardly to the side and observe as Edward continually assaulted him. His wounds were taking longer to heal with each passing session. Partly because the attacks became more and more brutal and lasted longer. He still wore the emerald tunic of the Northern Kingdom though it hung by mere threads on his shoulders. He refused to give it up. He fought for the Realm. He survived for the Realm. And he would die for the Realm. No matter the proposition by Edward, he would not join forces, whether real or false, with Lancer. He wished for his loyalty to be undeniable. He wished for Lancer to know that some men's hearts refused to bend to his will.

The heavy door creaked as a guard stepped inside and to the side as Edward entered wearing a grim expression. "It is time." He unlocked the door to Ryle's cell and waited as Ryle slowly stood and stretched out his limbs. Yes, the recovery was much slower from yesterday's beatings. He felt the pull in his muscles as he arched his back, and the slight sting in his side that lingered from the swish of Edward's blade. He did not let Edward see his ailments, however. Instead he held his head high and allowed the former prince to escort him down the hall without complaint. Once inside the chamber, he allowed Edward to bind his hands behind him as he sat in the now all too familiar chair in the center of the room.

"Good afternoon, Prince Ryle." Lancer greeted. "I trust you slept well."

The small snicker after his words irritated Ryle. The sport in which Lancer stood and watched his suffering disgusted him.

"Indeed. I find your accommodations quite pleasing." He watched as a small tick in Lancer's jaw showed his frustration beneath his false cheerfulness.

"I see. Well perhaps we should offer a change in venue then." Lancer nodded towards Edward. "Begin."

Edward turned and faced Ryle, his sword at the ready and regret in his eyes. Ryle stared into the prince, his sharp blue gaze never wavering as he felt the first pierce of the blade enter his side. He clenched his teeth and bore down on what little pride he possessed to restrain the scream that wished to escape his lips. He refused to give Lancer pleasure in his suffering.

"Now, Prince Ryle, where was I?" Lancer continued walking nonchalantly in circles around him as Edward continued to beat him and his blood seeped out of his wound and dripped to the floor. "I have a plan to bring you to the boundary line tomorrow. I wish to speak to your new queen and show her my new prisoner. I imagine she is quite worried over the loss of yet another prince. Though I had hoped to display another ally," he turned to Ryle to see if Ryle had come to his senses and wished to join forces with him. Ryle shook his head as he accepted the blow to the temple from Edward. His vision faded to black and his head fell.

"Edward!" Lancer complained. "I said not to knock him unconscious."

"Sorry, my Lord. That one must have slipped."

Lancer chuckled. "Yes, well he will come to in a moment and then we will continue. I have to say I am immensely pleased with the seriousness in which you take this task every day. I imagined it would be hard for you, but you seem to have taken to it quite well. I am impressed and gratified."

"Thank you, my Lord." Edward turned back to Ryle as a soft groan escaped the former prince's lips and his chin rose from his chest.

"Ah, perfect. He's awake." Lancer continued. "You alright there, Prince Ryle?"

"Never better." Ryle ground out behind clenched teeth.

"Good. As I was saying, I wish to display you as my newest prisoner in front of your queen. Perhaps then she will concede."

"She will never concede." Ryle stated on a laugh. "Do you seriously not understand? Are you that daft?" He looked straight into Lancer's fierce gaze. "You will lose. Your lands have never been in more trouble than they are now. You think by holding me prisoner, by killing me that those actions will stop what is going to happen to you? It won't. My life is forfeit. So be it. But your life will be too. It is only a matter of time. You are a fool if you think the Realm of Queen Alayna will give into your childish fantasy of domination."

He felt the sharp stab as Edward pierced his chest with the sword. Lancer walked closer to him and watched as pain marred Ryle's face. "We'll see about that." He snarled as he nodded to Edward again and the blade pierced Ryle from behind as Lancer stormed out of the chamber.

Chapter 2

Isaac groaned as Arnos worked quickly to change his bandages. "You have many visitors waiting to see you, my Lord." Arnos stated.

"I imagine so." He hissed as Arnos placed pressure against his side.

"I must warn you that you are not strong enough to be walking around or to leave this chamber for a few days." Arnos began, "No matter how tempting. You need to heal. This wound has penetrated your muscle."

"Thank you, Arnos. I'll do my best to be patient." Isaac stated as he leaned his head back against his pillows.

"Would you like me to send in your sister? She has been pacing outside the door."

Isaac's lips quirked into a small smile. "I imagine she has. A delicate heart does our Melody have."

Arnos nodded in agreement as he began gathering his supplies. "I imagine Princess Elizabeth and Prince Clifton have joined her by now, as well as King Samuel."

"You may send them all inside, Arnos. I would do well to allow them all to see me and cease their worry."

"Very well, my Lord." Arnos walked towards the chamber door and opened it to step outside into the hall.

Expectant faces met him and he nodded. "He is tired, but well. You may see him, though I must caution," before he could finish his sentence, the women had burst through the door into the chamber. Clifton softly chuckled. "I will make sure we allow him to rest Arnos, thank you." He lightly patted the older man's shoulder as he passed by him into the room. Elizabeth and Melody had already flanked Isaac on either side and doted upon the injured prince. Samuel walked beside Clifton and stood at the foot of the bed. Isaac met his gaze. "My thanks to your healer, Arnos."

Clifton nodded in acknowledgment. "He says you are well on your way to a smooth recovery. That is good news."

"That it is." Isaac grimaced as he pushed himself up in bed to lean against the headboard. "I must say I don't feel like my usual self at the moment."

"We've been so worried." Melody gripped his hand and her eyes held restrained tears as she stared at her brother. He kissed the back of her hand and smiled tenderly at her. "No worries, sister; it would take more than a blade to kill me."

"Well let us hope that is true." Elizabeth stated as she straightened the edges of his bedding. "You must rest and heal. You must not push yourself past your limits like you always do."

"Is that not the pot calling the kettle black?" Isaac and Clifton chuckled at the surprised expression Elizabeth flashed before lightly swatting Isaac's shoulder.

"You had us worried." She stated on a more serious note. "Don't ever do that again."

He met her concerned blue eyes and nodded soberly. "I do not plan on it. In fact, I wish to speak to my father about how Abner's army made it across the Western Kingdom. Has he arrived yet?"

Everyone looked from one to the other for an explanation that would suffice.

"Anyone?" Isaac asked.

"He has yet to arrive, Isaac." Clifton stated. "And we have all been staying close to the castle the last few days so no one has ventured out to check the Western Kingdom."

"Be assured that we will." Elizabeth offered. "We just have to catch our bearings. With your father out of contact and with Ryle missing, we have much to look into."

"Wait, Ryle is missing?" Isaac asked. "Since when?"

"Since the battles. He has yet to make it back. We aren't sure," Clifton's voice trailed off and he cleared his throat to push back his emotions. "We aren't sure what has become of him just yet."

"And Katarina?" He asked.

"She is resting." Melody provided with a smile. "She has sat by your side most of the time. I sent her to rest."

He sighed in relief. "Well at least there is some good news. Any word from Edward on how Lancer discovered our plan?"

"We have not ventured to the boundary line yet." Samuel explained.

"But we will. Soon." Elizabeth added.

"Not too soon." Clifton's tone held a soft warning for his wife to tamper down her eagerness, knowing Elizabeth wished to make the trip herself.

"And how is Alayna handling our latest defeat?" Isaac asked.

"She has yet to come out of the Council Room unless it is to her personal chambers. Only King Eamon has spoken with her thus far." Elizabeth explained. "Though I will be making a visit to her chambers this evening to see how she is doing."

"Well keep me in the loop on what is happening." Isaac stated. "Though I am confined to this bed for at least a few more days, I am not completely worthless."

"Now you see how it feels." Elizabeth baited with a smirk.

"Aye, and it is quite disagreeable."

"Perhaps we can send in Katarina. I'm sure her presence will perk you up." Elizabeth winked at Isaac and he laughed.

"Aye, maybe so, but perhaps another time. I am quite tired."

"We will let you rest then." Clifton added. "Come everyone, Isaac needs to sleep." He waved everyone to follow him to the door. Melody lingering to speak to her brother alone.

"I am happy to see you awake, brother. You had me scared."

Isaac softly brushed his knuckle over the tear that slipped down her cheek. "I will be okay, Melody. Don't you worry about me."

"And Father?" Melody sniffled. "It is not like him not to send word. I fear something has happened to him."

"I agree. Though we must not think the worst. I am sure he has a perfect explanation of what happened with Abner and is also just taking a refreshing breath after the battles. We must not worry over what we do not know. Understand?"

She nodded solemnly. "I will try to remain hopeful."

"Good. Now be on with you then. I need my beauty sleep."

She softly grinned as she squeezed his hand before departing.

Isaac watched as Melody's red dress slipped out his chamber door, her concern over their father's whereabouts disrupting his ache for rest. It was unlike his father to disengage during such times and his lack of interaction meant something was wrong. Isaac could feel it. Which also meant the Western Kingdom was vulnerable under the commands of his mother. Perhaps she did not realize his father was absent just yet. But the moment she did... he cringed. He prayed his body would rapidly heal so that he could tend to his kingdom before chaos reigned.

"Are you going to venture out of this room at some point?" Elizabeth poked her head into the Council Room and Alayna's blonde head popped up.

"Ah, Elizabeth, I'm glad you came by. I need to speak to your husband. We have much to discuss." She brushed a blonde curl behind her ear as Elizabeth squeezed through the doorway and shut the door behind her.

"What about?"

Alayna scoffed in surprise. "Why, about our retaliation of course."

"So soon? We have yet to catch our breath. Isaac is not yet healed. King Anthony is missing. We-"

Alayna waved her hands in dismissal. "I'm aware of our current circumstances. Now will you please tell Clifton I need to speak with him?"

"Why do you not summon the Council? We should all be a part of the discussion if it involves the Realm." She saw her sister make an effort not to lash out, but Alayna's stone cold expression spoke volumes as she made her way towards Elizabeth with fierce daggers in her brown eyes. "I have made my request, sister. You will convey my message." She opened the door and all but forced Elizabeth out into the hallway.

Elizabeth staggered in bewilderment as she stared at the wooden door before her.

"Elizabeth?" Clifton's voice drifted to her as he climbed the last of the main stairwell. He eyed her curiously as she continued to stand in bafflement. "Is something wrong, love?"

"I'm not sure." Her voice was quiet and edged with concern. "Alayna is not herself at the moment. She wishes to speak with you... without the rest of the council present."

"That doesn't seem so odd. I'm sure she just wishes to ask me about Ryle or Isaac."

"I don't think so."

Clifton entwined his fingers with Elizabeth's and then kissed her knuckles. "I will see what she needs. Why don't you go rest or see that Isaac is resting. I believe Arnos said he was having a hard time staying in bed. Melody is with him now as well."

Elizabeth silently nodded and made her way towards the stairwell. Clifton watched as his defeated wife retreated, her temperament surprising, he wondered what Alayna had said to upset her sister. He knocked on the door and opened it to find Alayna sitting at the head of the council table staring at maps before her.

"Elizabeth said you wished to speak with me." Clifton interrupted.

"Oh, yes, Clifton. Please come in and shut the door." She straightened in her chair and waited for him to fully enter. She waved to a seat adjacent to her and he sat. "We have much to discuss."

"Without the rest of the Council?" Clifton asked curiously.

"Yes. For now. I spoke with your father earlier, but he is not thinking clearly at the moment." Alayna waved away the despicable thought of King Eamon's reprimand from earlier and looked to Clifton. "We must retaliate soon. While the Unfading Lands is recuperating, we should launch another attack. They would not be expecting it."

Clifton slowly raised his hands off the tabletop to stop her from continuing. "Wait a minute, Alayna. We cannot discuss such topics without the rest of the Council. Especially something as big as war."

Alayna huffed. "We will discuss it with them, but right now I am discussing it with you. I wished to collect your thoughts on the matter and share my own. We must have a united front if we are to approach the full Council confidently."

"And what did my father have to say on the matter?" Clifton asked.

Alayna's gaze darted to the table again before meeting Clifton's sharp eye. "He feels it is too soon."

"And I must say, I agree with him. We are not ready. We have yet to even gather our remaining leaders and people. It would be a fool's errand to rush into another battle so quickly."

"I feel no one sees the benefits as I do. The point is, yes we are recovering, but Lancer would not be expecting us because he too is recovering." Alayna stressed her point by forcefully pointing at a map with a defined 'x' penned over the Unfading Lands.

"I say we send someone to the boundary line to converse with Edward first. We send someone to the west to inquire of King Anthony. And then, possibly then, we can decide our next move." Clifton stood and straightened his pale blue tunic. "We also should discuss plans with the rest of the Council before any action takes place." He turned to leave without further comment.

Alayna stood in frustration. "By week's end I will be sending troops over the boundary line and you will lead them. That is an order, Prince Clifton."

Clifton froze and his back stiffened. Alayna watched as his shoulders straightened and visibly she could see the deep breath he inhaled before turning. His green eyes fierce as he responded. "You are the Queen of the Realm, Alayna, and I respect your position. But it is my life and countless others that you would be gambling with. I will not willingly fight in a battle that has not been approved by the entire Council, order from the queen or not." He nodded that the conversation was over before turning and leaving.

Alayna sank into her chair in a huff as she wiped away a silent tear that trailed down her cheek.

"He appears physically weaker." Lancer commented as he took a generous sip of his favorite amber liquid and studied Edward's pacing.

"Physically, yes, but mentally he is stronger than ever, it seems. He refuses to join with us, my Lord. I am not sure I can break him."

Lancer set his glass aside and steepled his fingers and lightly tapped them against his lips as he thought. "Perhaps a visit to the boundary line is warranted to show him how separated from his loved ones he truly is. Perhaps that will lead his thinking in a more moldable direction. I am sure you have a spot convenient for conversing with your family from my last biddings?"

"I do. There is a small clearing we used prior to the last battle, but I do not know if anyone would dare venture there now."

"Go see. Continue to survey the boundary line and should you encounter someone make a request that we wish to interact with them the following day." Lancer ordered.

"And what should I say it is about?" Edward asked.

"Just tell them it is at my request. However you conversed with them last time will be sufficient enough. My message will be more visual anyhow."

"Yes, my Lord. I will see what I can do. Perhaps I can employ Cecilia's help in keeping watch on the clearing."

"That is a splendid idea. Cecilia is one of our greatest assets. Why, if it had not been for her warning me against the Realm's attack we would have been blindsided."

Edward froze. "My Lord?"

"Cecilia."

"Yes?" Edward waited with bated breath for Lancer to continue, his heart slowly constricting, as he feared what would spill from Lancer's lips.

"She found me as I patrolled the boundary lines and warned me that the Realm wished to plan a surprise attack while we were distracted by Abner's threat."

Edward eased himself into a chair. "How did she know of such a plan?"

Lancer waved his hand to dismiss the topic. "What does it matter? She sensed a threat. She was right. We won." He smiled, pleased with himself.

Edward's vision began to blur as anger bubbled within his heart at the brutal betrayal.

"Edward? Are you alright?"

Edward blinked and forced a smile. "Yes. Yes, my Lord. I am just surprised at Cecilia not coming to me first is all."

"Ah, I see." Lancer took a sip from his cup again and set it aside. "You are disturbed that she would go over your head with such valuable information and fear it makes you look bad. I assure you, Edward, I was only pleased. Her loyalty to me reflects upon your loyalty. She only wished to serve you and me with her knowledge. I am pleased with the relationship you possess. So yes, please ask her to keep an eye on the boundary line for us. She will report of any movement I am sure."

Lancer smiled and waved Edward away. His steps heavy, Edward slowly made his way towards the prison chamber. He and Prince Ryle had much to discuss. How could Edward have been so blinded by love for Cecilia, he did not see her two-sided face? He cringed and clinched his fists as he made his way across the castle. He needed to report this news to the Realm, but he needed to do so without Cecilia's knowledge. Her ease and availability to eavesdrop suddenly made sense to him. He always had her around when conversing with Ryle and Clifton. Though she had not told Lancer of his traitorous position, she still betrayed him and his blood ran cold at the thought. She was a problem now. And problems needed to be dealt with swiftly. Shaking his head in dismay, he entered the prison chamber to speak to Ryle.

"And then, she all but dismissed me by slamming the door in my face!" Elizabeth huffed as she paced at the foot of Isaac's bed retelling her encounter with Alayna. "Can you believe that?"

Isaac listened intently, propped up against his pillows as he watched Elizabeth march around his room. "It is a bit soon to be thinking of a battle when some of her strongest leaders are not accounted for."

"And not to mention you." Elizabeth waved his direction. "You are in no shape to ride a horse yet."

"Well thanks for the compliment of strength and weakness all in one comment." Isaac chuckled as Elizabeth rolled her eyes.

"You knew what I meant. Besides, I'm concerned about your father. We have not received one word from him yet and I fear asking Alayna to send a messenger to the West, because I know she will reject the idea. She wouldn't want to take the time. And Ryle…"

She paused and took a deep breath. "I don't have a good feeling about him either."

"That is the one that worries me most. My father could just be playing it safe like we are, but Ryle… he would be here now if he could. There would be no holding him back." Isaac admitted.

"That is my line of thinking as well." Elizabeth crossed her arms and squinted in thought. "We need to send someone to the boundary line."

"I agree."

"But Alayna does not want to send anyone. All she can think of is revenge right now." Elizabeth explained.

"Then don't tell her. Have someone go and speak with Edward to see how conditions are in the Lands. The information can only help us." Isaac shifted against his pillows and sighed in resignation. "There really is no comfortable position, is there?"

"No." Elizabeth smirked. "I would like to go to the boundary line, but Clifton would not have it, I'm sure."

"What about Samuel?"

"He would never go against Alayna, the queen, no matter if he wanted to."

"That's true." Isaac pondered for a moment. "What about me?"

Elizabeth stopped. "You are still healing."

"Yes, but I could easily go and no one would even realize I was missing." He grinned.

"And how do you expect to get there? You are not well enough to ride."

"I can manage." Isaac pinned her with a pointed gaze. "Let me do this, Elizabeth. I need to get out of this bed and this room before I go crazy. And no one else is going to risk upsetting Alayna. I am willing, more than willing on occasion, to take that risk. She already doesn't like me. What can she do? She has yet to even come to see me. She will not even know I am gone. I will simply tell Arnos that I wish to be alone so no one will come to my chambers. You can have the stable boy ready my horse. I will take it slow and easy so as not to overdo it, and will be back by nightfall."

"It is dangerous, Isaac." Elizabeth defended half-heartedly, both of them knowing she would go along with his plan. "Clifton will be upset you have pushed yourself."

"But he will inwardly be glad someone surveyed the circumstances."

"Yes, I think he would be. Okay, I will help you. However, I must say that I feel rather bad going against Alayna in secret."

"And is that not what she has been doing in the Council Room?" Isaac pointed out. "Besides, I have a stake in this too. I need to find my father. And if she is not willing to expend the resources to find some answers, I will."

"I wish to know who betrayed us." Elizabeth stated forcefully. "If it was Edward, I do not know how I will handle that news."

"I will find out."

"You risk much, Isaac."

"And so do you. If you begin to feel too guilty, you may share my whereabouts with Clifton."

"Thank you." She sighed in relief.

"But wait until after I leave. I will leave before dawn."

She squeezed his hand. "Be careful."

"Always." He winked at her as she slipped her hand from his grasp and left his chambers with burdened shoulders.

Clifton sat at ease as his father relayed his conversation with Alayna and his stance on her subject of retaliation. Crossing his right boot over his left knee, Clifton leaned into the cushions.

"She will not listen to reason." Eamon finished.

"I concur." Clifton added. "I had the same discussion with her. She attempted to order me to do her bidding, however, I did not take it to heart. I believe she is frustrated, overwhelmed, hurting, and scared, and I was an easy target for her lashings."

"I am concerned about Ryle." Clifton watched his father pause in his pacing to take a deep breath to contain his emotions. "It is not like your brother to disappear off the map without word."

"You think him dead?" Clifton asked softly.

Eamon shook his head. "Worse. I fear he is in The Land of Unfading Beauty." Eamon eased onto the chair opposite Clifton and placed his chin in his hand. Clifton had not seen his father distressed for some time, and his defeated demeanor worried Clifton.

"We do not know that for sure. Though, if he is in the Lands, perhaps he is still safe and gathering troops for us there in secret." Clifton stated, though his words lacked conviction.

"Lancer will not hesitate to kill your brother." Eamon began, his soft green gaze much like Clifton's looked away as he swallowed back his emotions. "I should have convinced your mother to allow him sanctuary all those years ago. If we had, perhaps the very creation of the Lands would never have happened."

"You had no way of knowing something like this would happen, Father. You must not wish for the past to play out differently. Changing one event would have compounded and changed a thousand others."

Eamon's lips slightly tilted into a small smile. "When did you become so wise?"

Clifton shrugged. "I contribute it to my wife."

Both men chuckled as the door opened and Elizabeth entered into the chambers. Her brows rose at the sight of the king and she smiled. "Did I miss a meeting of minds?"

"Not at all, love." Clifton waved her over to a seat and she lightly kissed him on the lips before sitting. "My father and I were just discussing Alayna."

Elizabeth huffed a frustrated breath and crossed her arms. "I do not know what we are going to do with her."

Clifton squeezed her hand. "Tell us what your thoughts are on the matters at hand, Elizabeth."

She inhaled a deep breath and sighed. "I understand her wish to launch an attack so swiftly. It is a good idea." She held up her hand to ward off interruption until she was finished. "However, it is only a good idea when we have all of our key players in line. Right now, we do not know up from down. We are missing people. Samuel's kingdom is hurting because yet again they have lost more troops. The Southern Kingdom can only give so much right now since it is in the stages of rebuilding. The Western Kingdom has gone silent. Ryle has disappeared. Isaac is hurt. There is too much taking place right now for us to make a successful attack. Do I feel we should attempt one? Yes. Soon? Yes. But not until these matters are resolved. Which brings me to my next point..." She trailed off and lightly threaded her fingers through Clifton's. "You are not to speak of this to Alayna or anyone else. In fact, I did not intend to share it with your father, but since he is here, perhaps it is best."

"Go on." Clifton prodded.

"Isaac is traveling to the boundary line tomorrow morning before dawn breaks."

"What?" Eamon sat up straight in his chair. "He is in no shape to make such a trip, no matter how short it may be."

"I tried to convince him otherwise, but he feels he is the best person for the job. Besides, he can disappear out of the castle without Alayna noticing. She does not wish to send anyone to the boundary line, or anywhere for that matter, but it needs to be done."

Clifton rubbed a hand over his face as he allowed Elizabeth's words to sink into his brain. "It is not wise."

"Yes, I know. He knows. But it is happening. He told me if I felt the secret too much a burden I could share it with you, but he did not intend to allow you to dissuade him."

Clifton nodded. "Very well. I will allow him the luxury of thinking he travels alone, but I will not be far behind. He is not strong enough yet, but I will give his ego a wide berth."

Elizabeth smiled in relief and hugged him quickly before hopping to her feet. "I also had another proposal I wished to share with you two. I want to find Anthony."

Both men studied her in surprise and she giggled. "You two look so similar at times." She mimicked their dumbfounded expressions before continuing. "And King Eamon, I wish for you to accompany me."

"Me?" He asked curiously, "whatever for?"

"Because should we encounter any problems in the West you can act upon authority more than I. Besides, you know your way around the Western Kingdom. I have never been."

"And what if Abner's guards remain in control over the West?" Clifton asked.

"We do not even know for sure if he gained control of the West. That is my point. We know nothing, and we need answers. I am ready for answers."

"And are you traveling in secret as well?" Eamon asked.

She shook her head. "No. I intend to inform Alayna of our plans. She will not be happy, but it needs to be done. And should she still seem resistant, then I will have to take my persuasion to the next level."

"And how would you manage that?" Clifton asked curiously with a small smile at his wife's confidence.

"I will simply give her no choice but to oblige or I shall tell her secret."

"Pesky little sister, aren't you?" Eamon chuckled.

"It's not much of a secret if everyone already knows." Clifton pointed out.

"Yes, but she does not realize people are aware of her feelings for Ryle. She honestly thinks no one notices." Elizabeth rolled her eyes and shrugged. "I hate to threaten that course of action, but she will do most anything to save face and guard her secrets."

"Perhaps it won't come to that, but if it must be done, so be it." Clifton nodded his assent and Elizabeth lightly ran her hand over his hair before turning to leave. "You two gentlemen begin plans for my journey." She called over her shoulder as she exited, the heavy doors closing behind her.

"Bossy little spitfire, isn't she?" Clifton asked his father in amusement and had his father laughing in agreement.

Chapter 3

Samuel made his way down the empty halls, his boots barely making a sound along the floor as he stealthily walked back towards his bedchamber. He had risen to a hollow stomach and though it was early, he had made his way to the kitchens for a small snack to tie him over until breakfast. Not a normal habit of his, but the late nights chatting with Melody had thrown off his system a bit. Not that he minded. He loved talking with Melody. She seemed to understand him better than anyone else, minus Clifton. But there was something else about Melody that intrigued Samuel as well- her quiet strength. He knew the others recognized it also, but Melody held herself with dignity and strength. The type of characteristics that rub off on those around her. He hoped they did him. He paused as he heard a door creak. Apparently he wasn't the only early riser. He heard muted footsteps coming from Prince Isaac's chamber. Perhaps Arnos made an early check up on the prince. Samuel rounded the corner and saw Prince Isaac silently shoving his arms into his red tunic. Samuel ducked behind the corner and waited. He eased his head around the side of the wall to peek and saw Isaac heading towards the stairwell. The Western prince moved at a slower pace, but his face was etched in hard determination. Samuel looked around him and spotted no one else and quietly followed.

What would have Isaac up so early? Where was he going?

Samuel hopped out of sight as Isaac stopped and turned abruptly as if he sensed someone following him. As his eyes surveyed the hallway, he shrugged and continued on his way. Samuel exhaled quietly and then continued to follow. The prince should not be out of bed yet, Arnos had yet to clear him. And the fact he was up before dawn rang warning bells in Samuel's mind as well. Samuel watched Isaac turn down the hall and stepped out to follow and he jumped in surprise as a firm hand clamped down on his shoulder. He stifled his gasp as Clifton's face came into view, a hint of amusement tilting his lips at having scared Samuel.

"What has you up and about Samuel?" He whispered quietly.

"Prince Isaac is walking up and about. He looked... up to something."

Clifton grinned. "That he is. I can take it from here. Go get some rest."

"Where is he going?" Samuel asked.

"To the boundary line." Clifton replied.

Samuel's eyes widened. "But why?"

"I will fill you in Samuel, but now is not the time. Please, go back to your chambers. And tell no one what you have seen or spoken." Clifton's voice held a soft warning and Samuel nodded.

"Yes, my Lord. Of course. Are you going to follow him?"

"Yes." Clifton nodded as Samuel retreated.

"Good. He should not be riding in his condition."

Clifton smiled at the young king. "You are kind, Samuel. A good man looking out for his friend. It is an appreciated attribute." Clifton squeezed his shoulder. "Now go. I will keep you informed, but I must hurry to catch up to him."

Samuel nodded as he watched Clifton stealthily weave his way down the hall and down the back stairwell.

Prince Isaac travelling to the boundary line, at this hour? He shook his head. Samuel sometimes struggled in understanding Isaac, and now was no exception. The fact Clifton knew of Isaac's purpose was surprising as well. There was more going on than met the eye and Samuel knew only one other person who would know. Elizabeth. He glanced out the window. *Not quite dawn.* He would head back to his chamber and dress for the day. By the time he was finished, it would be dawn and he would seek out Elizabeth.

Isaac panted as he eased himself off of his horse and his feet rested in the damp grass, as the morning sun was just beginning to peek over the horizon. The animals were starting their morning routines of foraging and the sound of leaves rustling in the early morning breeze. He inhaled deeply. He had missed being outdoors. Trapped in his chambers, the last week had been torture, and though he felt as if he were going to be sick, he still felt better in the fresh air. He grimaced as he reached up to snag the reins of his horse and began the walk through the trees and into Elizabeth's clearing. He tied off the horse on a nearby limb and made his way to the large stump that allowed one to sit and stare across the boundary. He eased himself down and watched as the small rabbit, called Thatcher, the usual messenger between lands, hopped out of his bushel awaiting a task. There was no letter tied around his small neck, and that told Isaac, Edward had yet to venture to the line. He did not have a message prepared, nor would he write one. He would wait.

As he sat he looked around, the familiar spot tinged with traces of dried blood and debris from the previous battles, he noted that shields, swords, and helmets still littered the ground. No bodies lingered, of that he was grateful, but the smell of blood in the air turned his empty stomach. Battles were ugly affairs, and Isaac had spent the last week reliving every second of the war against Abner. He knew there was nothing else that could have been done. But Abner's last words would not leave his mind.

"You have no idea what you have done."

What did Abner mean? Isaac ran a hand through his dark hair and rested his chin on his fist. Did Abner know a way to defeat Lancer and Isaac had ruined their chances of finding out? Was his father's absence due to Abner's veiled threat? Did Abner do something to his father? Or was the old king simply leaving the threat to torment Isaac as it currently did? He didn't know the answer, and that plagued him. Worse, he had killed Katarina's father. She had yet to mention it, but he knew she must be hurting despite the hardships the man gave her. But it had to be done. Surely Katarina saw the necessity of it.

He waved his hand as if dismissing his line of thinking. He did not need to think about Katarina at the moment. His focus needed to be on the Unfading Lands before him. Too many times had Lancer slipped through their fingers. There had to be a way to conquer the Lands without succumbing to the darkness. The darkness was the easy route. Isaac never liked easy. He thrived on the difficult and seemingly impossible. And Edward had enveloped the darkness and what good had it brought them other than the fact Lancer could no longer cross the boundary? Nothing.

Isaac glanced up as movement shifted on the other side and Edward hesitantly stepped into the clearing. Isaac's brows rose as he watched the former Northern Prince glance over his shoulder in paranoia. He offered a wave to Isaac and pointed to a letter in his hand. Isaac stood and grabbed Thatcher and nudged the small rabbit across the line to him. Edward hastily tied the letter around its neck and sent it across the line. He bowed to Isaac and quickly darted back through the trees.

Brow creased, Isaac untied the letter.

I am glad someone has ventured to the boundary line. I have been waiting.

There is much to discuss, but I only have a short time. I have discovered the source of the betrayal. The person who told Lancer of our plans was Cecilia. Yes, this cuts deeper than you know. I have yet to confront her or deal with the issue at present, but I intend to. Her motives, I'm sure, were not to harm the Realm, but only to keep the boundary line. She loves living within the Lands and did not wish to see the boundary line fall. The fact anyone would wish for this is foreign to me, but we must consider those that do not wish for the Realm to succeed and destroying the boundary. A factor, I do not believe, we paid much attention to previously.

Lancer wishes to meet with Alayna, here at the clearing. He told me that should I see someone here to have him or her bring her the following day. Therefore, we will be here tomorrow awaiting her arrival. I do not know more than that at the moment or what he intends to discuss, only that he wishes to show her something.

Please know that I remain loyal to the Realm and our cause to defeat the Lands.

Edward

Isaac folded the parchment and stuck it in his tunic pocket and slowly stood. He paused in his movements as he sensed someone watching him. Without hesitation he unsheathed his sword and swung around, the blade pausing within a breath of Clifton's neck. The Eastern Prince's eyes widened as he held up his hands in surrender. Isaac's shoulders relaxed and he lowered his breath.

"I could have had your head, Clifton." He put away his sword.

"I'm grateful you didn't." Clifton rubbed a nervous hand over the back of his neck.

"What are you doing here?" Isaac asked.

"Following you."

"Elizabeth." Isaac stated, knowing the princess had confessed his plan to her husband after all.

"Yes. She was worried."

Isaac smirked. "I figured as much. I try to do something heroic and selfless and you steal my thunder."

Clifton laughed. "Don't be so glum, Isaac. You are still heroic. You just aren't invincible. Now tell me, what did the letter say?"

Isaac handed it to him and watched as Clifton's green eyes scanned the page. "It will take some convincing to get Alayna to venture here."

"Aye. I agree. But we need a place to start. We are at that awkward moment of transition. Between battle and rest. Between rest and upcoming battle. We need direction. Perhaps her visit to the line and with Lancer will give us some direction." Isaac walked towards his horse and his lips tightened as he strained to lift himself into his saddle.

"You must recover first or you will be no good to anyone in the upcoming days." Clifton launched into his saddle with ease and Isaac bit back his envy.

"I am fine. Maybe a bit slower than usual, but I still almost caught your head at the end of my sword."

"That may be, but I was not trying to kill you." Clifton pointed out.

"Fair enough." Isaac grumbled as he slapped his reins and the two princes made the journey back towards the castle.

"So let me see, you wish to journey to the Western Kingdom with your father-in-law to check on the whereabouts of King Anthony while we wish to commence battle at week's end?" Alayna asked, the contempt in her tone not going unnoticed by Elizabeth or Melody as they both sat at the Council table.

"That is correct." Elizabeth replied. "Though the 'battle at week's end' part is still a bit vague."

"No it is not." Alayna stated in annoyance. She diverted her gaze towards the maps on the table and ignored the two princesses sitting before her. She would not be swayed, and Elizabeth wishing to pull King Eamon away from the North was her sister's subtle way of sabotaging Alayna's battle plans.

"Alayna?" Elizabeth waved her hand towards her sister. "We're still here."

Alayna glanced up as if just noticing her sister. "And what of you, Melody? What brings you to the Council Room?"

The Western Princess straightened in her seat. "Elizabeth asked me to join her."

"Ah. To double-team me, hmm? Two are stronger than one?"

"Not so." Elizabeth replied. "I asked Melody because my quest involves her kingdom and her father. I assumed she would like to know the plans King Eamon and I have conjured."

"My answer is no." Alayna stated. "Your request to journey to the Western Kingdom is denied until I say." She turned her attention back to the maps and avoided the open mouth of her sister. Elizabeth's cheeks flamed and she clenched and unclenched her fists.

"You are being unreasonable." Elizabeth replied combatively.

Alayna's head snapped up. "My answer is final, sister. Now please, leave me be."

Elizabeth looked at a shocked Melody who gathered her skirts and quietly made her way to the exit. Elizabeth stood and leaned against the back of her chair.

"You have been many things, Alayna. But you have never been selfish to the point of stupidity." She turned to walk away as Alayna jumped to her feet.

"What did you say?" She demanded.

"You heard me, sister." Elizabeth looked to Alayna with disappointment. "You wish to risk the lives of everyone for a foolish battle that cannot be won until we have our feet under us again. You rush this, and you do not heed counsel from those wiser than you."

"I cannot believe you are speaking to me this way. Has everyone forgotten that I am the Queen? That it is my decision that is final? You call me selfish," she pointed her finger at Elizabeth, "when you yourself are wanting to journey to the West no matter what I say. Is that not also selfish?"

"No."

"Oh really?" Alayna crossed her arms.

"Because I am going for the sake of our Realm. We are stronger knowing our situation in the West. The Western Kingdom could still be under Abner's rule, Alayna. Do you not wish to find out? King Anthony could be in trouble. We need the West if we are to battle against the Unfading Lands again. The trip is purposeful." Elizabeth explained.

Alayna shook her head. "You are all blind. Now is our time to defeat Lancer. We must kill him and destroy those lands."

"Lancer is not the enemy, Alayna. The darkness is. And we are not one step closer to figuring out how to rid him of it than we were last time. I think we realized the hard way that the Lands cannot be defeated without first defeating the darkness."

"I don't care about the darkness. I care about Lancer. He is the one holding the boundary line up. We kill him, and it disappears." Alayna waved her hand in finality.

"And what of the darkness? What about Edward?" Elizabeth asked.

"We will cross that bridge when it comes."

"That is folly." Elizabeth growled and clenched her fists at her sides. "Perhaps you should read Father's letter again, the one he wrote to you. If you will not listen to me, perhaps you will listen to him. Lancer is not our enemy, the darkness is. We achieve nothing if we kill him and let the darkness linger."

"I am aware of what Father's letter said to me. But things are different now."

"No, they are not." Elizabeth cut in and watched as Alayna's eyes hardened.

"Yes, they are. Besides, without my Captain of the Guard, it is up to me to make military decisions, as I see fit. I seek the counsel of no one on this matter until everyone agrees it is the best course of action."

"You dictate your choices, sister, and you risk killing us all. Perhaps it is best Ryle is not here to see this side of you. He would be as disgusted as I am." Elizabeth grabbed her skirts and spun on her heel as she left her sister glaring behind her.

"Cecilia?" Ryle asked in surprise as Edward ran a frustrated hand through his dark hair and nodded on the other side of iron bars.

"Yes. Lancer was quite pleased with her contribution. I have no idea what she told him, I have yet to speak to her until I have control over my emotions."

"That is understandable." Ryle scratched at the scruff that peppered along his jaw line as he pondered how to handle the news of Cecilia's betrayal. "Why would anyone wish to stay here?"

"I don't know, but if she is willing to betray me in order to keep the boundary, then there must be others loyal to Lancer as well. Perhaps they fear what their life would be like back in the Realm. I will admit that life here is much different than across the line. There are no stresses of time or hard labors as there are in the Realm. Time is limitless, and labors are not on a schedule. Perhaps they fear the Realm to be too constricting."

"It doesn't really matter what they fear, the fact is they are loyal to Lancer and that poses a problem, no matter their reasoning. Do you think she would tell you if your life was at risk?" Ryle asked curiously.

"Yes. From what I gather, she did not inform Lancer of my involvement. He seemed naïve as to what my role was in the surprise attack." Edward explained. "That tells me that her feelings are at least somewhat genuine. Though, thinking of her betrayal makes my skin crawl. I am not sure I could bear to look at her face at the moment."

Ryle smirked. "I think I would have a hard time as well."

"Prince Isaac was at the boundary line this morning. He seemed ill."

"I imagine he is nursing bruises of his own." Ryle lightly massaged a place on his thigh as Edward remembered the feel of his dagger through muscle he delivered there earlier that morning.

"I know I keep saying it, but I am sorry I am having to torment you each day." Edward leaned against the wall and crossed his arms. "Your wounds seem to be taking longer to heal."

"They are fine." Ryle looked up, his blue eyes hard. "Nothing I cannot handle."

"Until you can't handle them."

"I will and I must. Lancer can have you beat me a thousand times a day and I would still sit willingly in that chair and take it for the sake of the Realm."

"Your bravery is honorable, but it will also lead to your death should you not be wiser." Edward pushed himself off the wall. "Tomorrow Lancer will be meeting with Alayna at the boundary line, and I am sure some of the others. I will let you know how it goes. Until then, happy healing."

Ryle watched as Edward ducked out of the prison chamber and clambered up the stone stairwell that led out into the hall. So Cecilia had betrayed them. He had to admit part of him was not surprised at that revelation. There had always seemed something off about the young woman. Now he understood why. She was sneaky in her betrayal, he would give her that credit. They did not filter their plans in front of her, trusting Edward's affections for the woman. But affection did not make someone honest. And clearly not trustworthy either. He shifted on the uncomfortable ground, the dirt and hay sticking to his trousers as he pulled his knees up and leaned his head against them. He took several deep breaths as a pain in his side began to tinge and begin the process of fully healing. Edward was right; his body was taking longer to heal between tortures. However, Ryle knew he would never give into Lancer's demands or Edward's suggestions. He would die if need be. He did not wish to die, but he would gladly lay down his life for the Realm if he had to. He wondered if Alayna thought of him as much as he did her. Her face plagued his thoughts even in sleep. And he had convinced himself that just the sight of her would renew his strength. He feared her encounter with Lancer tomorrow. Would she bring Clifton with her? Isaac? His father? He needed to see them. He needed to see their faces and feel their quiet support. His body was weakening. The only strength that remained was in spirit, but he slowly felt the weakening in his resolve. He needed an encouragement. Perhaps Edward would accompany Lancer and share with him the happenings.

Stretching out his legs, Ryle leaned his head back against the stone wall and closed his eyes. Rest. He would rest while he could and save what little strength he possessed. He had a hunch that the outcome of Lancer's interaction with Alayna would determine his remaining treatment in the Lands. He prayed their meeting went smoothly.

Isaac sat in the Northern castle's gardens and watched as Katarina walked towards him. She was a beauty, but for the life of him he could not steer his heart towards her as more than a friend.

He had tried to feel for her as more, but she lacked certain qualities he knew he wished for. She was meek and sweet, but lacked an inner strength he came to find in others. She smiled at him as she approached and eased onto the bench beside him.

"Good to see you out and about, Isaac." She greeted warmly.

"Aye, likewise. It feels nice to be out and about. What brings you to the gardens?"

"You. I was hoping to talk with you."

He waved his hand for her to continue.

"It is about my father."

He noticed her divert her gaze to one of the yellow roses nearby, Elizabeth's favorite in the entire garden. He smiled at that thought and waited patiently for her to continue. When she did not, he spoke. "Are you wanting to know why I killed him?"

"Yes. I guess part of me is wondering. Would he not have been a better captive?"

"No. He was an evil man, Katarina. I apologize for speaking so plainly, but you must know that. You feared him yourself. Now you are free of him as well as the entire Realm. He can bully no one else."

"I did not ask you to liberate me." Her voice was quiet but sharp and his brows rose in surprise.

"I thought you would be glad to be free of him." Isaac stated.

"Part of me, yes. The other half of me is devastated. He was my father. At the end of the day, he was my father, Isaac. He did not deserve to be killed."

Isaac rubbed a hand over the back of his neck, not liking the turn in the conversation. Sighing, he turned towards her. "I will not apologize for my actions. The man was trying to kill Clifton. And me. He was also attacking the Realm. He would have killed everyone if I had not stopped him."

She shook her head. "There must have been another way."

Isaac motioned towards his side in frustration. "You see what he did to me. If Clifton had not been with me when this happened, I would have died right next to your father."

Katarina swallowed back her emotions though her eyes filled with unshed tears. "I truly am sorry for your wound, it's just… my heart is torn. I still grieve my father, even knowing what he did and has done."

"Understandable." Isaac said. "But if you are looking for an apology for my act, I regret to say, you will not find one."

She nodded. "Understandable."

His lips quirked at her mirroring his response.

"I wish to travel back to my realm as soon as Queen Alayna allows me to do so. I do not know what is to become of us now that my father is gone."

"Would the queen not rule in his stead?"

"I am sure she will. But my father was a hated man, I imagine there are plenty of strong-willed men wishing to overthrow him. Now is their chance."

"And you wish to return and face that?" He asked, surprised at her sudden gumption.

"I wish to return and aid the queen. Should she wish to step aside, rule would pass to me. It is my duty."

"And you would serve as queen?"

She held a faint smile. "I would try. Seeing Queen Alayna rule successfully has encouraged me quite a bit."

"That is good news. Too bad Lancer's family line is diminished. A strong alliance would be between your family and his. The two rulers of the Valleylands in a united front."

"Lancer?" Her brows rose. "Why would anyone wish to have his family rule over them again?"

"From what I gathered from King Eamon's stories, his father was a fair ruler."

Katarina's back stiffened. "Yes, but he was overthrown and his family line wiped out. My father made sure of that. So a merger would be impossible. And I must say I would not even consider the idea if it were possible."

"And why is that?"

"Because the Valleylands belong to my father. He fought for them and won."

Issac's brow furrowed at the tension in her voice. Katarina had to realize her father stole what was never meant to be his. She seemed to understand that clearly when he visited her prior to her coming to his realm. However, sitting before him now, a new Katarina had begun to take shape. A girl not much different than her father.

"You would not return the Valleylands to Lancer's family should there be an heir?"

"No. His family has long been out of rule. The Valleylands has changed considerably since his father was in power. They would be out of touch with the people."

"Bold sentiments from the girl who had never left the confines of the castle walls until just recently."

Her shoulders sagged. "It is different."

"I must say, Katarina, I am surprised at you. I thought you were wishing to be released from your father's controlling hand all this time. Did I misread your intentions of coming here? Or has your position just recently changed?"

"It changed when you killed my father." She stated. "For your realm to have the reputation of mercy, you did not think twice about killing my father and granting him mercy."

"Again," Isaac stood, straightening to his full height and tilting his chin, "your father was trying to kill me. Mercy was not on my mind at that moment."

"No. It was not. And it should have been. A future king should know when to show mercy." Katarina's eyes flared and Isaac scoffed.

"Yes, well perhaps you should speak of mercy to Lancer's family. I'm sure they would love to share with you how your father extended mercy to them. Oh wait, that's right, they are all dead. Because of your father." He took a step back. "One suggestion before I leave you." He held up his finger in thought. "Should these feelings of resentment continue to fester, you will find your way back to your realm without the aid of the Realm of Queen Alayna. As it stands currently, we wish to help you and your realm during this transition. You can be mad at me, Katarina. You have every right to be. But should you turn that anger towards the Realm, you will only be hurting yourself and those in your realm in the long run." Isaac rested his hand on the hilt of his sword. "You will lose the help we are offering. Think on that before you take your grievances to Queen Alayna."

He turned and began making his way back to the castle with a purposeful stride. His mind whirling at what he had just encountered with Katarina, her bitterness towards him surprising. Had he thought she would be grateful for him removing her evil father from her life? *Yes. He honestly thought so.* Had he considered that she would be upset by his actions, would the outcome have been different? *No.* He knew deep down within his core that he would still have killed Abner given the opportunity. With that decision settled, and his mind at peace with the results of his actions, Isaac entered the castle before allowing his body to relax. He made his way to his chamber, the day's tasks having utterly depleted what little energy he had stored up.

Chapter 4

The dining hall was steeped with tension as everyone gathered for the evening meal. The delectable ham was tasteless on Elizabeth's tongue as she forced herself to swallow. Alayna sat at the end of the table glowering. Isaac sat stiff-backed within his chair. King Eamon sat quietly brooding, and Elizabeth found herself struggling with each bite due to whatever had begun to ail her. She had felt poorly all day and had yet to figure out what had decided to sneak into her system. She did not have the need, nor time, for sickness, and she considered it a hindrance to her plans should she be sent to bed for days on end. So she kept her mouth shut and avoided the probing gazes of Clifton as he surveyed her face as if knowing she withheld something from him. If she even sniffled, he would guard her closely and not let her venture to the West. She squeezed his hand under the table and smiled so he would relax, the gesture giving him the satisfaction he sought. She heaved a sigh of relief as she turned towards her sister again. It was time to play dirty. She cleared her throat and everyone glanced her direction.

"So, Alayna, when do you plan on summoning the first Council meeting?"

Alayna straightened in her chair and rolled her shoulders back. "I have yet to decide, Elizabeth."

"I imagine there is much to discuss." Elizabeth glanced Isaac's direction and widened her eyes as if to signal him to share his news of the boundary visit. He did not interpret the hint and Elizabeth pounded her peg into his shin under the table. He jolted in his seat and a flash of annoyance crossed his face. He grumbled and then angled his body towards Alayna.

"If I may, Alayna," he began. She waved her hand to continue and Isaac set his fork aside. "I believe we should all gather after the meal to discuss current conditions and happenings in the Realm."

"Is that so?" Alayna asked, her words held a slight trace of bitterness at being, as she felt, told what to do. "What is there to discuss? We have yet to do anything of importance."

"I disagree with that statement entirely." King Eamon chimed in, his voice stern as if scolding her for childish manners.

Isaac sent a nod towards the king and then turned back towards Alayna. "There is much to discuss. Like, oh I don't know, my trip to the boundary line this morning."

The baiting worked and had several surprised glances flash his way. Alayna's brown eyes sparked. "You did what?"

"I went to the boundary line. And thank goodness I did, because Edward has been frantically awaiting us."

"He has?" Alayna's voice briefly softened.

"Yes. He gave me a letter and specific orders to share with you. So if the queen is willing, after dinner I wish to share it with the entire Council."

Alayna nodded. "Of course." Her voice quiet as her mind wandered to what her brother needed desperately to tell her. "We shall convene after dinner."

Elizabeth could not help the smile that spread over her face at finally, a step in the right direction. The smile was short lived, however, as she suddenly felt green. She stood abruptly, everyone watching her. "Excuse me a moment." She hurried out of the dining hall, grabbing the arm of her new attendant on her way out.

"What has gotten into her?" Alayna asked.

Clifton shrugged. "I do not know. She has been quite secretive today. I have a notion that my wife is feeling the beginnings of a bout of illness and refuses to tell me, as she knows I will worry."

Melody set her utensils aside. "Would you like me to check on her for you, Clifton?"

He nodded. "Yes, thank you, Melody. Perhaps she will allow someone else to aid her."

"If you didn't hover so much, maybe she would let you tend to her." Isaac teased.

Clifton smirked. "Your time will come one day and you will be accused of obsessing over your wife's well-being as well."

Isaac shook his head. "Nonsense." Though he grinned as he took a sip of his wine.

Melody knocked on Elizabeth's chamber door and her attendant answered. She waved Melody inside and her gaze found Elizabeth sprawled on the bed lying on her back.

"Elizabeth?"

Elizabeth glanced up with a weary smile. "Hello Melody."

"Are you feeling okay? You had us worried."

"I am fine. Just a bit of a stomach bug, I think. It will pass."

"Clifton is worried it is more serious." Melody explained as she eased onto the side of the bed.

Elizabeth grinned. "He always worries about me. I cannot but sneeze and he fears my other leg will fly off."

Melody giggled and Elizabeth crossed her eyes in jest.

Sighing, Melody lay on her back as well and both women stared up at the canopy draping over the bed. "But it must be nice to have a man worry about you so."

Elizabeth turned her head to face her friend and offered an encouraging smile. "It is, and you will know one day soon."

Melody turned to her and her smile faded. "I hope so."

"Hope is the best thing to do, Melody. Hope leads to faith. And having both hope and faith allows some pretty incredible things to happen."

"You make it sound so easy."

"It's not." Elizabeth added. "Trust me. But I have seen the results of hope in my own life, not just with Clifton, but with other events and people as well, and it never disappoints."

Melody smiled. "You are right. Thank you, Elizabeth."

"Of course." She squeezed Melody's hand and the Western Princess arose.

"We should probably head to the Council Room, if you are up for it."

Elizabeth sat up quickly and scooted herself off the bed. "Oh, I am more than ready for this meeting." Her smile widened as she lightly placed a hand to her stomach at the sudden movement. "I'm a bit queasy, but I would never miss a Council meeting."

Samuel passed by as the women entered the hall and he paused.

"Ah, King Samuel." Elizabeth bowed extravagantly and grinned as the young king flushed. "We were just headed to the Council meeting. Are you headed there as well?"

"I am, yes." He flashed a smile towards Melody and a hint of pink stained the Western Princess' cheeks.

"Perfect." Elizabeth linked her arm through his. "Melody, grab his other arm, we have an official escort of the highest caliber."

Melody slipped her arm in Samuel's and shyly smiled at him as he stood in surprise. Elizabeth looked up at him. "Well, are you not going to escort the two prettiest princesses in the Realm to the Council meeting?"

He caught the light of teasing in her eyes and smiled. "Of course. I shall be the envy of all as I enter with the both of you."

Elizabeth laughed as they walked down the hall and turned onto the main landing towards the large double doors that housed the Council Room and her sister's ill temper. "Deep breaths everyone." She stated, "For the next battle has just begun."

Alayna glanced up as Elizabeth entered with Samuel and Melody and watched as her sister accepted the quick kiss on the lips from Clifton before sitting in her seat. Clifton followed suit and sat next to his wife, tenderly swiping a hand down the back of her onyx hair before glancing across the table to Isaac for him to begin discussion.

"Now that we are all here, well, what there is left of us," Alayna began, "Prince Isaac, please tell us your news."

Isaac nodded and pulled Edward's letter from his trouser pocket. "Edward was at the boundary line this morning. He sent over a letter with pertinent information in regards to the person who betrayed the Realm. It was Cecilia."

Elizabeth gasped. "Cecilia? But why?"

Isaac motioned towards the letter. "According to Edward she is one of many who do not wish for the boundary line to fall. However, it does not seem like she betrayed Edward's allegiance to us. She just wished to maintain the boundary line and the life contained therein."

"I do not understand why anyone would wish to remain in such a place." Samuel stated.

"She may have had a difficult life here in the Realm," Melody added. "Perhaps she fears losing a life she loves and having to go back to what she was before she crossed."

"Good point." Elizabeth chimed in. "Still. Her betrayal is a tough pill to swallow. I cannot imagine Edward's heartbreak."

"His heartbreak is not the point of the message," Isaac continued and looked at Alayna. "Lancer wishes to meet with you at the boundary line tomorrow."

Alayna's brows slowly rose. "Whatever for?"

"He did not say. I do not think he knows, to be honest. He just stated that Lancer wished to speak to you and show you something."

"He intends to gloat, I'm sure." Alayna scoffed and crossed her arms. "I do not wish to go."

"You must." Elizabeth pleaded. "We must know what Lancer's feelings are right now. You, yourself, have wanted to launch an attack upon him thinking he was in recovery from the battles. This is your chance to see if he seems worried or confident."

"She has a point." Clifton tilted his head towards Alayna. "I will go with you, so will Isaac and my father."

Isaac nodded his thanks for being included.

"I want to go too." Elizabeth stated and had all men shaking their heads. Her shoulders slightly slumped in disappointment but she did not challenge their statement.

"Fine, I will go." Alayna uncrossed her arms and waved her hand. "Is there anything else we should discuss?"

King Eamon cleared his throat. "Elizabeth and I intend to travel to the Western Kingdom to check on King Anthony and the current conditions of the kingdom."

"So I heard." Alayna looked at her sister before turning her attention back to King Eamon. "When did you intend to leave?"

"We were hoping at week's end." He stated. "It will be a good day's ride to reach the kingdom, and should we intercept any hostility from Abner's people, I have guards from the East accompanying us."

Isaac sat up in his chair. "You are leaving to find my father?"

Elizabeth nodded with a smile. "It must be done. His silence is disconcerting, and we must find out what has happened in the West."

"Thank you." Melody chimed in and had King Eamon nodding towards her.

"I must share some information in regards to the Western Kingdom with you before you leave." Isaac explained to Eamon and Elizabeth.

"Why don't you explain it to the entire Council?" Alayna asked. "That is why we gather."

Isaac cast a cautious glance towards Melody and his sister nodded solemnly.

"Alright," Isaac began. "It's in regards to my mother, the Queen."

Intrigued, Elizabeth leaned forward and everyone held his or her breath in anticipation. No one ever mentioned the Queen of the West, Queen Isabella.

"You should know my mother is not well." Isaac stated.

"Should we send for a healer?" Elizabeth asked.

He shook his head. "No. A healer can do nothing to help her. Her ailment resides in her mind. Her memory is clouded and some days she may remember everything about you, and others she may not even know your face. Most days she acts as if she is a brand new bride just getting acquainted with my father and the kingdom. She cannot decipher the passing of time. We have guarded her condition because we feared should people find out, that people may think our family unfit to rule. Up until now, my father has kept close watch over her and her interactions within the castle. She does not leave the castle and few enter inside the castle walls. It is best that way. My fear, is that if my father has not returned to the castle since King Samuel's coronation... if he never made it back... my mother may be an issue."

"I am sure we can handle her with tenderness and care, Isaac. You have my word." Elizabeth stated.

His smile was faint. "What I'm trying to say is, should you arrive and my mother has begun to rule and make decisions, you must have her detained within her bed chamber. She rarely leaves her chambers, but should my father not be there to see her looked after, she begins to roam. And when she roams the castle, she may take liberties she does not need to. I fear my mother will realize she is still the queen and begin making unwise decisions in place of my father. We cannot trust her mind."

"I am sorry to hear of Isabella's condition." King Eamon lightly patted Isaac's shoulder. "Your father had spoken of her to Granton and me in the past, but we had no idea her mind had been lost to such a degree. We will handle her with diligent care, Isaac. You have my word."

Isaac caught Elizabeth's sympathetic gaze from across the table. "Thank you."

Alayna sat with an intrigued face and rolled her shoulders back. "Well, it sounds as if the journey to the West is happening, and though I wish for us to be in battle by then, I understand the need to check on the queen and the kingdom. I suppose battle plans can be postponed until we all reconvene again."

Elizabeth looked to her sister with gratitude.

"Now, once we have a status update from the West and I have spoken with Lancer tomorrow, perhaps we will have a better idea of what lies before us. Perhaps by the time you two return from the West, Captain Ryle will have returned as well. We will then be able to address the topic of war. If that is all, I believe we should all call it a night and get some rest." Alayna stood and exited the room, everyone quietly following and splitting off in different directions.

The morning air was cool, the dew still held fast to the grass and the air was still, a heavy dampness that permeated the clothes and chilled the skin. However, to Ryle, the morning had never been more beautiful. It had been days since he had been outside and smelled the fresh air. He promised himself he would never take it for granted again. He stumbled as his bound hands pulled in front him. Edward turned around to check on him as the rope pulled tight behind his horse. Ryle continued to be led, trying not to distract himself by his surroundings so as not to trip and fall. He was a prisoner being pulled behind Edward's horse on parade. As they made their way towards the clearing, several people cheered as Lancer and Edward journeyed through the castle gates and streets. Ryle felt several blows to the back as he passed through the markets, unsure of what items had been tossed his way, but knowing none of them were good.

As they neared the edge of the forest, all sounds of the people faded and quiet beckoned them further until the familiar clearing appeared before them. Edward stopped his horse on the edge of the tree line, Ryle unable to see through the foliage and make out who awaited them on the other side. He knew Alayna would be there, Edward had explained that much. He wondered if his brother would be as well. What he wouldn't give to talk with his brother again. He did not realize how much he valued his family and friends until he no longer saw them.

Edward dismounted his horse and turned to him. "I imagine it will not be long and you will get to see Alayna. Lancer wishes to wait and see how the discussion goes before allowing her to see you."

"I am not much to look at." Ryle looked down at his bloodied and bound hands, his shredded tunic, and dirty skin. "I fear the queen may be more disappointed than Lancer believes."

Edward's lips tilted into a smirk. "Trust me, the dirtier and bloodier you are, Lancer will find that better."

"Joy." Ryle grumbled as Edward patted him on the shoulder and stepped through the tree line and disappeared. With nothing else to do, Ryle sat upon a broken log and waited patiently soaking in his time outdoors for as long as it lasted.

"All hands ready." Isaac stated as Lancer and Edward appeared through the trees and emerged in the clearing. Lancer spread his arms wide and smiled as if greeting them to his presence. He bowed with gusto at Alayna and motioned to Edward.

"Bow, Edward." He ordered and smiled broadly as Edward bowed towards his sister. She acknowledged them both with a hard stare.

"Do not stand too close to the boundary line, Alayna." Clifton warned and placed a hand on her forearm to restrain her from stepping closer.

She shrugged his hand away and lifted her chin. She held her hands out to her sides. "Well?" Though she knew her voice did not carry through the fog, she knew Lancer could interpret her message.

Lancer turned towards Edward. "Do you have the first letter we prepared?"

Edward nodded and handed it to Lancer. "Now how do you get it to cross the line?"

"We normally use a rabbit, however, now that objects can pass through the line, we could easily tie it to a rock." Edward reached for the letter and tied a small rope around a medium rock and tossed it gently across the line.

Isaac bent to pick it up, his side pinching and he pulled back quickly, the rock remaining on the ground. "Yep, yep, yep, yep." He grimaced and tried to walk off the pain. "That is all you, Clifton." He placed his hand on his side and walked to clear away the pain that drifted over him.

Clifton bent over and picked up the rock, untying the letter and handing it straight to Alayna.

She began to read aloud.

Queen Alayna,

I am pleased to see you made it through the last battles unscathed. I am surprised your realm survived the threat of Abner. I hope you can now see why I created The Land of Unfading Beauty. It was because of that man. He destroyed my kingdom. My family. I am sorry for annihilating your troops that you deviously sent into my Lands to try and overcome me. You see I will never be overthrown again. It did not sit well with me last time. And now that I have the power to protect my kingdom, I will not let it happen again.

I imagine you are tormenting yourself trying to think of ways to combat with me and retaliate. Don't bother. You cannot defeat me. I have a power on my side that no man can match. Not even through secrecy. Your plans of a surprise attack were thwarted by your very own brother's significant other, Cecilia, my loyal resident here in the Lands. She is not the only one who wishes to keep the boundary line in place. There is much resistance to your plan. Should you attempt to overtake my kingdom again, I will kill you all.

And most importantly, I will start with him.

Alayna glanced up as Lancer waved Edward to disappear into the trees to grab Ryle. As he pulled the rope through the trees,

Clifton darted forward as Ryle appeared, blinking against the brightness of the sun as he emerged from the shadows.

Alayna gasped and tightly snagged Clifton's arm before he ran across the boundary line.

"We must save him." Clifton fought back his emotions as his gaze carried over to his father, King Eamon, lingering behind as he studied his former brother-in-law and hated the pleasure he saw in Lancer's face.

Lancer saluted towards Eamon and laughed as he pointed to Edward and nodded. Edward unsheathed his sword. Ignoring the silent implore from Ryle's eyes, he drove his blade through the prince's side and watched as he crumbled to the forest floor.

Alayna covered her distress and stepped forward, her toes humming from the boundary's electricity.

Lancer stepped forward as well. Toe to toe. The fog the only separation between the two and he smiled. She studied his face closely.

"He is a handsome man, is he not?"

"He what?" Isaac asked in horror. "You're staring into the face of a killer and all you can say is that he is handsome?"

She smirked in return. "It is odd seeing him so up close. He is not nearly as scary as I imagined."

Her eyes softened as she continued to peruse his face and she noticed a change in Lancer's demeanor as well as he watched her. He became less confident, fidgety, as if her close study unnerved him and he did not know how to handle the attention. She lifted her hand and lightly fanned the fog in front of her, but not crossing through and Lancer watched.

"It's odd that this energy is the only invisible foe separating us from them."

"Invisible foe, indeed." King Eamon chimed in and stepped towards her. "There is a bigger and darker threat beneath the surface. His eyes seem kind, but remember what is hidden in his soul."

Alayna nodded in understanding and then glanced at Ryle. He lay upon his stomach, his eyes watchful, his blood spilling upon the green grass. Yet, his wound had begun to heal. She saw the pain, the determination, and the longing in his blue eyes, and she offered him a sympathetic smile. There was nothing she could do for him. Not from where she stood. She took a step closer and now stood halfway inside the fog. Clifton grabbed her elbow and pulled her back, the tug breaking her trance and causing her to fumble. Lancer grinned on the other side and shook his finger at her.

"Your sister seems tempted to cross, Edward." Lancer turned in amusement towards Edward and his smile turned into shock as he felt the sharp stab of a blade pierce his stomach. He turned back towards the line and saw Alayna's bold glare as she pulled back Clifton's sword and dropped it to the ground. Lancer placed a hand over his wound and stumbled backwards, Edward catching him as he fell to the ground. The wound had already begun to heal, but Edward could see the sheer terror in Lancer's eyes.

"You will be fine, my Lord." Edward gripped Lancer's hand as the man heaved for more air. As he bled, Edward's gaze narrowed in on the blackness that seeped from Lancer's side and began to creep along the ground.

"You must claim it Edward. You must claim it before it is lost." Lancer strained as he panted.

Edward quickly sliced his hand and closed his eyes. Instead of calling the darkness into himself, he placed his open wound over Lancer's and summoned all his strength into the healing. Blood to blood. The darkness crawled around them, the eyes of everyone across the boundary line widened in fear as they watched the events unfold.

Ryle spotted Isaac creeping towards the boundary line and waving him over. The Western Prince attempting to draw him back into the Realm. Ryle slowly pulled himself to his knees, the effort consuming all his strength as he moved slowly across the ground in a crawl. His hand brushed the fog, but he could not pull away from the Lands. He was tied to a tree and out of reach of any blade or rescue. He shook his head at Isaac and caught Alayna's desperate gaze. He tried to smile, and mustered a slight grimace in her direction. Her distraction with Lancer was to retrieve Ryle, and he could not escape. His father held his hands clasped in front of his face as he silently willed his son to cross the boundary, but Ryle could not. He shook his head and Eamon's head dropped.

Edward stood as Lancer's breathing became even, his body weak, but healed. Edward had escaped the temptation and the need to absorb the darkness by summoning it back into Lancer. He had not known if the action was possible, but he did it. Alayna's brown eyes studied him as he rose to his feet and helped Lancer to his. Lancer brushed a hand over his stomach and smiled in relief. Though pale, Lancer stood strong and healthy, his eyes blazing with fury as he turned towards Alayna. She took a retreating step back as he walked slowly towards the boundary line.

"You wish to send another letter across?" Edward asked, reaching into his trouser pocket.

"No." Lancer held up his hand to stop Edward. "We will leave. I think our statement has been made. We are unstoppable and invincible. And she just killed her prince. Retrieve him. We leave now."

Lancer turned and walked back through the forest as Edward reached for Ryle's rope and untied him from the tree. He saw in the prince's eyes that he was contemplating an escape and he just shook his head. "Not now, Prince Ryle. Save your strength. I promise I will not let him kill you."

Ryle shook his head in disbelief. "After what I just saw, I am not sure I trust you."

Edward tugged on the rope to encourage Ryle to start walking. "You should," Edward continued. "That darkness would have found the next available target, and that would have been you. I stopped it for both our sakes."

Ryle glanced towards his family and friends one more time before disappearing through the trees.

Alayna leapt forward. "Fight!" She yelled. "Why is he not fighting?!" She ran along the boundary line towards the spot Ryle disappeared and felt the tears begin to stream down her cheeks. "What is he doing? Why is he letting them take him?"

"He does not have the strength, Alayna." Isaac offered softly.

"But they will kill him." She turned towards Clifton, her eyes silently pleading for him to do something and he just shook his head. "We must wait, Alayna. I am sorry. But we cannot rescue him now. Edward will look after him."

"No he won't!" She screamed. "Did you see what my brother did? He saved him! He saved Lancer! Why would he do that?"

"I do not know, but we cannot dismiss his loyalty just yet. Edward will inform us of Lancer's plans. We just have to wait." King Eamon stepped forward and pulled Alayna into a hug that for once she did not attempt to escape. Instead, she felt the sobs shake her shoulders and she enjoyed the feel of a father to comfort her. Ryle was a prisoner, and it was her fault.

Chapter 5

Elizabeth sat on the parapet, her eyes focused on the edge of the horizon for sight of Alayna and the others. She longed to hear what news Edward had to share and how the encounter with Lancer unfolded. A throat cleared behind her and she turned, careful to balance herself on the ledge.

"Oh, hello Samuel."

"I am sorry to intrude on your quiet time, Princess Elizabeth, but I found myself wandering the halls with nothing to do."

Elizabeth smiled and patted the spot beside her and Samuel hopped up on the ledge to join her, swinging his legs over the side to dangle along the parapet.

"I feel as if I should be contributing somehow, but I'm not sure how."

Elizabeth nodded in agreement. "I understand the feeling. I've been struggling as well. We just have to learn that sometimes our role is to be here. Sometimes we are the anchors instead of the sails."

Samuel rubbed his chin in thought and shrugged. "I'm not sure I quite like being an anchor."

Elizabeth giggled. "I'm surprised at you Samuel."

"Why is that?"

"You seem to have blossomed into a king overnight. You wish to be proactive in the protection of the Realm instead of on the sidelines."

"Indeed. I received a letter from Mosiah just this morning. The Southern Kingdom is doing fine in my absence though we have suffered more casualties and loss. I am here to serve and to aid the Realm and yet I'm sitting on a parapet." His words trailed off in disappointment at the end and Elizabeth reached over and squeezed his hand.

"I'm glad you are just sitting on a parapet. You bring me company when I need it." Sighing, she closed her eyes as the wind lifted the wisps of black hair that escaped her braid.

"Are you still feeling ill?" Samuel asked curiously.

"A bit, but not as bad. Not ill enough to prevent me from my journey to the West."

His scrutiny made her laugh. "Trust me. I learned my lesson the first time. If I do not feel up for a journey, I will not take it."

Samuel's lips twitched into a smile. "Was my concern that obvious?"

"I know you are Clifton's eyes when he is absent. Don't think I am not aware of you two scheming behind my back."

Samuel feigned innocence and Elizabeth laughed even harder. "You are my guard detail, are you not? Clifton probably asked you to keep an eye on me while he was gone."

"He did." Samuel confirmed. "Though I am not sure it was about your health or the fear he thought you would follow them."

Elizabeth tilted her head at his statement and nodded. "Yes, I could see how he would worry about that. I was tempted, to be sure. But I also knew this was not my encounter. Mine will come. This was for Alayna."

Samuel straightened as he watched four horses and riders appear in the distance. "They are almost back."

Elizabeth followed his gaze and smiled at the sight of Clifton riding confidently next to his father. "They seem all in one piece."

Samuel swung his legs around and stood. "Shall we go meet them at the entrance?" He extended a hand to Elizabeth and she accepted the help to gain her footing, her peg leg still slightly unstable on the outer landing stones. "Thank you."

They began walking at a leisurely pace through the castle doors and into the main hall. Melody reached the top of the stairwell. "Have they returned?" She called down, her sweet voice echoing against the walls.

"Yes." Elizabeth called up to her. "We are meeting them on the steps."

"I'll be right down." Melody's blonde head disappeared as she ducked back towards her chambers to gather herself. Elizabeth watched as Samuel's gaze lingered on the spot Melody just vacated. "Have you told her yet?"

Samuel looked down at Elizabeth. "Told her what?"

"That you have feelings for her."

The young king's face flushed and he stuck a finger in his collar and tugged as he fought his embarrassment. "You do not have to be embarrassed, Samuel. We all think it would be a great match." Elizabeth explained.

"I am too young at the moment."

"At the moment." Elizabeth agreed. "But you won't always be."

"Yes, but I am King of the South and she is a princess from the Western Kingdom."

"And? What does that have to do with anything?" Elizabeth asked.

"I am not sure King Anthony would appreciate his daughter aligning with the South. We do not exactly have the best reputation in the Realm."

"That is over." Elizabeth's voice hardened. "You have proved yourself loyal to the Realm time and again, Samuel. You are not your father and brother, and we see that. Besides, King Anthony presided over your coronation. I do not think he would have accepted that responsibility if he did not wish to make the South a strong kingdom again."

"I do not know." Samuel's self-doubt shadowed his face and Elizabeth nudged him with her shoulder.

"You do not give yourself near enough credit, Samuel. Not even close to enough. We all see the way you look at her." Elizabeth held up her hand. "I am not saying that to embarrass you, I'm just pointing out the fact we see you have eyes for Melody. We also see her look at you the same way."

He turned to her in surprise and Elizabeth rolled her eyes and smiled. "Surely you are not that blind?" At his vacant stare she continued. "Or maybe you are… clearly I have sprung some news on you. I apologize for speaking so frankly, but I do not wish to see you undermine your importance to this Realm or the fact any princess would be blessed to have a husband like you."

"Husband?" His voice croaked and she chuckled.

"Again… in the future. I see I have officially terrified you. We will let the matter drop for now, but should you need someone to talk to, please know that Clifton and I are all ears."

They rounded the corner and the castle doors opened and Alayna rushed inside, followed by Isaac, Clifton, and King Eamon. Her gaze found Elizabeth and Samuel and she rushed towards Elizabeth and swallowed her in a huge embrace. Elizabeth's eyes widened and she glanced over her sister's shoulders to see Clifton's weary gaze as well.

"Ryle?" Elizabeth asked. She felt her sister nod between sobs. "Is he... dead?"

"Not yet." Alayna sniffled and pulled away, accepting the white handkerchief Samuel offered and wiped her eyes. "But I am sure it will happen. I made the worst mistake." Elizabeth rubbed her sister's arms as Alayna pulled away and blubbered over her words, her face strained and full of terror.

Elizabeth looked to Clifton and noticed her husband's tight jaw and his green eyes full of grief. Elizabeth looked back to her sister and pulled her into another hug. "He will be okay, Alayna. You mustn't lose hope. She rubbed a hand over her sister's back. "Let's go to your chamber and we will send Jessa for some hot tea." She began leading Alayna away from the doorway and sent a firm nod to Clifton that she would see him in a few minutes. Guiding Alayna into her room, Elizabeth sat with her on a sofa and watched as Jessa replenished the fire and set out tea.

"Now, tell me what happened today." Elizabeth clasped Alayna's hand and waited as her sister dabbed her swollen eyes and inhaled a calming breath.

"It was awful." Alayna began. "Ryle looked..." she shook her head as if the image in her mind was too much to bear. "Edward stabbed him in front of us and he just collapsed. His clothes were torn to pieces, wounds were still healing from what I can only imagine was hours of torture. He was dirty and bleeding. Oh Elizabeth, they are torturing him to death."

Elizabeth's blue eyes flashed sympathy as Alayna continued. "And we couldn't save him. Isaac tried to usher him across the line while I distracted Lancer, but Edward had tied him to a tree. He was so close, yet we could not save him. And it is my fault."

"How is his capture your fault?" Elizabeth lightly brushed her sister's hair from her face as Alayna wiped tears from her eyes. "I-I stabbed Lancer and h-he will surely take revenge by k-killing Ryle."

Elizabeth's eyes widened. "You stabbed Lancer? Alayna!" She grabbed her sister's shoulders and shook her. "That is amazing!"

Alayna looked at Elizabeth with selfish disgust. "No it is not, because I inadvertently put Ryle's life at risk."

"Tell me everything. What happened when you stabbed Lancer?" Elizabeth patted Alayna's hand. "Alayna, this is important. What happened?"

Alayna cleared her throat and sniffled to gather her composure. "He fell. Edward caught him as he fell. And this black mist began pouring out of him onto the ground. Edward helped put it back into him. That was it. He healed."

"It poured out of him? From his wound?"

"Yes."

Elizabeth's brow furrowed as she considered her sister's words. "So as Lancer was injured and weakening, the darkness fled from him."

Alayna rolled her eyes. "Yes, Lizzy, that is what I said."

Elizabeth clapped her hands together. "This is good news."

"What is?"

"The fact that Lancer can be killed. The darkness is a coward. As soon as its vessel is injured it is already looking for an escape. This also means that Lancer can be saved. Think about it, Alayna. If we were to seriously injure Lancer and the darkness seeps out of him and then we heal him, without Edward forcing the darkness back into Lancer, then Lancer will be saved from the darkness."

"You make it sound so easy."

"I've been hearing that a lot lately." Elizabeth grinned. "And it sounds easy, because it is. Well, the concept of it is. Father said that the real enemy is the darkness, not Lancer. And that if we ever came across a way to save him, we must. This is it. You figured it out." Elizabeth smiled and rubbed her sister's shoulders.

"I hate to tell you, sister, but the last thing on my mind after seeing Ryle is saving Lancer. What he has done to the Realm, to people, and to Ryle... I do not think he deserves to live." Alayna stiffened as she rose to walk towards her vanity table, Elizabeth boring holes into her back.

"That is not for you to decide."

"I am the Queen. It is my decision."

"You're the Queen, yes. But you make decisions for the good of the kingdom and the Realm. You do not choose which people live and which people die. That is certainly not your role."

"It is now." Alayna's eyes glimmered with restrained anger as Elizabeth stood and made her way to her door feeling defeated. "Well I am glad you made it back safely, sister. And I am glad you have discovered a new attribute of the darkness. Get some rest. I will see you later." As she shut the door, she leaned against the smooth wood and took a deep breath. Alayna had a success today, she should be happy. Instead, she worried about Alayna's obsession with killing Lancer and ignoring the fact that not only could they save the Lands, but he too could be saved. Lifting her skirts and turning towards her own chambers, she decided to seek out her husband and offer comfort to him next. No doubt, Clifton struggled seeing his brother in such a condition.

"He forced the darkness back into him, you said?" Samuel asked.

Isaac nodded stoically. "Yes, he stood right over him and it was as if he summoned the darkness back inside Lancer."

"That must take great power." Samuel stated with concern as he studied Isaac's thoughtful demeanor.

"That is my thinking as well. What if our focus has been on the wrong person?"

"What do you mean?"

"Well, we have all been so worried about Lancer and his power, but Lancer was taken down with a single sword wound. Edward was the one with the real strength today. It was effortless for him to wield such power. What if he is now stronger than Lancer?"

"It is a possibility. But you said he also seemed pleased to see all of you."

"And I'm sure he was. However, the struggle within him is still there. All I'm saying is, that kind of power takes great strength. Edward has struggled with the darkness from the beginning. How much more can he handle if he has to perform such tasks again? And would he want to give up the darkness after wielding such power? It is a great temptation that I think many a man would have a hard time relinquishing."

"Do we even give him the choice?" Samuel asked.

"It is always a choice. It was his choice to succumb to the darkness, it must be his choice to give it up." Isaac stated. "The darkness will not want to leave a willing vessel."

Samuel sighed as he leaned back against the chair in the conservatory. "I pray he is wise."

"Me too."

"And what of Captain Ryle? Did he seem... different?"

Isaac shrugged. "Not really. He seemed tired, injured, and frustrated. But he did not seem as if he had inwardly changed. It was great relief in his eyes when he saw us. I feel terrible I could not reach him. His body-" Isaac trailed off. "I don't know how much more it can take."

Samuel swallowed the news of the Captain down with his emotions and tried not to dwell on the sad status of his friend. He needed to think like a king. "We must save him then."

"I believe that is the plan, eventually." Isaac glumly placed his chin in his hand as he sat, his mind turning circles over the idea.

"The question is how." Samuel added. "I will think on it. Perhaps the way to rescue Prince Ryle is the attack Queen Alayna needs to convince the Council to go to war again. Maybe if we focus on a small task first then we will be able to accomplish our larger goal of defeating the Lands."

"Small task?" Isaac's voice held doubt.

"I did not say easy." Samuel emphasized. "I said small as in our main objective only being one thing. To rescue Ryle. We worry about defeating the Lands on another day. But the rescue of Ryle will give us insight into the layout of Lancer's personal space that we can use later on."

Impressed by the young king, Isaac leaned back in his seat and flinched as pain shot up his side. He shifted to find comfort and crossed his arms over his chest. "Okay, I'll play along. So how do we rescue our dearest Captain?"

Samuel smirked and rubbed his hands together as if he had patiently been waiting for someone to ask. "I have given the matter great thought."

Isaac waved his hand to continue.

"Me."

"What?" Isaac asked, his brows rising in surprise.

"Me." Samuel grinned. "The last person anyone would expect to come into the Lands is me. I would blend in well with all the Southern guards that remain there. I could slip in almost unnoticed. I could team up with Edward to sneak me into the castle. I could free Ryle, and then we would be back before the sun rose."

"You think it would be that easy?"

"No. I am just hoping there will not be any unnecessary risks involved. It should happen quick and smooth. The less people know about it, the better."

"You are forgetting one thing," Isaac pointed out. "You will be stuck in the Lands."

"There is that." Samuel added. "But then I would be there to rally my guards for the sake of the Realm when the real battle should begin. I will serve a purpose on both fronts."

"You would willingly cross into the Lands and be stranded there should things not go according to plan."

"Yes." Samuel stated without hesitation.

"You realize every female in this castle would fight this plan, correct?"

Samuel flushed. "I do. I know everyone still sees me as too young to contribute much, but I can do this, Prince Isaac. I know I can."

"You have contributed much, Samuel. For the record, the Northern Kingdom would have been lost if it had not been for you and your army in the previous battle. Do not undermine your worth. My concern is that the Southern Kingdom would be losing their king."

"I would not be lost. You would come and save me along with the rest of the Lands in the following battle. Mosiah can lead my troops from the South, they are familiar with him."

"I am glad you have confidence in my abilities of a heroic rescue." Baffled, Isaac chuckled.

"I do. I am not kidding around when I say these things, Isaac."

The lack of formality in the young king's tone told Isaac Samuel was indeed not kidding and his dark eyes held a solemn determination. "I have seen you save Elizabeth and you have saved Clifton twice. And by killing Abner, you saved us all. I know you will save me."

Isaac reached over and nudged Samuel's shoulder in brotherly affection. "Thank you for that confidence. But if you were to cross and stay in the Lands I would have no choice but to save you. Otherwise my sister may never speak to me again."

Samuel's reddening cheeks had Isaac laughing as he rose to his feet. "I like your line of thinking, Samuel. Perhaps we run your idea by Clifton and see what his thoughts are on the matter."

"Thank you, Isaac."

"Of course. It's a crafty idea. I'm surprised I didn't think of it myself." He winked as he slapped Samuel on the shoulder on his way out of the room.

Elizabeth looked up as Katarina made her way through the gardens to where she sat on a stone bench in front of Mary's grave. She did not wish to be disturbed, but the princess looked as if she had much on her mind. She smiled warmly and Katarina did not return it.

"Hello, Katarina."

"Elizabeth." She greeted as she sat with a heavy sigh.

"You seem rather distraught today, Katarina. What is the matter?"

Katarina studied Mary's grave and then faced Elizabeth. "You really miss her, don't you?"

Elizabeth nodded. "She was my best friend."

"She was your servant." Katarina's voice held a sharpness that had Elizabeth slightly taken aback.

"It never seemed like it."

"To you maybe, but I am sure it felt that way to Mary."

Elizabeth stiffened at the tone Katarina's voice held and turned to her. "Do not speak for her. You did not know her. Now please tell me what brings you out here in such a state or dismiss yourself immediately."

Katarina's face fell. "I am sorry, Princess Elizabeth. I... I am just having a hard time dealing with the loss of my father."

"I can understand that."

"Can you? Your father was loved by everyone and mine was hated. How could you possibly understand?"

Elizabeth took a deep breath for patience and then offered as understanding a smile as she could muster. "It is still a loss, Katarina. Whether he was evil or not, he was your father. We are not so blind to the fact that you must have some good memories with him as well as the bad. It is difficult losing a father. I have yet to fully let mine go."

"Really?"

"Of course. Sometimes I feel as if I still hear him shuffling down the halls, his heavy robes dragging on the floor. It was always a comforting sound and I miss it." Elizabeth admitted. "But he is gone and I must learn to accept that. As should you with Abner."

"He was just," Katarina paused as if to formulate the right way to convey her heart. "I feel he was just taken from me so abruptly. I was not prepared for that. My father was invincible it seemed, and for Isaac to take his life in a moment just seems so... surreal."

"I know what you mean." Elizabeth waved her hand towards Mary's grave. "Watching Mary die will haunt me forever. But I also know she would want me to be happy and move past the pain."

"My father would not want me to move past his death. He was about revenge. He would wish for me to seek revenge." Katarina admitted.

"But is that your character?"

"I am not sure anymore. Before I would have said no, but now, I am left feeling confused and hurt. I understand Isaac felt he needed to kill my father, but to act upon it without consulting others still irritates me. I should have been given the chance to intervene for my father, and I was robbed of that."

"War does not leave room for much except victory and defeat. There is no time to decipher diplomatic ways to maneuver. It's kill or be killed, and if you hesitate or make one wrong move, you're killed. Isaac was protecting the Realm, himself, and I believe, you."

"If he would have spoken to me beforehand he would know I would never have wished my father dead."

"But would you wish Isaac dead? Because that is exactly what would have happened to him if he had not struck your father. Clifton would most likely be dead as well." Elizabeth added.

Katarina shrugged. "Like I said, I am struggling with making sense of it all. My heart is torn. I feel I should return to my realm and see the state of things, perhaps then I may feel more like myself."

"We will arrange it. King Eamon and I will be traveling to the Western Kingdom at week's end. You can journey with us there and we will send letter to your realm to meet us at the western border."

"I think I would like that."

"With your father gone, will the queen seek to rule or will the crown pass to you?"

"It will pass to me. The queen has no desire to rule and never has."

"So should we need you in the future for battles against the Unfading Lands, would you consider coming to our aide?"

Katarina bit her lower lip in consideration. "Yes, I suppose I will. You all have been good to me in my stay, and I see the threat the Lands pose to us all. Should it be necessary, you have a friend."

Elizabeth nodded. "Good. Then prepare to leave by week's end. Now if you will excuse me, I need to seek out my husband." With a small bow, Elizabeth hustled out of the gardens, her lavender skirts sashaying behind her as she headed to find Clifton.

Clifton flung his dagger at the straw target and grunted with the effort, the small blade piercing through the center of the bull's eye. He retrieved the weapon and walked back to the line he had carved in the grass and stood. Lining up his free arm with his target, he focused, his green eyes narrowing, and then he threw the blade with all his strength once more. This time the dagger passed straight through the bull's eye and landed a few feet behind the target.

"Nice one." Elizabeth complimented with an impressed smile as she walked down the sloping hill towards the small clearing next to the stables. "I wasn't sure I heard Tomas correctly when he said you were down here practicing. That seems more Isaac's activity. You must have come to think much like I was doing in the gardens."

Clifton bent and picked up his dagger. "That was the plan."

"Should I leave?" Elizabeth asked.

"No. I think I am almost finished for today. I just needed to clear my thoughts." He smiled as she walked towards him and placed her hand on the side of his face. "They still aren't clear, are they?"

Clifton smirked. "You read me too well, love."

She grinned. "I'm your wife. It's my job."

Chuckling, Clifton grabbed her hand and squeezed it before draping it through his elbow. Sighing he brought her to the foot of the hill amidst some flowers and the shade of a large tree and sat.

"I am worried about Ryle." He admitted, his voice low as she watched him swallow and attempt to remain under control of his emotions. "He did not look well."

She lightly brushed her fingers over his forehead, tucking away the rogue curl that seemed to escape whenever he worked up a sweat. "I know. Alayna told me. She is having a hard time as well."

He nodded grimly.

"What course of action are you planning now that you have seen him and have spoken with Edward?"

"I am not sure. It is not up to me, but the entire Council. It's just that seeing him today, like he was... he will not be able to withstand much longer."

"Well he cannot die just from being injured. He will continue to heal, even if it takes more time."

"Unless they kill him. Which could very well be a strong possibility after today."

Elizabeth turned his face towards hers. "You know what else happened today?"

"What is that, love?"

"You found out that Lancer could lose the darkness. As he grows weaker, the darkness flees from him. From what Alayna told me, Edward is the one to have placed the darkness back inside Lancer."

"He was. Which is another concern all in itself. That much power?" Clifton held out his hands as if wondering what such a thing would feel like. "I am concerned about Edward now as well. He possesses more darkness than we know."

"Perhaps you should continue trips to the boundary line so that Isaac may heal. And you can converse with Edward and study his condition. If he is not trustworthy, you are the best judge. We must learn now before we involve him in our future plans. Besides, there is Cecilia to consider."

Clifton shook his head. "The penalty for treason is death. But the thought of killing her does not sit well with me."

"Me either. But something tells me Cecilia is not our problem to handle."

"What do you mean?" Clifton asked curiously.

"Well, Lancer likes her now for being loyal, but what happens to her when Lancer finds out Edward is the true traitor to the Lands? I do not see him standing for her knowledge on the matter, even though she helped him in the past."

"You are right." Clifton replied. "One less person to worry about."

She squeezed his hand. "How do you feel about my trip to the Western Kingdom with your father?"

"I think it necessary, though I do not like the idea of you traveling."

"Why?" Elizabeth asked defensively. "I'm completely healed. I fought in a battle for goodness sake."

He laughed and pulled her towards him, claiming her lips in a swift but passionate kiss. "I only meant I did not want to be without you, love. You are more than capable of such a journey. I will miss you is all."

"Oh." Elizabeth flushed and kissed him sweetly on the lips as she maneuvered her peg leg in order to push herself off the ground. Standing, she extended a hand to her husband. Rising to his feet, Clifton pulled her in his arms and Elizabeth listened to the strong steady beat of his heart. "Promise me you will not approve a war while we are gone?" Her words muffled against his chest and he soothed a hand over her silky hair.

"You have my word."

"Good." Pulling away from him, she spotted Isaac at the top of the hill waving his arms for their attention. "Looks like we are being summoned."

Clifton turned and spotted Isaac, Samuel stepping up beside him. "Two of them. This should be good."

Elizabeth giggled as they made their way up the hill towards their friends, curious as to what the two princes conjured during their own meeting of minds.

Chapter 6

Edward waited, his fingers drumming upon his knees as he sat anxiously awaiting Cecilia in the Uniters' camp. She had ventured out with a group earlier in the day to gather supplies and had yet to return. He knew she would shortly, and his angst stemmed from the deep sorrow of betrayal. He clenched and unclenched his fists, his veins protruding from his skin as he tried to control the darkness that dared to try and seep out of his every pore. He could control it. Up until saving Lancer he had rarely used the darkness. Now knowing what he was capable of, Edward struggled balancing his thoughts and reactions. His body automatically wished to lash out while his mind attempted to convince him to maintain control. The darkness tempted him. Every day. Every hour. Slowly seeping into his mind and heart like curling fingers that brushed his very soul. The grip tightening and his control slipping. He heard a rustle in the trees and shook his thoughts away as Cecilia stepped into the clearing.

"Edward." She smiled in greeting and kissed his cheek. Uncertainty flashed across her face as she studied his tense posture and firm gaze. "Is something wrong?

"Please sit." He motioned to the log and sat beside her.

She reached for his hand and he moved it out of her path. "I have words for you Cecilia. And I am finding them quite hard to say, though I need to. And I need to know why you did it."

"Did what, Edward?"

"Why did you betray the Realm and inform Lancer of their plans of attack?"

She inhaled deeply and slightly raised her chin. She sensed his displeasure, but wished for him to know her true feelings. "I did not inform Lancer of your role, Edward. I simply told him the Realm was planning a surprise attack while he was distracted by Abner."

"Why?" Edward asked. "Why would you do such a thing?"

She bristled and stood, her small frame bowed up in a tight stance of defiance. "Because I wish to stay here."

His eyes widened, as he stood baffled. "I do not understand. We have talked about this. About us. About our life and what it could be in the Realm."

"No. You spoke of such things." She pointed out. "Not once did you ever ask if I wished for that life. Not once, Edward. If you had, then perhaps you would have known I wish for the Lands to remain."

"But why? There is nothing here."

"Nothing?" Cecilia's eyes sparkled as she laughed coyly. "Edward, here there is everything. We do not have to worry about aging, about losing those we love. We do not have the daily stresses of life that exist beyond the veil. Life is beautiful here."

"We lose the ones we love in the Realm." Edward corrected. "My family. Your mother. They will all perish and we will have to watch them slowly disappear."

"And life will go on." Cecilia added. "I have never regretted my decision to cross the boundary line. Not once. Lancer has provided me a life better than I could have hoped for in the Realm. I would never have met you in our old realm, Edward. We would never have crossed paths. And yet, here we are."

Edward ran a hand through his dark hair and sighed. "You have placed me in a dire position, Cecilia. I love you. I do. But I feel completely betrayed. And what is worse is that I have to torture one of my own every day. A good man. A noble man. A prince. Your choice has brought him under severe punishment."

"As it should." Cecilia countered.

Edward stood to his feet and his eyes flashed as he felt the darkness rushing through him. Cecilia must have noticed a change in him as well. She backed away a few steps. "Edward." Her voice was quiet, fearful. She reached to touch him and gasped as she pulled her hand away, his body hot to the touch. When he spoke, his voice was low and angry. "I do not tolerate betrayal, Cecilia. You could have cost me my family." He swung his arm out in frustration and a tree limb overhead snapped and fell to the ground. Her eyes widened.

Edward stepped towards her and she retreated another step, but he gripped her shoulders as he peered down at her. His blue eyes now black as night. "What is wrong with you, Edward?" She stammered.

"This," he paused, as he tilted his head back and forth to control the power and anger coursing through him. "This is the power that maintains the boundary. Do you like it now?" His smile was sardonic and left Cecilia terrified. He lifted her off of her feet and tossed her over his shoulder. She screamed and Edward lifted a fist in the air, and her voice silenced. She gripped her throat at the invisible vice that stole her sound. He carried her away from the clearing, away from her friends and the life they shared together. And before she knew what was happening, he tossed her into a dank cell, the sounds of chains and iron echoing in the dark. She tried to scream out, but her voice remained absent and she cupped her throat as tears streamed down her face. Edward was gone and with him, her voice.

"You sure you have everything you need?" Clifton asked, as he helped Elizabeth into the carrier, tucking her skirts around her. He climbed in after her and shut the door. She laughed. "You do realize you are not escorting me on this trip?"

He grinned. "Of course. I just wish to have a moment with my wife before she leaves for weeks on end."

"It should not be weeks, Clifton. I have high hopes we shall be back in a week."

"That may be, but I would still like my moment."

She waved her hand for him to continue and her smile grew as he snatched her hand and pulled her towards him and into his lap. He hugged her close and burrowed his face in her hair inhaling the faint scent of rose that was always Elizabeth. "Please be careful." He whispered. He pulled back and stared into her ice blue eyes.

She cupped his face and kissed him gently on the lips. "I will be. I will also have your father looking out for me. I am in good hands."

"I know."

Elizabeth could tell Clifton hesitated on allowing her to leave. Part of her did not wish to leave him as well, but she knew her quest was to find King Anthony. "Promise me you will not allow Alayna to do anything rash?"

He nodded. "I believe my task might be harder than yours'."

She laughed. "I imagine it will be. Though you will have Isaac's help. And Samuel's. Look out for Samuel. His idea to cross the boundary worries me. Though his intentions are noble and smart, I fear for him as well. I do not wish for him to be stranded in the Lands."

"Neither do I, but we are at a point where tough decisions need to be made and our actions must progress our purpose. His offer to infiltrate the Lands may be the catalyst to a future success. It is our best option for now."

"I agree." Elizabeth sighed. "But it does not mean I am still not worried about him. And Isaac is still healing. Please make sure he rests. And Melody-"

Clifton cut her off by placing his finger over her lips. "I will see to your ducklings, love." He winked at her and she flushed.

"I just-" She trailed off and tightly wound her hands in her lap. "I wish to take this journey, but I too, am finding it hard to leave everyone."

"I know, love." He kissed her temple and nudged for her to take her seat. When she comfortably sat, Clifton rose to exit. "I had better hear from you every few days or I will send a search party."

"I will write." She smoothed a hand over her skirts as he leaned forward and kissed her heartily.

A throat cleared as his father waited with a knowing smile at the now open door. "I believe you are in my seat, son."

Clifton pulled away from Elizabeth and lightly ran his fingertips over her cheek before stepping out of the carrier and allowing his father to step inside. "No worries, Cliff, I will take great care of your bride." He flashed a tender smile at his son as Clifton took a slow step back. Elizabeth leaned through the window and waved once more as the carriage began pulling away from the castle steps. Clifton felt the weight in his chest grow heavier as he watched his wife and father disappear out the castle gates, and he took a deep breath for composure. Elizabeth had not been feeling well, and yet he was watching her leave. He rubbed a hand over his face as he turned to walk back into the castle and caught Isaac standing on the top steps watching him. "Shouldn't you be resting?" Clifton asked, his voice sharp.

"I am. I am resting against the wall as I watch you pitifully say good bye to your wife." He smirked.

"Pitifully?" Clifton asked with slight offense. "If you mean struggling to watch her leave, yes. But pitifully, I would think not."

Isaac shrugged. "Perhaps I should have said hopelessly. You are a strong man, Cliff, but Elizabeth is the chink in your armor."

"As any great woman should be." Clifton added. Again, Isaac shrugged. "She risks much by travelling to the West. I have the right to worry."

"I did not say you didn't. Though I believe she will be fine. She is in good hands with your father. Besides, King Eamon knows that should anything befall your wife while she is in his care, you would possibly kill him. Family ties aside." Isaac grinned as Clifton ignored his comment and continued to storm through the castle, Isaac like a parrot on his shoulder.

"Do you not have somewhere to be?" Clifton asked.

"So you may mope in peace?" Isaac countered.

Clifton growled in frustration as he climbed the steps towards the Council Room. "I am following you, my friend." Isaac continued. "You look as if you are on a mission, and my curiosity seeks to know what it is."

"Curiosity could be the death of you." Clifton tossed over his shoulder.

"Wouldn't be the first time." Isaac added as he and Clifton entered into the Council Room to find Alayna talking with Samuel about his journey of crossing the boundary line. She looked up and her eyes flashed sympathy towards Clifton as if she knew he was missing her sister. Clifton held up a hand in greeting. "We are here to help plan."

"Are you sure you are up for it?" Alayna asked.

"Why wouldn't I be?" Clifton looked confused and then rolled his eyes. "My wife left on a journey. I am fine. I miss her, that is all. I am not so delicate a man that I cannot continue on my way in her absence."

"I'm not so sure." Isaac mumbled and accepted the punch in the shoulder on a laugh as he pulled up a seat next to Clifton.

Alayna smiled at her brother-in-law and then turned towards Samuel. "Well, I think Samuel and I have sought out a plan."

Both princes waved their hands for her to continue.

"We will send him across the boundary first thing tomorrow morning, but we will not be sharing that news with Edward until we for sure know the status of his allegiance. Samuel will seek to find that out first before pursuing Ryle. We will meet with Samuel daily in the clearing. Clifton, I am naming you for that position because you can cross freely should the need arise."

Clifton nodded in acknowledgement.

"And what of me?" Isaac asked.

"You are healing." Alayna finished.

"I am better."

"No, you are not." Alayna narrowed her gaze upon him and her look of disbelief had him forfeit. "Okay, so I am not completely healed, but I am well enough to play messenger."

"I intend for you to partner with Clifton, yes." She continued. "Together you two will oversee the guards and prepare them for Ryle's rescue as well as our battle against the Lands. You two are now the Captains of the Realm's armies. Mosiah will oversee the Southern Kingdom in King Samuel's stead."

"Fair enough." Isaac stated.

"Are you sure you wish to do this?" Clifton turned towards Samuel and asked. "Should things not turn out as we plan, we have no idea how long you could be stranded in the Unfading Lands."

"I am aware of the risk." Samuel affirmed with a quiet confidence. "I know that I can be of service no matter the length of time."

"Aye. Alright then." Clifton nodded that he understood Samuel's determination.

"Then preparations should be made, Samuel. Tomorrow you cross the veil. Tonight we will honor you at dinner." Alayna waved her hand in dismissal and the three men stood. Clifton and Samuel exited while Isaac stood to the side.

"Was there something you needed?" Alayna asked.

"I wish to speak to you about Katarina."

"She left today in a separate caravan along with Elizabeth and King Eamon." Alayna stated.

"I know." Isaac added.

"You did not see her off." Alayna pointed out curiously.

"I did not."

"Why?"

"I did not wish to." He added as if the matter were simple.

"I see." Alayna leaned back in her chair and watched him as he crossed his arms over his chest and stood firmly against the wall. "Then what is it you wish to discuss?"

"I wish for us to keep an eye on her and the conditions of Abner's Realm. Her last words to me were not… encouraging. I do not know if Abner's Realm will be forgiving of his death."

"They should be." Alayna mumbled.

"I agree, but Katarina was upset with me for my part in his death."

"I know. Elizabeth told me. Apparently she and Katarina had words as well."

"I did not realize that."

"Do not fret, Prince Isaac. I have sent eyes to keep watch over our 'friend.'"

"You mean a spy."

"Obviously." Alayna smirked. "I never trusted her. Why should I let my guard down now that she has departed? She is the daughter of an evil king. Perhaps she is of kind character, but I wish to make sure. I also intend for us to keep open relations with her should she be the next ruler. I want her to know that our realm is ever present. Our guard is never down."

"You think she would attack us?" Isaac pushed himself off the wall. "I realize Katarina was upset, but I know enough about her to know she does not have the backbone for such a feat."

"She may not." Alayna added. "But I do not wish to give her the slightest confidence in her strength."

"You wish to keep her scared of our realm?"

"I do."

Isaac smiled. "I do not believe I am going to say this, Alayna, but for once, I believe I agree with you and your plans."

"There is a first time for everything."

Nodding his approval of her sarcasm, Isaac bowed dramatically. "On that note, I will leave you to your wiles, my Queen." He ducked out of the room leaving Alayna smiling in her seat.

Lancer grinned as he and Edward stood in the Reflection Chamber and summoned the darkness. The lights faded to their normal hue as he inhaled deeply and sighed a contented sigh. "Now that was extraordinary." Lancer grinned happily. "I am so pleased at the power within you, Edward. You are only growing stronger and together we can accomplish much. Why, the Land of Unfading Beauty could possibly double in size. Before we know it, we will be our own realm." Pleased, Lancer slapped Edward on the back and waved towards the empty chair surrounded by dry blood. "How is our prisoner doing?"

"Weaker." Edward replied. "His wounds are taking longer to heal yet his inner determination is only growing stronger."

"Pity." Lancer added. "I had high hopes we could turn Eamon's son against him. Perhaps we chose the wrong one." He chuckled at that and then nodded towards the chair again. "Keep up the routine. I do not wish to cave into laziness of our task. Eventually they will send someone for him."

"I am not sure about that, my Lord. I believe Alayna will think him dead by now."

"Then we must inform her he is not." Lancer stated. "I wish to parade him as a prisoner. Wave him like a drenched rag in front of her face until she makes the unwise decision to attack again."

"I will do my best at breaking him, my Lord."

"Do that." Lancer agreed. "Now tell me this, how did you summon the darkness back into me? That was great power." Lancer's greedy eyes held a spark of intrigue and hunger at the answer.

"I do not know, my Lord. I just willed it and it happened. I am still new to this power. Perhaps you can enlighten me."

"I cannot." Lancer shrugged his shoulders. "I have had many great powers over the years, Edward. The ability to cross the boundary line, the ability to move objects with a wave of my wrist, the ability to transform objects. But never have I been able to summon the darkness into another target. It is always about free will. They have to choose to possess it."

"Perhaps since you already do possess the darkness is why I was able to direct it back to you." Edward pointed out. "And did you say transform objects?"

"I did. Why?"

Edward grinned. "Just curious as to how that works. I hadn't thought to try anything like that yet."

Lancer laughed. "It is quite fun. I had just mastered transforming faces when I was suddenly weakened."

"Faces?"

"Yes. Meaning I can turn a simple guard into anyone I wish. Do you wish to see Queen Alayna? A wave of the wrist and I can turn the guard outside the door into Alayna. In appearance only, of course. Everything else would remain the guard. But you would be surprised how handy that power is. I cannot be everywhere at once, therefore I would create duplicates of me for appearances sake."

"Fascinating." Edward rubbed his chin in thought.

"Indeed. Though sadly I must say I no longer have that ability. Until we understand why I am weakened, I cannot perform such a task. Should you master it, let me know. We could use the skill in our favor during the next battle."

"Yes, we could." Edward added. He felt his heart race at the prospect of using multiple decoys of himself and Lancer in the next battle. Though he knew the skill could also serve the Realm, the idea of helping the Realm in such a way did not hold the usual excitement. He shook away the thought and turned back towards Lancer. "Well, I will go retrieve our prisoner."

Lancer walked towards the door with him. "I will be in my chamber. Let me know if our Captain changes his mind about joining us."

Edward walked down the hall towards the prison cells and aimed to introduce Ryle to the new knowledge of his potential capabilities. Perhaps, knowing the amount of power he could potentially possess, Captain Ryle would find the darkness a bit more tempting.

Ryle jolted from a deep slumber as he heard an iron door slam closed and the sound of footsteps scurrying into the prison chamber. He blinked adjusting his eyes to the light provided by a small lantern hanging along the wall and noticed another form in the cell next to him. A woman. Edward standing over her. He prayed it was not a woman from his realm and cleared his throat. The woman's head jerked around and his gaze collided with Cecilia.

"Cecilia?" He asked in surprise. Edward turned to him and stalked towards his cell. Cecilia ran towards the bars and attempted to yell but no sound came from her mouth.

"Edward, what is this?" Ryle asked as Edward stormed towards him, his gaze dark and his fists clenched at his sides. "She is a traitor."

"Does Lancer know of this?" Ryle asked.

"No." Edward looked at Cecilia with contempt. "And he won't. He never comes down here."

Cecilia cried out Edward's name, tears streaking her face as she remained silent.

"Why can she not speak?" Ryle looked to Edward, the Northern Prince's jaw tightened. "Why can she not speak, Edward?" Ryle's voice held warning and Edward leaned in closely to his face. "Because I stole her voice." His blue eyes blackened as the words dripped from his mouth like poison. Ryle stepped closer to him and reached through the bars, grabbed the front of Edward's tunic and pulled him forcefully against the bars, the prince's cheek smashed against the iron bars. "Give her back her voice, Edward." Ryle's voice descended to a threatening octave and he retained his hold on

Edward until the prince's eyes transformed back to their normal blue. Edward reluctantly raised his hand and unfolded his fist one finger at a time and flicked his wrist in Cecilia's direction. Her struggled gasp proof her voice had been returned. "Now release me." Ryle eased his grip and Edward pulled away. "Do not forget what she has done, Ryle." With his words echoing in the chamber, Edward spun on his heel and left.

Cecilia studied him warily. "Prince Ryle."

Ryle, surprised that the Northern prince would go to such lengths to protect the Realm, scooted closer to the barred wall separating his cell from Cecilia's. "Yes."

Cecilia's chin rose and her eyes flashed with pride. "What are you doing here?"

"I was captured during the battle." Ryle stated, his appearance coming into the light. His condition, his body, his inability to move swiftly, shocked her.

"I do not wish for your realm to destroy the boundary line. I like it here." She answered. "I told Lancer of your plans."

He contemplated her answer as if he knew nothing about her betrayal.

"Is Edward responsible for your current condition as well?" Cecilia asked.

"He is." Ryle replied.

"I am surprised he is treating you so badly."

Ryle shrugged. "He has to in order for Lancer to continue thinking he is loyal to the Lands."

Cecilia leaned forward, her small hands gripping the rails in front of her. "But he tortures you?"

Ryle nodded. "Once, sometimes twice a day until I give into their offer."

"What offer?"

"To join them here in the Lands and become a part of their resistance towards the Realm. But I will not."

"Why not?" She asked.

"Because my home is not here. My home is in the Realm. I do not wish to live forever. That is unnatural. In order for my life to have a purpose, I have to actually have a life that is lived. Staying the same age, living for myself and my desires is not a life."

"You make us all sound so selfish."

"I believe it is."

"So you would rather die?"

"Yes. We are meant to die. That is part of life. You cannot have life without death. You cannot have light without the dark. It is a balance that is meant to be."

"I do not wish to die."

"That is you." Ryle simply pointed out.

"And you are willing to die? To leave the ones you love behind?"

"If it comes to that, yes."

"But they would be heartbroken." Cecilia added.

"And they would move on. It would take time. It would take grief. But they would move on."

"And that does not bother you?"

"Why should it? I only want what is best for them. That is part of the reason I'm in my current situation. The easy choice- the selfish choice would be to team up with Lancer so that I might live forever, but my life and my heart is on the other side. What quality of life would I have here if all I longed for was to be over there?"

"That is how I feel about the Lands. Edward does not understand."

"Because he still has people on the other side that he loves." Ryle explained.

"But he also loves me." She pleaded. "Or he did, I am not so sure now."

"Only time will tell."

Cecilia sat on her haunches as she surveyed Ryle and his appearance. "You are trapped in here because of me. Why are you being kind to me?"

Ryle shifted and hissed as a wound in his calf continued to heal from the stroke of a blade. "I am trapped in here because of my decision to cross into the Lands. My decision had nothing to do with you. It is my own fault."

"Do you think Edward will forgive me? Or do you think he is capable of torturing me like he has you?"

"I do not know." Ryle's honesty dispirited her shoulders. "Edward has a struggle all his own. The darkness and power that pulls at him is a dangerous temptation."

"I did not know he possessed the same darkness as Lancer until today. I saw it in his eyes." Cecilia explained. "He changed."

"He battles with it daily. He consumed the darkness in order to weaken Lancer so that the Realm may have a fighting chance at victory. Course, we all know how that played out... thanks to you." Ryle nodded towards her. "Now he is trapped in the Lands even longer, still having to possess pure evil, and he is to complete horrid tasks of torture every day. That would pull on any man's soul."

Cecilia nibbled on her thumbnail as she leaned against her cell wall. "What I just witnessed in his eyes was not the same Edward. I fear for him."

"As you should. Perhaps now you understand his desperation in bringing down the boundary line. Should we not succeed, Edward is lost."

Ryle let his words sink in and watched as Cecilia folded in on herself in reflection. He leaned his head back and closed his eyes again, his strength slowly returning, but not near fast enough for his taste. Cecilia. He admitted to himself that Edward's arrest of her surprised him. The fact she saw the darkness within him without him speaking of it was a bad sign. The Northern Prince was losing control over his ability to restrain it. Ryle could see it each time he lashed another sword through him. Edward's eyes would darken, his breathing labored, and he used increased force with each blow. If the boundary line did not fall, Ryle feared Edward could not be saved. If the boundary line did not fall, Ryle also feared Edward would not want to be saved as well. Tuning out Cecilia's soft whimpers, he faded into a deep sleep praying for relief.

Chapter 7

Samuel stood at the edge of the boundary line, the sparks of electricity flowed through him as he took a deep breath. He turned to Clifton next to him, the Eastern prince crossing with him to ensure he made it safely to the Uniter's camp. Isaac stood behind them; hand on the hilt of his sword, watchful.

"Ready?" Clifton asked.

Samuel nodded, though he swallowed passed the lump in his throat.

"Wait!" A voice called out from the tree line and had all men turning.

"Melody!" Isaac yelled, his sword pointed in her direction. "I could have stabbed you." He sheathed his sword and glowered at his sister. Melody rushed passed her brother towards Samuel and enveloped him in a tight hug. When she let him go, her eyes searched his face. "Be careful, King Samuel. You will be missed." She handed him a folded letter and ignored the small smirk Prince

Clifton held as he turned back toward the boundary line. Samuel squeezed Melody's hand. "Thank you, Melody, for seeing me off. But I will not be gone long." He soaked in her image for several long seconds and then turned back towards the boundary line. Clifton stepped through and Samuel followed. When he reached the other side, he exhaled in relief and grinned at Clifton.

"Not so bad." Samuel stated.

Chuckling, Clifton patted him on the back as they turned and waved at the Western royals. "Follow me."

"That was one dramatic goodbye." Isaac teased as his sister nervously wrung her hands together watching Samuel and Clifton disappear into the trees.

"I did not receive the chance to see him off at the castle."

"And was that a love note you handed him?" Isaac asked, receiving the annoyed glare he was expecting.

"It was an encouraging note. Not that it is any of your business, brother." Melody turned towards Isaac as soon as she lost sight of the other two men. "He is brave to cross with the future so uncertain."

"He seems certain about it." Isaac countered. "Because Samuel is an optimist. He sees the good in everyone and every thing."

"Not always." Melody pointed out. "The young king witnessed enough bad people and events before the Southern revolt. The fact he can even see good in anything anymore is a testament to the type of man he is."

"I see." Isaac smirked at his sister's defense. "I am sure your presence meant a great deal to him today, Melody. He cares for you."

Melody's cheeks flushed as she began walking back towards the tree line. "I will leave you to your task. I had only wished to see

Samuel across the boundary, now that he has gone, I will head back to the castle."

Isaac nodded at her retreating back as he heard her horse begin its steps along with whom he could only assume were castle guards riding alongside her. His gaze wandered over to the other side of the boundary and he waited for Clifton to return.

Elizabeth jostled in her seat as the carriage traversed over roughened paths through the Western Kingdom her face glued to the passing scenery. "So far I have not seen any guards of suspicious character."

"And you have been watching." King Eamon jested as she eased back into her seat with a grin.

"Well is it not our job to make sure the Western Kingdom is not overrun with Abner's guards?"

"Yes. However, we have our own guards keeping an eye out for now." Eamon added. "Relax while you can."

Elizabeth sighed as she attempted to calm her nerves. She shifted uncomfortably and held a hand to her queasy stomach.

"You alright, dear?" Eamon asked.

"Yes. I'm fine. Just a bit of a stomach bug lately." She wiped the back of her hand across her forehead to clear away the sweat that beaded along her brow.

"Are you sure?"

Elizabeth nodded, her face paling as she leaned forward and placed her head between her knees. King Eamon tilted her chin up and tsked his tongue and a wide smile spread over his face. "I believe I know what ails you, Elizabeth. Perhaps when we reach the Western castle their healer can take a look at you."

Shelving her pride, Elizabeth leaned back against the carriage cushions and closed her eyes, praying she would not lose her breakfast at the feet of the king.

The carrier halted and Eamon held up his hand for Elizabeth to remain seated. A guard opened the door. "My Lord, we are at the gates but the guards refuse to open the doors."

King Eamon sighed. "Isabella." Shaking his head, he climbed out of the carriage. "I will take it from here. Thank you."

"Greetings friends," he offered to the guards. "I am King Eamon from the Eastern Kingdom. I am here to visit with your King and Queen."

The two guards flanking the door looked at one another. "King Anthony is not here, my Lord, and we are under strict orders not to allow visitors during his absence."

"I understand. However, we have the blessing of his son, Prince Isaac, your future king."

The guards talked amongst themselves and nodded at Eamon. "We will have the Captain meet you at the doors."

Eamon flashed a friendly smile and made his way back to the carriage.

"Well?" Elizabeth asked.

"Anthony is not here." Eamon reported. "That is not a good sign. I warn you, Elizabeth, the Queen may be-"

"Out of sorts, I know."

"Alright. Perhaps just leave the talking to me. She will know who I am."

Elizabeth nodded in obedience as the carriage pulled to a stop outside the castle steps. A man, dressed in his Western military tunic stepped forward as Eamon climbed out and extended his hand to Elizabeth. She eased herself to the ground and gazed upon the looming castle before her. The Western Kingdom settled within the mountains and the castle protruded from the rocky edifice giving a polished finish to the rough terrain.

"My Lord," the guard bowed. "I know you have travelled at great lengths to visit with the King, but he is not here. We were under the assumption he was still in the Northern Kingdom."

Eamon shook his head. "A word in private would be best, Captain."

The Captain nodded as the castle doors opened and an older woman dressed in Western formality stood with her arms outstretched. "Eamon!" Her smile slowly faded and she squinted at the king. "My goodness you are old."

Elizabeth held back her snicker as Queen Isabella of the Western Kingdom enveloped King Eamon in a warm hug of welcome. The queen's amber eyes travelled to Elizabeth. "Why Rebecca, you haven't aged a day!" She gleefully clapped Eamon on the shoulder as she bypassed him and hugged Elizabeth to her. "What are you doing travelling with Eamon? Does Granton know of this escapade? How is Granton?" Queen Isabella began dragging Elizabeth through the castle doors asking question after question and Elizabeth attempted to maintain a smooth stride. When they entered the castle, Isabella released her hold on Elizabeth and placed her hands on her hips, her face stern. "Now I don't want you two to think I am not happy to see you, but if there is a scandalous affair taking place, I must know. Anthony will not be pleased being placed in the middle."

Eamon smiled. "Actually Isabella, this is not Rebecca. This is her daughter Elizabeth."

"Her daughter?!" The queen gasped placing her delicate hand over her breast. "Eamon! She is but a child. Now I know you were upset when Erica passed, but to marry Granton's daughter?! You have sons her age."

Elizabeth could not help the giggle that escaped as Eamon's face flushed with embarrassment at the queen's assumption. "I assure you, Isabella, there is nothing between the princess and me. She is married to my son, Clifton."

The queen's shoulders relaxed. "Ah. I see. That's better then. You are a beauty, child, did you know that? Have you met my Isaac. I bet he would love a girl like you." She linked her arm with Elizabeth, and began leading her to a large room with comfortable furniture and sat. "Have you met him?"

"I have met Isaac, my Queen. He is a good man."

"Of course he is." The queen waved her hand in the air as if she knew her son to be the greatest man alive. She turned towards the doorway as Eamon entered. "Eamon! When did you arrive?!" She walked towards him and hugged him tightly. "My goodness you are old. How long has it been?" Isabella chuckled as she led him into the room and sat. "Come, sit with Rebecca and me. We were just waiting on Granton and Anthony."

Elizabeth looked to Eamon as they both realized the queen's mind had wandered already and Elizabeth felt sympathy for the confused woman.

"Hello, Isabella. I am curious about Anthony, is he around?"

"Oh heavens, I do not know. The man travels here and there so much I am unsure where he is. He hasn't been home in weeks. Though that other man was sure kind enough to offer to help find him."

"Other man?" Elizabeth asked curiously.

"Yes, our neighbor. King Abner. Nice man that one. He offered to find Anthony for me."

"He did?" Elizabeth asked. "When?"

Queen Isabella patted Elizabeth's hand and smiled. "Weeks ago, Rebecca. Do not fret. Anthony will turn up soon. He is never gone for too long. Let me see if I can find my children, you will not believe how much they've grown." She stood and walked towards the doorway and began yelling for Isaac and Melody.

"What do we do?" Elizabeth whispered to Eamon. The king ran a hand over his face, a gesture much like Clifton's that made her miss her husband instantly.

"Leave it to me, dear." He stated quietly as Queen Isabella made her way back into the room.

"They seem to have disappeared again. Teenagers." She mumbled. "So tell me, what brings you two here?"

Eamon cleared his throat and finally sat. "We have come to find Anthony as well, Isabella. He left the Southern Kingdom after King Samuel's coronation and no one has heard from him since. We were worried."

She waved her hand and laughed. "Oh Eamon, you always were a worrier. Anthony is fine. Why he was just here this morning."

Elizabeth cast a quick glance at Eamon, frustration starting to mar her face as they were not getting anywhere in their conversation with the queen.

"Well would you mind if we stayed for a few days? Elizabeth has been feeling poorly, and I had hoped your healer could take a look at her." Eamon motioned to the princess and Isabella's eyes squinted. "Oh yes, Princess Elizabeth of the North. So you married Eamon's boy, Clifton, hm?"

The queen's mind seemed to catch up and Elizabeth sighed in relief. "Yes ma'am. I did."

"Ah, the blush of a newlywed. Is he a handsome boy?"

"He is. Very much so." Elizabeth smiled sweetly as her cheeks brightened.

"And is he good in-"

"Ah, Isabella," Eamon interrupted, awkward with the queen's turn in conversation. Elizabeth stifled a laugh as the queen shrugged her shoulders.

"Apologies Eamon, girl talk." Isabella winked at Elizabeth before standing. "You two shall have the East wing of the castle. I seem that only fitting. I will have our healer sent to you, my dear." She squeezed Elizabeth's hand. "Now I must go change, these rags are not near appropriate for dinner with friends. See you in the main dining hall tonight." Like a light breeze, she left the room and Elizabeth chuckled at her father-in-law's bewildered face.

"This may be a harder task than anticipated." Eamon waved for Elizabeth to follow him as they made their way up the steps towards the East wing of the castle.

"At least we know Abner visited." Elizabeth pointed out. "Which is odd."

"Indeed. I am curious about that as well. Perhaps we can pull more information from her on that topic at dinner. In the meantime, I wish for you to rest, dear. I will send the healer in shortly."

"I am fine, King Eamon. Really. It is just a bug."

Eamon smiled mischievously again. "I do not believe it is, Elizabeth. But we shall know soon enough." He bowed his head towards her and exited with a slight pep in his step.

Samuel relaxed as the Uniters welcomed him with open arms of gratitude and surprise. Several Southern guards stepped forward and bowed and Samuel waved for them to rise to their feet. "That is not necessary. Please."

Clifton stepped forward and held up his hand. "A word."

Everyone silenced.

"King Samuel is here for a specific purpose. His arrival is to remain secret."

"All of us live here in secret." One guard stated.

"No." Clifton continued. "His presence is to remain secret even from Prince Edward."

Mumbles carried throughout the clearing.

"Should his presence be leaked to Edward, Cecilia, or Lancer, our purpose will be moot. It is vital that he remain hidden among you for a greater purpose. Do we have your word?"

Everyone in the clearing slowly began to bow to their knees. Pleased, Clifton gripped Samuel's shoulder. "We can do this, Samuel. We can do this."

Samuel nodded in awe as he watched the sea of people fall to their knees in respect. "I will meet you at the boundary line in the morning at dawn." He turned to Clifton in dismissal and Clifton nodded with a wide grin. "I will see you then, my friend."

Samuel watched as the Eastern prince found his leave and men and women slowly began to rise to their feet. He inhaled a deep breath for courage and then set about introducing himself to his fellow Uniters, eager to find several trusted men to accompany him to Lancer's castle to rescue Ryle.

Clifton stepped back across the boundary and Isaac became alert. "About time. I was getting antsy over here. How did it go?"

"He seemed quite comfortable and the Uniters seem quite pleased and honored to have him in their mix. We shall see if his presence goes unnoticed by Edward or not. Everyone seemed on board, but we will not know for sure. Only time will tell."

"Samuel is smart. He will play his role well whether discovered or not." Isaac stated confidently. "I have high hopes for him."

"Me too." Clifton lifted himself into his saddle and clicked his reins, as the morning sun was warming the earth and erasing the morning dew. Isaac's pulled back on his horse. "Is there a reason you are moving at such a slow pace?"

"Hm?" Clifton turned to him as if he just realized he was not alone. "Oh, I am sorry."

Isaac laughed. "You, my friend, are at a loss without your woman."

Clifton turned to him and shook his head. "I do not know what you are talking about. I was not even thinking of Elizabeth."

"Sure you weren't. It is written all over you, Clifton. Perhaps you are riding so slow because there is no one waiting for your arrival at the castle?"

"Not the reason at all. I was just admiring the morning." Clifton gestured towards their surroundings and Isaac continued to laugh.

"Right. Well when I decide to believe you, I will be sure to let you know. However, I am quite starved, so I will be leaving you in my dust if you continue to meander at such a pace."

Clifton's eyes narrowed and he gripped his reins and tapped his heels into his horse's flanks as he sped past Isaac, the two princes racing back towards the castle.

Alayna pushed aside her maps and ran her hands over her face as fatigue settled into her shoulders and the morning's events weighed upon her. Samuel had now crossed into the Unfading Lands and here she sat, perplexed on how to move forward with battle plans. *She was so sure of herself a week ago, why was she questioning herself now?* She stood and stretched her back before walking towards the open window and looking out over the grassy hills, the wind causing seas of green to billow in the sunshine. It was a beautiful day. She should be grateful and leave this dark room for a spell and enjoy it. Clifton and Isaac would find her upon their arrival. She could surely take a moment for peace. She made her way through the castle in stealth so as not to be stopped by anyone; her mind focused upon the gardens and the fresh air. When she made it safely to the castle doors leading outside she spotted Melody rounding the corner.

"Doors." She ordered quickly for the guards. She slipped through hastily, not that she did not wish to speak to Melody, but that her hopes of a private moment sounded too glorious to have any interruption. When she stepped outside and the doors closed behind her, she took a deep breath and relaxed her shoulders. The pond. That is where she would head first. She made her way through the gardens, stopping every few steps to smell a bloom or pluck a blossom and continued on her way. The last time she had walked these gardens was before the attack on the castle. Elizabeth had rushed out to retrieve her and then their entire world had changed. More war. More chaos. More loss. She sat upon a bench beside the water and watched the ripples float across the surface as the wind whispered around her. She wished Ryle were here to enjoy the day with her. The thought saddened her. He risked much for the Realm and now he sat as a prisoner of Lancer, if he were even still alive. She shook away the thought of him not surviving. He was alive. She felt him deep down and knew he lived. She prayed Samuel was successful and continued to think of ways to utilize the young king from within the veil.

"Excuse me, my Queen." Her attendant, Jessa, stepped forward. "Prince Clifton and Prince Isaac have returned and are asking for you."

"Of course." Alayna stood, noting Jessa's regret for interrupting her time of reflection on her face. Alayna patted her on the shoulder as she passed and handed her the flowers she had plucked. "Thank you, Jessa." As she turned towards the castle, Isaac emerged followed by Clifton, both princes looking wind swept and eager to fill her in on their news.

"Gentlemen." She greeted. "How is our Samuel?"

"Successfully ensconced in the Uniters'." Clifton reported. "They welcomed him openly."

"And Edward was not there?"

"No. He was not around."

"Good. Now we wait for news from Samuel tomorrow morning I suppose."

Weeks passed and Clifton held in his hand the last letter Elizabeth sent the prior week. Another letter should arrive today if his calculations were correct. She and his father were no closer to finding King Anthony than when they left and Samuel's work in the Unfading Lands was a slow process as well. Action. Clifton needed action, and he found himself wandering down towards the stables where his targets were set up. He would practice again. Much like he did yesterday and the day before. To say his boots were itching for action was an understatement. The fact that all of them were stirring around, short of temper, and avoiding one another proved that the last few weeks were wearing on everyone. He topped the hill and spotted Isaac using his practice targets and inwardly groaned. He only wanted time alone to his thoughts. Isaac paused and raised his sword. "En garde, Clifton. I need to duel."

Clifton unsheathed his sword and gladly took his stance as the two princes collided blades and parried back and forth. He blocked a blow to his shoulder and barely missed Isaac's side as the Western prince dodged his blade. "Careful now, Clifton, I am beginning to think you are not just playing." Isaac grinned as he struck a blow with his elbow into Clifton's gut, the satisfying grunt making him laugh. He felt the brunt of Clifton's shove and flourished around with a swipe of his blade, the tassel upon Clifton's shoulder falling to the ground.

"Am I to take it you two are out to kill one another?" Melody's voice drifted to them as she emerged from the stables with a smile. Isaac paused, turning to his sister. "I see you are pleased. You must have gone to visit Samuel at the boundary line."

"I did."

Isaac grunted as Clifton dove towards him, shoulder slamming into his stomach and taking him to the ground. Melody gasped as the two princes rolled around punching one another. Fists and kicks flying, Melody watched as her brother bested Clifton and the Eastern prince slammed upon his back in the green grass, chest heaving from exertion.

"Promise me you will not kill one another?" She asked in passing.

"Promise." Both men uttered between breaths. Melody rolled her eyes and continued on her way to the castle, the letter from Samuel hiding in her surcoat pocket. She had met Samuel at the boundary line every few days for the last few weeks, their letters growing in length and detail of his current situation. He seemed to be making great strides in the Lands, and his hope for a rescue from the Realm never wavered. As she entered the castle, Alayna paused in the hallway. "Afternoon, Melody."

"Hello, Alayna."

"I trust our Samuel is doing well?"

Melody blushed. "Yes. He is."

Alayna nodded with a knowing smile. "Any news that needs to be reported?"

"No, not yet. He said Edward appeared in the camp yesterday evening, but Samuel was not recognized. He said Edward conversed with several guards and then left. He was not sure of specifics."

"Very well." Alayna sounded disappointed but offered a small smile.

"Have you witnessed the shenanigans of our princes?" Melody pointed to the doorway. "I fear Isaac and Clifton are growing restless. They have taken to battling one another."

Alayna walked to the doorway and the doors opened for her. She walked with Melody to the edge of the hill as she watched Isaac dive towards Clifton on the ground, but Clifton kicked his feet up, flipping Isaac over him, the Western prince landing on his back. "Oh my." She said.

"Yes. I fear if they keep at it, they will harm one another. Isaac should not be taking such blows."

"Are you sure they are just jesting back and forth? It looks more serious than that." Alayna asked.

"Yes. I stopped them earlier and neither seemed ill tempered."

"Well that is good, I suppose. I feel almost as restless. I pray we have news soon that encourages progress." Alayna watched the two men battle out their agitation for a few more minutes and then turned to walk back to the castle. Melody followed but remained silent. "Has Samuel said anything about Captain Ryle?" Alayna asked curiously.

Melody shook her head. "No, he has not. Though he did say he befriended two guards that work within the castle. He is hoping they can provide cover to sneak him inside when the time comes."

Alayna perked up. "That is good news. That also means Ryle is still alive if the guards are willing to put forth such effort. They would not if he were already dead."

"Yes, that is what I gathered as well. There is still hope." Melody smiled tenderly as she placed a gentle hand on Alayna's arm. Alayna, not comfortable with displaying her feelings so openly, forced a smile and then stepped away from the kind gesture. "Well, until dinner, Melody." She curtsied and walked away leaving the Western princess contemplating the queen's struggles as well as the two men outside.

Chapter 8

Edward dragged an unconscious Ryle back to his cell and leaned him up against the stonewalls.

"Edward, what have you done to him?" Cecilia's worried voice drifted from the other side of the prison chamber and Edward spun. "It is not your concern, Cecilia."

"But he is bleeding. Badly." She scooted over to the bars separating her cell from Ryle's and studied the Eastern prince looking for signs of life.

"He cannot die." Edward stated. "His wounds are already healing. I just hit him harder than I intended and he is unconscious."

"Every day you punish him. Do you not see his body cannot take anymore?" Cecilia leaned her forehead against one of the bars and silently pleaded for Edward to show mercy to Prince Ryle and herself.

"What concern is it of yours?" Edward barked. "He is in here because of you. This is all happening because of you. I HAVE TO DO THIS BECAUSE OF YOU!" His eyes flashed as he turned away from her to gain his composure.

"You are not yourself, Edward. The man I know would not allow Lancer to seek such injustice on an innocent man."

"So now you take the side of the Realm? When did your loyalties change?"

"They haven't." Cecilia confirmed. "I just do not like to see a kind man being tortured for no reason."

"Lancer believes there is a reason, Cecilia. Again, this would not be happening if you had not betrayed them. His blood is on your hands, not mine." Edward nudged Ryle's foot as the Eastern prince groaned and slowly blinked his eyes open. He rubbed a hand over his head, his fingertips staining with blood. "Must you always go for the head?"

"It stopped it, did it not?" Edward asked, his patience wearing thin with everyone questioning him.

"True." Ryle straightened against the wall and coughed, blood spurting from his lips as he tried to contain the pain the action initiated.

"The offer still stands, Prince Ryle. Should you agree to Lancer's terms, then the torture will stop."

"I will not."

Edward sighed and dropped his hands down to his sides. "I assumed as much. You realize this weighs heavily upon me, do you not?"

"I do. I am sorry, Edward. But I will not give in. I do not want any part of these Lands or that man."

"Weeks ago I would have continued to respect your choice, but now it is plain foolish. Look at you." Edward studied Ryle closely, sympathy disappearing from his face and a stone façade replacing it. "I cannot help you anymore. Your denial makes me look bad. The punishments will grow tougher every day. Lancer ordered it. I cannot continue to beat you senseless each time. Soon Lancer will give into his desire and kill you altogether. What then? What good will your imprisonment have been then?"

"You could always release me." Ryle pointed out.

Edward shook his head. "We've been through this. I can't. My role would be jeopardized if I let you go."

"Then how about her?" Ryle nodded towards Cecilia.

"She is a traitor. She remains."

"I believe you have made your point. I doubt she will betray you to Lancer, even now. Let her go. She should not have to suffer."

"Did you not hear me?" Edward closed Ryle's cell door and locked it. "She is a traitor. I do not tolerate betrayal." He flashed a dangerous gaze Cecilia's direction. "If I allowed the darkness to decide, she would be dead already."

"You mean the darkness would kill a person loyal to the Lands?" Ryle asked. "That seems counter productive."

Edward growled. "The darkness has no loyalty to these lands. It is loyal to people. If you embrace it, it follows you no matter where you are."

"I see. So even if the boundary line falls and all is well in the world, you will carry the darkness with you when you leave?"

"I pray not." Edward stated, though his voice sounded hesitant.

"It is part of you now." Ryle pointed out.

"I will rid myself of it."

"How?"

"I DO NOT KNOW!" Edward shouted and then clasped the hair at his temples. "Stop pushing, Prince Ryle. Please." He attempted to compose himself and bit down on his bottom lip as his hands tightened on his hair and his eyes swirled between blue and black. Ryle watched him battle against the darkness' power and caught Cecilia's nervous look and her scurry to the far corner of her cell. When Edward's hand fell to his sides, his eyes were normal and his face strained. "I will figure it out." His voice was low and defeated.

"I will help you." Ryle added. "Just remain strong, Edward."

"I am strong." Edward hissed, his eyes swirling again at his taking offense.

Ryle held up his hands in forfeit and Edward backed away and hurried out of the chamber.

"He is not well." Cecilia's voice drifted from the darkness and she appeared in the lamplight.

"No. But there is no way to help him if he does not contain the darkness within him."

Elizabeth signed her name and folded the parchment and dipped a dollop of wax on the seam. She had delayed in writing Clifton not knowing what to tell him of her journey in the West. So far, she and his father had yet to find out any news of King Anthony, and King Eamon was hesitant on sending out search parties for fear of causing a kingdom-wide panic. She could understand, but she felt as if she were not putting forth as much effort as she should. She sighed as she scrolled Clifton's name across the front of the letter. She had news for him, of that she was certain, but not news she wished to share in the letter. She patted her stomach. A baby. That was what the healer had told her. Her sickness was no stomach bug, and she had slowly started feeling the difference between a normal sickness and the common ails of a baby. She could not believe it. She and Clifton were to be parents to a child. She shook her head in disbelief. To say the timing was less than perfect would be an understatement, but the joy a baby could bring helped ease her fears.

The fact King Eamon had maintained a constant state of glee over the matter had shown her that much. Now here she sat, twiddling her thumbs, as he handled the search for Anthony. *So much for her quest.* She heard the shuffling of footsteps and Queen Isabella emerged in the doorway.

"Rebecca." She greeted warmly.

Elizabeth inwardly prayed for patience as the woman's mind struggled with catching up to the current time.

"Hello Queen Isabella. How are you today?"

The queen waved her hand in annoyance as she sat. "Dreadful. Absolutely dreadful. Anthony has decided to disappear again. And so has Isaac and Melody. I cannot seem to keep a grip on my household. Do they think a kingdom can run itself?"

"I am sure they will return shortly." Elizabeth added, playing along. "Do you know where they went?"

Shaking her head, Isabella rested her chin in her hand as she stared out the window. "Heaven knows. I'm sure Anthony is checking on that blasted prisoner, and Isaac is probably chasing tail somewhere, and Melody is more than likely off daydreaming."

Elizabeth smirked at the description of Isaac before she realized what the queen had said. "I'm sorry, prisoner? What prisoner would the king be tending to?"

"That one in the hills. The one Abner asked for me to keep guards on. Didn't I tell you?" She turned from the window and looked at Elizabeth. "Oh never mind. I'm sure he is just another criminal that stole from the market."

"But why would Abner wish for you to watch him here and not take him back to his kingdom?"

"How am I to know, Rebecca? You and your questions. I honestly do not know how Granton deals with you all the time. Questions are pestering."

"I apologize, Queen Isabella. I did not mean to offend."

"Oh pish posh, don't apologize for asking them. They annoy, Rebecca. I did not say they were pointless."

Elizabeth looked up as King Eamon entered the room. "Eamon," Isabella greeted. "You look well today. Did you sleep okay?" Knowing it was now well into the evening, Eamon reacted as if he had just awoken. "Slept fine, Isabella, thank you."

"King Eamon, " Elizabeth began. "Queen Isabella was just telling me about a prisoner in the hills." Her voice had a leading tone and she narrowed her gaze at her father-in-law to silently plead for him to ask more questions.

Eamon straightened. "A prisoner? What type of prisoner?"

"My goodness," Isabella shifted her crimson shawl and folded her hands in her lap. "Do you not have prisoners in the East? The both of you, goodness, carrying on as if I discovered a new realm. I was just telling…" she paused and focused upon Elizabeth as if to figure out whom she was.

"Elizabeth." Elizabeth offered.

"Of course, Elizabeth. How are you dear? How's the baby? Oh to think, I am going to be a grandmother!"

Elizabeth deflated. The queen was losing track of her thoughts.

"The prisoner, Isabella." Eamon prodded, ignoring the queen's confused ramblings. "What of this prisoner?"

"Oh, right, of course. Abner asked that he be able to keep a prisoner in the hills. His prison chambers were too full and he asked me for the extra housing."

"Did he say what this criminal was responsible for?"

"No. I did not ask. Anthony was gone and I just granted his request thinking Anthony would see to it when he returned. Where is

Anthony? Did he go out to the gardens? I should go find him. Excuse me." She stood and wandered off before either of them could respond. Eamon looked to Elizabeth and she nodded. "I think we found him."

"I will find the Captain." Eamon stated, excitement lacing his voice.

Samuel nodded to the guard ahead of him as the man ushered him to move through the castle hall quietly behind him. Dressed in the uniform of an Unfading Lands guard, he moved silently through the stone halls, careful to avoid contact with any others. He heard footsteps up ahead and darted into an alcove, as the footsteps grew louder. He prayed the person was not heading toward the doorway he blocked. He shifted as close to the wall as possible as a man walked by. Edward. He watched as he carried on down the hall and entered a room at the end. His personal chamber, he assumed. He waited a few breaths and then continued his journey down the hall. His fellow guards emerged from their own hiding places and followed behind him. When he reached the prison chamber, he motioned for his guards to stand at the door and he entered alone.

It was dark, the only light coming from a small lantern in the far corner and the room smelled of stale blood. He heard a gasp and Cecilia's face appeared behind the first cell.

Samuel continued walking until he spotted a man's form leaning up against the wall in the far cell. "Prince Ryle." He whispered, his voice sounding like a scream in the quiet room.

The man's boots shifted and he pulled himself up. "Samuel?" Ryle moved to the light and the door of his cell. A wide smile appeared on his face as Samuel stepped closer.

"What are you doing here? Ryle asked.

"I'm rescuing you, of course." Samuel grinned as Ryle stood dumbfounded.

"How did you- why would y-" His questions tapered off as he stood in complete shock at the Southern king's sacrifice to come to his aid. "You crossed?"

"Obviously." The young prince stated with a small shrug. "Now, where does Edward keep the key?"

Ryle pointed to a hook across the room by the door. Samuel hurried over and began filtering through the keys to try and find one that fit the lock. He unlatched Ryle's door and opened it. The two men embraced in a brotherly fashion, surprising Cecilia.

"I cannot believe it." Ryle's eyes held restrained tears and his gaze wandered to Cecilia. He bowed his head and stepped away from Samuel. "I cannot go with you."

"What? Why?" Samuel asked. "The whole point of me crossing was to rescue you. Everyone has been so worried. Queen Alayna has been completely lost without you."

Ryle sighed and rubbed a hand over his face. "I am sorry, Samuel, but if I were to escape with you, Edward would know the Uniters attempted a rescue without informing him. He is not stable. He could then turn Lancer's guards against the entire camp. We cannot lose our only chance of an army."

"Edward would kill them? Has he been lost to the darkness?"

"Not completely." Ryle continued. "But it is a struggle. I do not wish to give him any reason to take that final step. Making him look bad in front of Lancer would definitely be the final step. I cannot go with you."

"But what do I tell the others? Alayna? Isaac? Your brother?"

"Tell them exactly what I have told you." Ryle explained. "They will have to understand. When the time is right for the battle against the Lands, then and only then can you come for me. I will be waiting."

"But-"

Ryle held up his hand to ward off Samuel's protest. "Do not let your attempt be in vain. Rescue her." He motioned towards Cecilia and to her surprise and Samuel's, Ryle pulled his cell door closed.

"But she betrayed us." Samuel whispered. "How can I show up with her and not you?"

"I believe she still has a part to play." Ryle looked to Cecilia. "You will leave with him and should Lancer ever approach you for information about the Realm you will be ignorant of such matters. Understood?"

"What of Edward?" She asked.

"I will handle Edward. You must go. Hurry Samuel."

Samuel filtered through the keys once more and found the one fitting Cecilia's lock. She waited impatiently at the ready. Before he clicked the lock open, he peered into her face. "Should you betray us again, Prince Edward will be the least of your worries." Her eyes widened at the young king and she nodded hastily.

"I will return for you." Samuel reached through the bars and shook Ryle's hand.

"I know. Now go. Be safe. And give," he paused and ripped off the Northern seal from his tunic, "give this to Alayna."

Samuel pocketed the seal and nodded. He grabbed Cecilia by the elbow and ushered her forward and out the door.

"So see Edward, it only makes sense that we move the training grounds further to the West. With Abner gone, and the state of that kingdom potentially weak from his armies trailing through, our boundary may expand further in that direction." Lancer pointed to a map before them and Edward nodded.

"But why not the East? The king and his other son are still in the North. We have Prince Ryle in our custody, surely they are weak as well."

"No. Not like the West." Lancer answered.

"But if we-"

Lancer slammed a fist onto the table. "You are trying my patience, Edward. Do you remember who I am?"

Edward pulled back his shoulders and raised his chin. "Of course. I am only trying to be helpful, my Lord."

"Well I do not like it. I am the leader of these Lands. You are my subordinate. When I say where we will expand that is where we will expand. Do I make myself clear?"

"Yes, my Lord. Apologies."

"Now. How is our prisoner?"

"Still maintaining his allegiance."

"You must not be trying hard enough."

"Trust me, my Lord, I am doing everything in my power to torment and convince him, but he refuses."

"Excuses, Edward. You know how I feel about excuses. This is our opportunity to take a record expansion while the Realm is weak. If he turns then we will have enough strength to take half of the Western Kingdom into our possession. But only if he turns."

"I am trying." Edward stated. "He is stubborn."

"Of course he is. He is Eamon's son. I could have told you that, Edward." Lancer chuckled, releasing a portion of the tension in the room. "However, should he not turn, we may need to take drastic measures."

"And what might those be?"

"Perhaps he will be of better use to us dead." Lancer offered. "Nothing speaks more clearly than death."

"But how would that give us strength?"

"Loss and devastation are powerful attributes to our success as well. The boundary line moves when the Realm is weak. A loss of a prince would definitely weaken them."

"But he is captured and there has been no change in strength." Edward clarified. "His death will not move the line any more than his capture has. And I also know that his death will only make the Realm grow stronger because they will seek retribution."

Lancer rubbed his chin and smirked. "Fine. Then bring him to me."

"I'm sorry?" Edward asked.

"I said, bring him to me. If you are so convinced his death will not strengthen us, then I will try other ideas."

"But what do you want with him?"

"Edward!" Lancer growled. "Again with the questions! I am your leader. Just because you saved me from losing the darkness does not mean you have the upper hand. This is my realm. Now do as I say." He walked to his favorite seat and poured himself a glass of the tasteless concoction Edward loathed.

"You wish for me to bring him to you now?"

Lancer did not respond, his eyes said it all as Edward immediately exited to retrieve Ryle.

Four guards accompanied King Eamon to the back entrance of the Western castle, the Western Captain of the Guard in their company. Elizabeth stood to the side, arms crossed, and waited.

"With the cover of darkness we will be able to move across the mountains freely without the fear of being seen. Should we come across any of Abner's guards we know we have reached our destination."

"This entire kingdom is full of mountains." Elizabeth cut in. "There has to be a way to narrow the search. Are there any caves?" She looked to the Captain.

He nodded. "There is one I suggest we look into first. It is an abandoned cave we used to confine our most vicious criminals inside. We have not used it in decades, but perhaps Abner discovered it."

"Where is it?" Elizabeth asked.

"Towards the North."

"That would make sense." Eamon stated. "Abner would need a place in between here and his route to the Northern Kingdom. We check there first. Full breastplates, gentlemen, we must be prepared for anything."

"I am going too." Elizabeth untied her skirt and pulled it aside revealing the trousers Mary had previously made for her to use during her swordsmanship lessons.

The guards looked at one another and then to their captain. King Eamon shook his head. "It is too dangerous, Elizabeth. You must remain here."

"I am going." Elizabeth waved her hand and her attendant stepped forward carrying her sword. "I promised Isaac and Melody that I would find their father and I intend to do so. I will not be rash."

"You cannot participate this time, my dear. Not in your condition." He motioned towards her stomach.

"I will hang behind until you give me the all clear, and then I will retrieve Anthony. Please. I have to be there."

She watched as her father-in-law debated with himself before finally nodding. "You do not move unless I say, understand?"

She jumped for joy, her peg leg's clatter echoing down the hall. She noticed the guards look down in surprise. She kissed Eamon on the cheek as she followed closely behind the Captain.

The ride through the mountains was rough and the moonlight only allowed a few feet of visibility. Elizabeth trusted the horse beneath her and prayed for safe travel. The sound of hooves crushing against rocks filled the night until suddenly the Captain quietly called back to them for no movement. They had been riding for several hours and Elizabeth felt fatigue from her head to her toes. Her legs burned from riding in the saddle, an irritation confirming that she was out of practice. She refused to show it, however, because she was determined to find King Anthony. She owed it to Isaac.

"Up ahead. I saw a light." The Captain spoke into the night and though Elizabeth could only see shapes of the men before her, she knew the Captain rode up front. "I will go investigate." He dismounted. "I will return before making a move." He slipped into the night as Elizabeth dismounted with the rest of the group and stretched out her back.

"How are you feeling, dear?" King Eamon lightly tapped her elbow.

"I am fine."

"You would tell me if you were tired?"

She smiled, though she knew he could not see it. She lightly squeezed his hand. "Yes. I would." Hearing his sigh of relief, Elizabeth said a silent prayer of thankfulness for a caring father-in-law as they heard the Captain returning.

"There are only two guards at the mouth of the cave. I could not see inside, but I do not believe there are any others. Could be the reason we never noticed them here. Few in number are easier to hide."

"If Abner only left two guards, you can bet they are two of his best." Elizabeth stated.

"Aye. I agree." The Captain motioned for two guards to come forward. "Circle around the backside of the cave and only approach if I call for you." They nodded and slinked into the darkness.

"King Eamon, Andrew, and myself will approach from the front. Princess, you hang here until we give the all clear."

Elizabeth forced a nod though she bit her tongue in protest. She gripped the hilt of her sword and followed wordlessly behind them at a safe distance. She would not miss this fight.

Chapter 9

Clifton waited in the clearing for Samuel to appear on the other side of the boundary line. The light breeze drifted over him and calmed his restless heart. He had not heard from Elizabeth in over a week, an issue he struggled with pursuing. *Should he travel to the West to check up on her?* He shook his head. *His father was with her, there was no need to worry.* And yet he did. Sighing, he watched the Rollings River flow by him, the sound peaceful, yet the pace in which it moved held unrelenting turmoil hidden beneath the calm glass surface. He heard a thud and turned towards the veil to see Samuel standing on the other side pointing to the rock he had tossed across the line. There was no letter attached to it and Clifton realized he was only making himself known. Clifton could cross freely, and so he stood, straightening his pale blue tunic, the horse emblazoned seal over his heart taut over his muscular frame. He walked towards the line and stepped across on a deep breath.

Samuel smiled. "It is good to see you."

"You as well." Clifton accepted the firm handshake Samuel offered. "Any news?"

"Much. Do you have the time?"

"Of course." Clifton motioned towards the log that had served as a meeting spot for several months now and he and Samuel sat.

"I attempted a rescue of Captain Ryle." Samuel stated.

Clifton's brows rose. "Attempted?"

"I would have been successful but he refused to come with me."

Dread filled Clifton's stomach and he gritted his teeth against the bad news he was sure to hear. His brother had given into the darkness or to Lancer's demands.

Samuel's knees bounced as he spoke as if he tried to contain the anxiety that rushed through him. "It is not what you think, Clifton. He has not betrayed us."

Clifton's shoulders did not relax so Samuel continued. "When I arrived in the prison chamber, he was not alone. Edward had arrested someone else."

Tilting his head in interest, Clifton waved for him to continue. Samuel hopped to his feet. "Ryle refused to let me rescue him, instead wanting me to rescue her." He walked to the tree line and leaned through the thicket. "Come." His young voice held a new authority Clifton had not heard from the young king. Cecilia emerged slowly with trepidation in her steps. Clifton stood. "Her?"

Samuel nodded. "Edward arrested her for betraying the Realm, and Ryle feared for her safety."

"He wished to set her free over himself? She is a traitor." Clifton's kind eyes stormed with restrained anger. "Why would he do such a foolish thing? Let her receive what is just."

"Those were my thoughts as well." Samuel gripped Cecilia's arm as she attempted to walk away and forced her to stand in the clearing. "But Ryle feels she may have a part to play in the near future."

"As if she would." Clifton motioned towards Cecilia. "Do you have any idea what you have done? What your actions have cost us?"

She lowered her head.

"Look at me." His voice was fierce and she fearfully raised her gaze. Clifton stood resolute as he forced Cecilia to witness his anger. "You have cost the Realm multiple lives. You have cost my brother his freedom-"

"I only wished-"

"Do not interrupt me." Clifton ordered. "Your actions have cost the Realm all of these things. And Edward, well, you may very well have cost him his soul. You are a traitor and you deserve every punishment worthy of such a crime."

Tears streaked Cecilia's face and Samuel's hold on her arm released. She used both hands to cover her face as she sobbed.

"However," Clifton began, causing Cecilia to slowly look upon his stern face once more. "My brother wishes to show you mercy, so I will. If he feels you may be an asset to us I will trust his judgment. For now. But should I hear one word of you betraying us again, I will handle your punishment personally." He looked to Samuel. "Am I clear?"

Samuel nodded. "I will keep my eyes upon her, Clifton."

"Very well. Now leave us." He ordered Cecilia. She gathered her skirts and rushed through the clearing with no hesitation.

"Any ideas on how we may utilize her?" Clifton asked.

Samuel shook his head. "Not yet. Though perhaps we may use her in the same way she betrayed us last time. An informant to Lancer."

Clifton rubbed a hand over his face. "Possibly."

"He was okay, Clifton." Samuel offered, knowing the prince still worried about his brother. "His body is badly injured, but his heart remains strong."

"That is good to hear."

"He worries about Edward. He said the Northern prince struggles fiercely with the darkness and only grows more powerful. He feared should I rescue him that Edward would retaliate due to wounded pride. I do not believe we have an ally in Prince Edward any longer. If we do, it is merely temporary. Therefore, I suggest we keep all of our plans secret from him." Samuel reached into his trouser pocket. "Ryle wished for the queen to have this." He handed over the Northern seal from Ryle's tunic. Dried blood and dirt smudged the image of the crown, but the symbol remained. Clifton gripped the fabric in his hand. "Thank you, Samuel."

"I will see you tomorrow, Prince Clifton. I wish to hear more news from the Realm, but I do not wish to leave Cecilia without my supervision for too long."

"I understand." Clifton shook his hand. "You serve us well, Samuel."

Samuel bowed in response and then darted through the trees.

Katarina walked through her father's castle with an air of leadership she had not known she possessed. Her chin up, she faced the guard before her. "I wish to enter."

He nodded. "Yes, my Queen."

Queen. The title had yet to settle upon her with comfort, but the last several weeks had been pleasing. The people of the Valleylands had rallied behind her in support, the previous queen glad to relinquish the responsibility. Though she did not wish to serve the Valleylands like her father had, with a stiff-arm and fear, she did wish to maintain a strict hold on loyalty. Her father, though a harsh man, remained loyal to his family and his lands. It was through this loyalty that King Abner had left her a special gift. As if he had known his potential fate in the last war and knew she would take his position as the crown of authority. She smiled to herself as she stepped into the dark room. A precious gift. A gift of choice. A flirtation in her mind to satisfy her vengefulness or to acclimate to a friendship of support to the Realm of Queen Alayna. She was just not sure which choice she preferred. Until she did, she maintained her secrecy and silence.

As she lowered the stone steps, she heard the sounds of screams echoing off the walls making her cringe. She was not cut out for torture and she had called a stop to it as soon as she was queen. It seemed her guards had other ideas and she walked into the room to a bloody mess. Shaking her head at the limp body before her, she turned to the guard. "Who gave you such an order?"

The guard had the nerve to look sheepish. "I realize you were ordered to do these things under my father. Perhaps even worse things. But as for me, I will not have such treatment, no matter the prisoner. Take him back to his cell, and report to the Captain at once. He will hear of your disobedience and will deal with you accordingly."

The guard bowed and quickly unchained the unconscious man from the posts before her.

Ryle stepped into the light as Edward cleared the steps and emerged in the prison chamber. His eyes darting towards Cecilia's cell with a passing glance before it settled upon Ryle. "It's that time, Prince Ryle."

Ryle slowly stood to his feet, biting back the groan that wished to escape his lips. He offered a smile to Edward.

"You seem cheerful for someone who is about to be tortured."

"I have had a good day."

"Really?" Edward's sarcasm and disbelief evident in his tone.

"Indeed."

"I guess there is much to do down here in the dirt."

"Sometimes." Ryle baited.

"And what has you in such a good mood, Prince?"

Ryle nodded towards Cecilia's cell and Edward followed his line of vision. "What about her?" Edward asked.

Ryle tilted his head towards her cell again and Edward released his chained hands and walked towards the cell. "Cecilia, come out here?"

No sound.

"Cecilia." Edward called again. He turned to see Ryle's smug smirk. "Where is she? Did Lancer find her? Did he come down here?" Edward's words were laced with panic.

"Are you worried he found out you arrested his loyal servant? That would definitely look bad on your part." Ryle continued.

"Do not mock me, Prince. Where is she?" Edward's eyes darkened and Ryle sighed.

"She was rescued."

"What? By whom?" Edward stepped closer and gripped the front of Ryle's tunic in his fist.

Ryle shrugged.

"You will tell me!" Edward yelled.

"Let's just say someone found her services to be useful elsewhere." Ryle added. "For your sake, it is best she is gone."

"Oh really?" Edward asked. "Why is that?"

"Because looking at her fills you with anger, and with your anger comes the darkness. Perhaps removing her from the equation will allow you to keep your senses."

"I am in complete control over my actions." Edward defended. "I grow more powerful by the day and it has no effect upon me."

"I believe it does."

"Well you are wrong."

"Am I? I watched you replenish Lancer's source of darkness with my own eyes. I watched you throw the woman you love into prison. Even now, you struggle, your very body rejecting reason." He motioned his head down towards the firm grip Edward had on his dagger that aimed at Ryle's chest. "Though I have wondered why you have yet to attempt destroying the boundary yourself. You obviously have the strength."

"I cannot take it down." Edward growled, stepping away from Ryle.

"Why? Is it because you inwardly wish for it to remain?"

Edward spun around and narrowed his gaze. "Never. I crossed into these Lands to destroy them. If I could, I would. The boundary was sealed with Lancer's blood, not mine. Only his blood can take it down."

Ryle rolled that thought around in his head. "I see."

"Do you?" Edward asked, walking up to Ryle and standing a mere inch from his face. "The fact that I risk my very being for the Realm seems to be forgotten. I will destroy these Lands as best I can, but I cannot do that when you secretly plot behind my back."

Ryle felt the tug on his chains as Edward began leading him out of the cell and towards the reflection chamber. He tried to muster strength for what he knew would be a debilitating day ahead.

A twig snapped and Elizabeth cringed, pausing in her secret pursuit of her father-in-law and the Western guards. None of the men noticed her presence behind them and continued onward towards the cave. She took a deep breath and tread even more carefully behind them as they neared the entrance. Still two guards. She watched as the men in front of her unsheathed their swords and she too, pulled hers silently from her side. The Captain lunged out of the darkness, the two guards turning in surprise as they scrambled to find their weapons. As the Captain attacked one guard, King Eamon and the other Western guard followed and clashed blades with the other man. It did not take long for the two guards to fall.

The Captain slipped his sword into its sheath and turned towards the others. "That wasn't so hard. Now, let's go find our king."

Before anyone could step further towards the cave, a blade pierced through the Captain's chest, his eyes bulging with surprise and then fear. Elizabeth covered her mouth from the shrub she stood behind and watched as five more of Abner's guards emerged from the cave. The two extra Western guards ran onto the scene with cries of vengeance and blades at the ready as they watched their Captain fall lifelessly to the ground. Eamon battled the largest guard of all and though he was skilled with the blade, felt himself losing ground. Elizabeth surveyed the surroundings. It was five against four. If she joined in the fight, they would be evenly matched. She took a deep breath and stepped from her hiding place.

She watched as Eamon was pinned against a boulder, his blade and his opponent's blade inches from his neck. Elizabeth ran forward and thrust her blade through the man's side, surprising both men. The guard attempted a swing in her direction, but she ducked out of its path and kicked him to his knees as her blade withdrew from his side. He fell to the ground, his eyes glazing.

Eamon grabbed her arm. "I did not call for you. You cannot be here." His voice was cut off as two guards darted towards them and had them both dodging swords. "Cliff would have my hide if something happened to you!" Eamon yelled as he nailed a kick to the man's chest and sent him stumbling backwards.

Elizabeth spun as she avoided a sword to the arm and rotated back around, her sword finding her target of the man's stomach. She wrenched her blade free as he fell to the ground and ran towards Eamon. She reached him just as he brought the guard down with a single blow. Panting, he gripped her arm. "You will leave. Head back to the horses."

She shook her head. "No. We have them beaten."

"There may be more guards inside."

"There isn't."

"You do not know that." Eamon's jaw remained firm as he led her to a small thicket and shoved her down behind it. "Do not move." He ordered. Elizabeth huffed in frustration as she watched him and the other guards finish off Abner's small army. Eamon grabbed a limb from the fire and walked towards the mouth of the cave. Slowly, he and the other guards disappeared and Elizabeth waited impatiently.

"Come on, come on, come on." She whispered as she slowly began to let her worry take her over. *They should be back by now.* As she stood to defy her father-in-law's orders to check on them, he emerged at the entrance and waved her over. "It is not Anthony." He stated with disappointment.

"What?" Elizabeth walked towards the dark as figures emerged. Beaten, weatherworn, and half-starved Western soldiers emerged.

"It is Anthony's royal caravan." Eamon explained. "They have been here since their journey home from Samuel's coronation."

"That was months ago."

Eamon nodded. "Come, we must take them back to the castle. They are struggling."

Elizabeth stepped forward and draped a man's arm over her shoulders as she gripped his too thin waist. He moved slowly, his limbs weak with lack of use and he smelled of urine and blood. She battled against her reflexes and kept her dinner in her stomach, though she did not know how she managed. She watched as he climbed upon her horse, another guard behind him as she walked towards Eamon's mount and he hoisted her behind him.

Alayna rushed towards the front of the castle as the Eastern carriages pulled to a stop. Clifton darted past her, his shoulder brushing hers as he rushed to the door of his father's carriage. The footman opened the door and he all but dove inside as he reached for his wife and pulled her into his arms. She heard her sister laughing as she pushed her husband out of the carriage and stepped out. She then let him sweep her into his arms and spin her around. As they reunited, King Eamon stepped from within with a smile on his face as well, until he gazed upon Alayna. He shook his head.

"You did not find him?"

Everyone froze and looked to the king. "No. I am afraid not. We shall fill you in once we are inside."

Clifton cupped Elizabeth's face. "You are alright? I was worried. I did not receive a letter this week." He kissed her heartily on the lips.

She grinned. "I am more than fine. Your father took great care of me. As well as Queen Isabella." She looked over his shoulder to Isaac and Melody, their shoulders slumped in disappointment, but still happy to see Elizabeth and Eamon. Elizabeth squeezed Clifton's hand before walking towards Isaac.

"I am sorry, Isaac."

A muscle in his jaw ticked as he nodded. Clearing his throat, he motioned towards the castle. "I wish to know everything."

She reached for Clifton's hand as they entered the castle and Alayna ushered them quickly to the Council Room. "Sit, sit, sit. Please, tell us everything. What happened? In your last letter, you seemed hopeful that you had found him."

"It was not him." Eamon reported. "Turns out Abner had convinced your mother that he needed extra prison space for some of his criminals. So she agreed to let him use a cave in the hills."

"Yes, I know that cave." Isaac said. "We have not used it in years."

"That is what your Captain reported as well. When we approached there were two of Abner's guards standing guard, but there were more inside the cave. The ambush was swift, and though we lost your Captain, a fine man, we found victory. However, the prisoner inside was not your father."

Isaac slammed his hand on the table in frustration and then ran his hand through his hair. "Then who was it?"

"His caravan." Elizabeth cut in. "All the men that travelled with him from Samuel's coronation. They never even made it back to the Western castle. They were ambushed by Abner on his way to the North and he took your father hostage. They did not know where Abner took him."

"So those poor men have been living in a cave these last few months?" Melody asked in horror, her hand over her heart.

"Yes." Eamon replied. "We now have them back at the Western castle and Queen Isabella is seeing to them quite diligently."

"How was... how was my mother?" Isaac asked.

"She is fine." Elizabeth lightly patted his hand. "Confused a bit every now and then, but still fine. She has not grasped the fact that your father is missing. She sees him as being away on travels. For her sake, we let her keep believing that until we know for certain his whereabouts."

"Thank you." He tapped his finger on the back of Elizabeth's hand and nodded. "Thank you for handling her delicately."

"Of course."

"So now we are back to square one in regards to King Anthony." Alayna sounded disappointed. "It seems our plans of recuperating have slowed considerably. Any reports from Samuel?"

Clifton shifted in his seat. "Some. He attempted his rescue of Ryle."

Alayna held up her hand. "You're just now telling me this?"

"I debated telling you at all." Clifton reported truthfully.

"So I take it his efforts were unsuccessful?"

"No. He was able to reach Ryle, however, Ryle did not wish to be rescued just yet."

"What?" Alayna stood to her feet, her chair teetering on its back legs. "Why?"

Clifton held up his hand for her to calm down and she began pacing about the room as he continued. "Samuel rescued Cecilia."

"Cecilia?" Elizabeth asked. "What was she even doing there?"

Clifton sighed and ran a hand over his face as if the story was too much to explain. "Edward arrested Cecilia for betraying him though Lancer does not know that. Ryle wished for Samuel to rescue her instead of him because he feared Edward would kill her and then he would truly be lost to the darkness. Ryle also feels we can utilize Cecilia later on. Did I leave anything out?"

Elizabeth patted his leg under the table and he threaded his fingers through hers.

"But- He- What?" Alayna studdered. "I do not understand why he would not wish to be free? He is beaten every day. Does he know that his life could be forfeit?"

"Yes. He seems to know his circumstances quite well." Clifton replied and reached into his trouser pocket. "He told Samuel to give you this." He slid the Northern seal across the table and Alayna picked it up, her eyes immediately clouding and her thumb slowly brushing across the emblem. "Ryle remains loyal to the Realm, but he wishes to play a role there in the Lands. I say we let him."

Alayna shook her head and Eamon lightly tapped her arm. "He must have a plan, Alayna, or he would have come. We must trust him."

"I'm glad to hear someone has a plan, but we need action. What of Edward? Have you conversed with him?"

Clifton shook his head. "Nor do I intend to for a while. Ryle claims Edward is slowly retreating into the darkness. He is not stable for us to use as an ally. We must operate without him. Samuel's position in the Lands is now more vital than ever."

"And what of King Anthony?" Alayna asked. "He has to be somewhere? Where would Abner take him?"

"He could have killed him." Melody's voice was quiet and Elizabeth shook her head. "No. I do not believe he did. Why would he keep Anthony's caravan alive? If he kept them alive, I have no doubt your father is still alive as well. It is just a matter of finding him. I believe Abner knew we would hunt for Anthony. Why else would he manipulate your mother? It is a game to him, even after his death. A wild game of treasure hunt. King Anthony is alive and he is being held somewhere, we just have to keep looking."

"I will take that task." King Eamon volunteered. "In the meantime, I will oversee the Western armies while my Captain commands the East. That way, Isaac and Melody may remain here and aid in whatever plans take place."

Isaac nodded. "I agree with that plan. Without a Captain, the Western armies will need a leader. I will lead them if necessary, but I believe my place is here for now, if Eamon can be there in my stead."

Alayna agreed. "Of course. So are we all in agreement that we must move forward in our plans then? That we must direct our attention to defeating the Lands?"

Everyone nodded.

"Good. Meeting adjourned. Once we have more word from Samuel in regards to the Lands, we will begin gathering twice a week. King Eamon we will keep you informed via messengers. I will also be sending a letter to Katarina in the Valleylands of our plans so that should we need her aid, she is ready."

"I do not trust her." Elizabeth blurted out. "I mean, not fully... anymore." She shrunk back as if regretful of her outburst.

"I am cautious too, but right now we need allies, and she is all we have."

"But to ask an army that we just defeated to actually fight with us... how do we plan for that to go over? I am almost certain some of those men may hold grudges." Isaac pointed out.

"They have a new queen." Alayna stated. "They will follow her orders."

"The guards in the West did not even realize Abner had died." Elizabeth explained. "How do we know if Katarina has even made a mark or a change yet?"

"We ask her." Alayna answered. "It is that simple. I will not rely upon her if she does not seem confident in coming to our aid or joining in our fight. But I feel it necessary to have her involved."

"Very well." Elizabeth waved her hand in acquiescence.

"Isaac and Clifton work with the soldiers. When you feel we are fit and ready for battle, we will coordinate with Samuel. We have waited long enough. It is time for us to move forward." Alayna reached over and lightly brushed Elizabeth's hair with her hand. "It's good to have you back."

Elizabeth smiled as everyone began their movements to exit. She stood and allowed her husband to lead her away. Alayna watched them go, and her heart sighed at the thought of ever having such a relationship. Clifton cared for her sister, deeply. It was evident that both of them truly loved the other. And though she had found it amusing to see Clifton wander aimlessly about the castle the last month not knowing what to do without his wife, she found herself glad that his other half returned along with his sanity.

Chapter 10

"I honestly do not understand you, Prince Ryle." Lancer walked about the reflection chamber with his hands clasped behind his back and his red tunic crisp and spotless. Edward lingered to the side of Ryle's chair, his bloody sword hanging by his side.

"In another life you and Prince Edward could have been brothers." Lancer chuckled. "I mean, that is if Queen Alayna wished to marry you or perhaps the other one. What's her name again, Edward?"

"Elizabeth."

"Ah yes, Elizabeth. Must have been painfully embarrassing for your younger brother to snatch one of Granton's daughters instead of you. Now your brother is heir to not only your father's throne, but heir to the throne of the entire Realm as well." Lancer chuckled. "I can see why you crossed into my lands."

Ryle sat stiffly, not willing to defend himself or to encourage Lancer's bantering.

"You know how easy it would be for you to take what you wanted if you joined with us? Ask Edward. Why, since he's embraced the darkness a whole new world has opened before him. Right, Edward?"

Edward nodded. "Yes, my Lord."

"Edward's strength is testament to his belief in the power that the darkness contains." Lancer continued. "Though I do not share the darkness with just anyone, Edward has proved quite brilliant."

Ryle snarled at Edward and Edward's eyes flashed and he backhanded Ryle across the face. Lancer paused in his walkabout and studied them. He smirked and continued on his journey about the room. "Even the love of his life serves me." Lancer smiled at Edward and Ryle watched as a brief semblance of pain washed through Edward's gaze.

"You could have that too, you know." Lancer grinned as he walked towards Ryle. "Get the door, Edward." Lancer pointed to the wooden door in the corner of the room. Edward opened it and a servant walked inside, her head bowed.

"Why, yes, it would not be Queen Alayna completely, but perhaps in part?" Lancer waved his hand and nothing happened. He looked to Edward. "A bit of help, Edward? I do not believe I'm back to full capacity just yet."

He and Edward waved their hand towards the servant and she transformed into Alayna. Ryle's heart hammered in his chest at the transformation and though longing filled his heart, the terror of that sort of power filtered through him.

"Ah, he's intrigued now Edward. Do you see?" Lancer laughed and rubbed his hands together. He knelt in front of Ryle and tapped his chest where the seal of the Northern Kingdom used to reside. "Hm, oh dear. Seems you lost something there, Prince Ryle. A sign of your true identity. Did you erase your tie with Queen

Alayna's Realm as a symbol of your conversion?" Lancer turned towards Edward with a sly tilt to his lips. "You are more than ready than I imagined. Edward," Lancer motioned to the side of Ryle. "Let us try to convince the Prince once more."

Lancer closed his eyes and extended his hands out and Edward mimicked his pose. Lancer peeked one eye open and then opened his eyes and rolled them in annoyance. "Edward." Edward opened his eyes. "Yes, my Lord?"

"My hand, Edward."

"Oh yes, apologies, my Lord." Edward slipped out his dagger and cut along Lancer's palm and did the same to his own. He then reached for Ryle's hand. Ryle gripped his hand into a fist, but Edward slowly unfolded his fingers enough to slice through his palm. Ryle did not flinch as fear began to overcome him at what possibly may consume him. "Bring the girl closer, Edward, and slice her palm as well." Lancer motioned to the servant who now looked like Alayna. She stood silently in front of Ryle.

"Look at her Prince Ryle. She could be yours." Lancer whispered as he closed his eyes. Edward did the same as Ryle studied the woman before him. Her eyes were Alayna's eyes and her hair was the mirror image of Alayna's as well. He found himself wishing he could touch the blonde curls, just to see if they felt the same way as the real Alayna's. The lanterns along the wall erupted and light flooded the room as the eerie black smoke slinked across the floor and began swirling around their feet. Ryle watched as Lancer breathed it in, the black billows seeping into his palm, his mouth, and his nostrils as he consumed the addicting source. Edward stood firm, his arms outstretched as if welcoming the flood. Ryle stared at the woman before him and her eyes held fear. A fear he knew matched his own. He closed his fist as blackness swirled around his legs and arms tightening him to the chair like ropes. His chest felt constricted and he closed his eyes and mouth to prevent any opportunity for the darkness to seep in. What seemed like hours was only a few minutes. He opened his eyes and saw the girl enveloped in the blackness. Lifted off of her feet and in a trance. When she settled upon her feet again and opened her eyes, they were black as night. The lights faded and Ryle watched the darkened Alayna. The woman exhibiting strength she did not possess before. To see the onyx storm in Alayna's eyes made him jolt.

"Pity." Lancer leaned towards Ryle's face and shook his head in disappointment. "I truly thought this might convince you. Look at the power you two could hold." He motioned towards the dark Alayna. She stood bravely next to Lancer and before she could mouth a word, Lancer brandished his sword and cut off her head. Ryle and Edward both looked on in shock.

Darkness crawled out of the woman's body, her appearance remained as Alayna, and Ryle wished to never see Alayna experience a death so bitter. He turned his head away and Lancer grabbed his chin forcing him to watch the woman's body bleed across the floor. The darkness hovered, circling around the room before slithering across the floor and seeping into Lancer's palm. His eyes brightened at the contact and he breathed in as if savoring a pleasant aroma. "Ah, that's better." He patted Ryle's shoulder. "Take care of the body, Edward. And take care of our Prince."

Katarina unfolded the letter, Queen Alayna's wax seal intriguing her to the letter's contents. She began to read:

Katarina, or shall I now say, Queen Katarina,

Congratulations on your coronation. I know you had intentions to wear the crown, but to hear you officially do is quite encouraging. I am happy for you.

I write to you with grave news. King Anthony has yet to be found, but we did find his royal caravan trapped in the Western hills, watched by a few of your father's guards. Guards who did not realize your father had passed. Unfortunately in our rescue attempt, none of these guards survived. Also, we unfortunately did not discover King Anthony. We are deeply saddened by this, Isaac and Melody most of all, though Isaac refuses to show his emotions on the matter. With this weakening in the West, King Eamon from the East will be overseeing that kingdom while his kingdom is taken care of by his Captain of the Guard. We are rallying our troops to begin preparations for battle against The Land of Unfading Beauty.

The time has come. The time for that blasted boundary to be destroyed, and I am writing to ask for your help. We do not know the status of your armies, but we wish to be able to call upon them if necessary. I await your word.

Queen Alayna

Katarina sighed and tucked the letter into her surcoat pocket as she continued down the hall. She turned to the guard standing outside her prison chamber and nodded. He opened the door and stepped aside as she began descending the steps.

Would she help the Realm defeat Lancer? Could she forget about her father's death and move forward? And what of Isaac? He held no remorse for killing her father. And though he claimed to be acting in self-defense, his action still poisoned her heart. She reached the bottom of the stairs and lit the lantern hanging above the farthest cell. Her secret. Her temptation with turning out like her father, sat before her, dirty, thin, mangy, and worn and despite the horrid appearance, she still struggled with giving into her revenge. King Anthony stared back at her with eyes much like Isaac's and she felt her anger bubble up within her.

Darkness and the trail of smoke billowed in the still air as she huffed out the light and quickly retreated out of the room. Just gazing upon the King of the West hastened her steps to reply to Alayna. The stakes of this upcoming battle had changed. And she was about to lay claim to what was rightfully hers.

Dearest Queen Alayna,

I will promise you my aid in the upcoming battle against Lancer and The Land of Unfading Beauty. The Lands plague us all. However, I have conditions. Conditions that I do not think you are going to like, and conditions that I am sure will change the way your realm prepares for this battle.

My father left me something. He was always planning for any unexpected event, and perhaps he foresaw the outcome of the last battles before they happened. Either way, he gave me an opportunity to show my strength while also avenging his death. I have your King of the West, King Anthony. He is in my possession. Yes, I said possession. He is mine. Prince Isaac killed my father and I find it only fitting I receive the same courtesy. King Anthony's life is in my hands. My father left him for me as if he knew Isaac would betray me and have him killed. How fitting it is that I now hold the life of Isaac's father in my hands, when he so willingly took my father's life. So here is my proposal and my offer of aid.

I will send troops to aid in your fight against the Lands. But should we all fail once more, your king's life is forfeit. I will keep him in my possession until the fate of the Lands has become known. Should we have victory, I will release him. Should we fail, he will die. I do not risk the lives of my armies without cost. King Anthony is the cost. I suppose this time you will have a clear plan on how you wish to defeat the Lands. Best to make them count.

I await YOUR word.

Queen Katarina

Elizabeth sat on the edge of her bed waiting for Clifton. She knew he was wrapping up a conversation with Isaac in the hall and she anxiously wound her hands in her lap at what she was about to tell him. *Would he be excited? Would he be scared like her?*

"Of course not." She whispered aloud. *He is not scared of anything.* As she mentally debated, Clifton opened the door and shut it behind him.

"I imagined you would already be in bed. You have had a long day." He leaned over and kissed her as he headed to the washbasin and began washing his face.

"I am quite tired." Elizabeth's voice was quiet and had him turning in suspicion.

"Is everything alright?"

She shook her head and a tear ran down her cheek. He hastened to her and knelt in front of her, gripping her hands in her lap. "What is the matter?" He kissed her knuckles and she sniffled, using one hand to wipe her dripping nose. Clifton watched as her blue eyes sought his. "I have news for you, and I am scared."

"You? Scared?" His brow furrowed. "Alright. I'm sure it is not as bad as it seems." He nervously pulled a chair towards her and sat, still holding her hands. "Tell me what is plaguing your mind, love."

She took a deep breath and looked up at him. "We are to have a baby."

She watched as the meaning of her words seeped into his mind. His eyes held confusion, glee, and then concern. "Are you not happy about this?" He asked.

"I am very happy." She confirmed. "I am just terrified."

He chuckled as he pulled her into a tight hug and kissed the top of her hair. "You have nothing to be terrified about, Elizabeth. This is exciting!" He pulled her away from him and kissed her heartily. "You will be an amazing mother. And I," he paused as if his next statement was unbelievable. "I am to be a father." A wide smile spread over his face as he kissed her again. He lifted her from the bed and spun her around the room, Elizabeth finally releasing a small giggle as she allowed him to sweep her off her feet. When he settled her back to the floor, he tilted her chin up to look into her beautiful face. "I am most pleased, Elizabeth. You have given me a great gift. I love you."

She smiled despite her tears and wrapped her arms around his waist and laid her head against his chest. His heartbeat strong and rhythmic soothed her nerves.

"Have you told Alayna?"

She shook her head and looked up at him. "Only your father knows."

"My father? You told my father?"

"Well, he sort of figured it out while we were in the West. And I guess you could say Queen Isabella knows, but I fear she will probably forget or assign my child to someone else entirely."

They both chuckled as he gently held her face in his hands and brushed his thumbs over her cheeks. "You are amazing, have I told you that?"

"Not lately." She replied with a grin.

Laughing, Clifton pulled her into another hug. "I say, I believe I am too worked up to go to sleep. I feel like shouting the news to everyone."

Elizabeth backed away and motioned towards the door. "Go ahead."

He grinned and darted out into the hall, standing along the landing and shouted down to the floors below, his arms outstretched. "I am to be a father!"

His words drifted down the halls as he repeated the phrase over and over until doors began opening and people began emerging from their private chambers. Elizabeth stood in the doorway and shook her head as she watched him. She wished to memorize the moment. Clifton, arms wide, radiant smile, and hopeful heart shouting his news to the world.

Edward walked through the Uniters' camp and sensed an imbalance. He could not tell for sure, but he sensed everyone treating him a bit differently. *Was it just his imagination?* He was not certain. The darkness tainted everything nowadays. What was real and what was not real was growing more difficult to decipher. His eyes roamed familiar faces, Cecilia nowhere to be found among them. He had asked around and no one had seen her. Who helped her escape? If it was not one of his Uniters, then who? Did someone loyal to Lancer know of his split loyalties and save her? The idea made his skin crawl. It would not be long before Lancer found out about his true allegiance and then what help could Edward be? He circled his neck around to loosen his muscles and the constant ache he had been carrying since his last encounter in the reflection chamber. Ryle was to be killed. He had not completed the task yet, but he would have to do it in order for Lancer to not question him. *Could he do it? Yes. No. Yes.* He shook his head, willing the darkness away as best he could, but the temptation to feel Ryle's life seep away from him and through his bare hands was dancing within Edward's mind.

He lifted himself into his saddle and caught sight of a familiar face. He recognized it, but could not place it. The young man turned before he could catch a second look. Shrugging, Edward turned his horse towards the castle. As he pulled into the stables, he handed his reins to the stable boy and set about his plan for Ryle. He walked straight to the prison chamber with purposeful strides.

He knocked his fist against the bars on Ryle's cell as he entered. Ryle slowly stood. "Is it that time already? Have you come to kill me?" The prince did not seem turned off by the aspect and Edward felt as if he were testing him.

"Shut it, would you?" Edward stated as he grabbed the key ring from the wall. "I am not going to kill you."

"Why not?"

"Because I am still loyal to the Realm. Why would I kill one of their princes?"

"Their?" Ryle asked.

"You know what I mean." Edward barked as he unlocked the cell and opened the door. Ryle still wore the shackles and walked slowly out, watchful of Edward.

"Do not look at me like I am insane." Edward nudged him towards the stairs. "Up."

"Where are you taking me?"

"I do not know. I intend to keep you hidden. Perhaps then you will see I am trustworthy."

"Why not send me back over the boundary? Lancer would not see me, and I could retreat back to the North."

"No. You remain here."

"Why?"

Edward's grip on his arm grew tighter and the Northern prince blew a hot stream of air as he attempted to maintain his composure. "Just trust me, okay?"

Ryle, not wanting to seem ungrateful for the pardon, kept his mouth shut. However, in his mind's eye he kept the fact that Edward was not releasing him at the forefront. He remained a prisoner, only this time, instead of being Lancer's prisoner he was Edward's.

Edward shoved him out the doorway into the stables, the stable boy just about to unmount his horse. "Leave it." Edward barked. He hoisted Ryle up onto the horse and covered his head with a saddle blanket. He then saddled up behind him and slapped the reins.

"Is this necessary?" Ryle asked under the heavy blanket, as the smell of sweet hay and horsehide flooded his nostrils.

"Yes. Now keep quiet." Edward rode fast and hard putting as much distance between the castle and himself as possible. When he felt comfortable, he dismounted and pulled Ryle down beside him, the Eastern prince stumbling to gain his footing. When he righted himself, Edward whipped back the saddle blanket, Ryle blinking against the bright sunlight.

"Where are we?"

"That is no concern of yours. All you must know is that this is where you will remain until the exact moment I need you."

Edward extended a rope around the base of a tree. "This should give you enough length to gather water at the river and to find shelter should it rain." He tied the rope to the shackles at Ryle's wrists.

"You are not removing these?" Ryle asked.

"No."

"Come now, Edward." Ryle clinked his wrists together. "How am I to live outdoors with my hands bound? Can you not tie it to my feet?"

"You will just untie it." Edward nervously ran a hand through his hair. "At least this way, your hands cannot untie the rope. I will check on you daily, so you do not need your hands for hunting purposes any way. Here." Edward cinched the rope tightly. "You're welcome."

"For what? Leaving me to live outside like a wild animal? You're right, I am so thankful." Ryle's sarcasm caused Edward's hand to lash out and slap him across the face. Both princes stood in surprise at the action. Edward looked at his hand as if it betrayed him. "I am sorry. You cannot speak to me that way."

"Why? Or the darkness will apparently manipulate you into lashing out?"

Edward clenched his fists. "You do not know the struggle, Prince Ryle. I am trying my hardest."

"Are you though?" Ryle asked. "I mean, you only grow stronger, and it seems you like it."

"I only like that I am stronger than Lancer. That is all."

"Are you sure?"

"Are you baiting me? Do you want me to kill you? Because that is what the darkness wants. It wants me to kill you, and I am trying really hard to fight that urge."

"Go ahead." Ryle stood with his hands in front of him. "But something tells me you are not so much of a coward as to kill an unarmed man."

Without a word, Edward abruptly turned, jumped into his saddle and rode away.

"My allegiance has not changed." Cecilia planted her hands on her hips as she glared at Samuel. "I will remain loyal to these lands. You cannot force me to follow your cause."

"Actually, I can." Samuel pointed out as he laid the basket of food before her. "Here is a supply for you for now."

Cecilia did not move to take the basket.

Samuel sighed and sat upon the nearest boulder and looked to her. "Prince Ryle saved you because he feels you are an important asset to us. We can utilize you in the upcoming battle."

"Prince Ryle does not know me."

"He does." Samuel challenged. "He is not blind. He sees where your ties remain. However, if he says we can use you, I trust him. Therefore, I will do my best to keep you hidden until that time."

"I should not have to hide." Cecilia spouted. "I am perfectly safe in these lands from Lancer."

"True enough, but you are not safe from Edward. He will kill you if he finds you. And I am sorry, Cecilia but we cannot let that happen."

"Edward loves me. He would never kill me."

"He did love you, yes. But you betrayed him. He threw you in prison, Cecilia. I do not think he cares for you any longer. Ryle believes he will kill you given the first opportunity."

"I would think your Realm would wish me dead. I betrayed all of you, not just Edward."

"I did not say we didn't." Samuel stood and walked towards his horse. "Should Edward kill you, we lose him. We do not wish for that to happen. It is not for your sake we wish for you to live. Think on that."

"So are we all to be pawns in the Realm's games? You yourself are a pawn, living here in secret? What if I tell Edward of your location? Will he kill you? Will he kill me then?"

"You will not have the chance to spoil any of the Realm's plans. If you do, I will kill you myself. You will remain right here." Samuel's words, though not as forceful as the other men she encountered, still made her heart drop to her feet. The young king was willing to do anything to protect his realm, even kill her if necessary. Did he not realize she was willing to do the same for her home?

She walked towards the basket and sifted through the food and supplies. She refused to believe her life was forfeit to the plans of the Realm of Queen Alayna. She loved the Lands. She would not aid the Realm in any way. If what King Samuel said was true, Edward did not love her anymore. She refused to believe that as well. She was the reason he crossed the boundary in the first place. She was the reason Lancer found him to be worthy of Captain, and it was her loyalty that brought Lancer's trust in Edward to new heights. If Edward or his realm thought they could brush her aside, they were sadly mistaken. Cecilia had worked too hard to be where she was, and she would not allow them to take her life away. Even a life in the Lands without Edward was still better than the life she would have in the Realm. She needed to figure out a way to sneak away and talk with Lancer. He had to know about Edward's true allegiance. And he had to know about King Samuel's purpose in the Lands.

Chapter 11

"A baby?" Isaac shook his head in disbelief.

"I know." Elizabeth stated. "It is quite overwhelming news."

"Clifton seemed thrilled last night." Isaac grinned as they both reflected upon Clifton's shouts of joy throughout the castle. The Eastern Prince had walked around telling everyone the news, even the servants.

"He is quite excited." Elizabeth confirmed with a tender smile.

"But you do not seem to be." Isaac's brow furrowed as he studied her. Her long sigh cluing him in even more so.

"I am excited." Elizabeth stated without much enthusiasm.

"Is this what excitement looks like?" Isaac jested.

Elizabeth's nervous laugh had him narrowing his gaze. "Tell me what bothers you, Elizabeth. Are you not happy?"

She nervously bit her bottom lip. "I am happy. I am just nervous is all. I mean… a baby changes everything."

"I've heard that." Isaac agreed.

"What if I'm not ready for things to change?"

"You have quite a while." He pointed out. "I hear it takes months before the baby actually arrives." He winked at her and he saw a small tilt to her lips that told him she was slowly coming out of her stupor.

"I know that. I just- I just want to be of use when the time comes for us to take on the Unfading Lands. Now that I am with child my role has changed. Clifton would not have me fighting. I am too delicate."

"No one would have you fight."

"Exactly my point!" She waved her hands in frustration. "It is not like me to be cast aside when a battle is waging. I wish to fight alongside everyone. I always fight. It's my purpose."

"Not anymore." Isaac watched as she pushed herself off the bench and began to pace.

"How would you like it if you were no longer able to participate in battle?" She asked.

"I would assume there would be another role offered to me. A different way I could be of use. You should consider that as well. You are not useless now that you are carrying a child. You have other strengths besides your fighting."

Elizabeth thought back to her father's letter and the words he penned to her about her strength. She brought people together is what he said. And she helped others see the strength within themselves. *Was that still true?*

"All I am saying is that you may find a place here that is more beneficial this time around. This battle will be different than the others. We risk everything going into the Lands. We need you here in the Realm should the worst happen. It is important the Realm maintain strong leadership should Clifton or I not return."

"You plan to cross the boundary?" Elizabeth looked to him in shock. "You cannot. You cannot cross back freely. You would be trapped."

"Not if we win." Isaac pointed out.

"But what if we don't?" Elizabeth seemed horrified at the prospect. "You are the future King of the West. You must stay on this side of the veil."

"It did not stop us from sending Samuel. The King of the South is currently in the Lands serving us. Imagine what two of us could accomplish."

Elizabeth shook her head. "No. We will have to think of other ways. Perhaps Clifton can lead the armies into the Lands. He can always cross back. You can guard this side of the boundary. Like last time."

"And we see how well that turned out." Isaac waved his hand as if he held a solid point. "We cannot repeat the same battle plan twice, Elizabeth. I know you realize that. With great victory comes great sacrifice. I'm willing to make that sacrifice if it means the boundary line falls."

"If the boundary line falls. If." She paced and flexed her fingers next to her sides. "We are not prepared for such a fight. Your father is still missing. Ryle is rescuing traitors. I'm with child. Edward is losing himself to the darkness. Samuel is in the Lands. Cecilia is free. What else could possibly come about?"

Elizabeth looked up as her sister ran towards them, Alayna's heavy skirts dragging against the small pebbles along the path through the gardens. "Prince Isaac! Elizabeth!" She called to them and waved a letter their direction. "Council Room at once!" She turned around swiftly and sprinted back towards the castle.

Elizabeth looked to Isaac in confusion as he stood. "I believe we are about to find out the answer to your question, Elizabeth."

Ryle twisted his wrists and pulled with all his might. Nothing. The rope Edward had tied to the center of his shackles would not budge and he could not find enough slack to wrench it free. He walked around the small alcove and hunted for something that might help him. His eyes landed on a sharp rock. Walking over to it, he sat on the plush grass and began raking the pointed rock over the rope. He heard hooves approaching and immediately climbed to his feet and walked away from what could be his savior as Edward hopped down from his saddle. He carried a linen sack and tossed it on the ground. "Your meals for the day." He turned to leave.

"That's it? You come and dump food at my feet and then leave?" Ryle asked. "Any word from the Realm?"

"No." Edward continued on his way towards his horse.

Ryle watched as he rode away.

"Unbelievable." He muttered, as he bent over to retrieve the supplies. Three small dinner rolls resided in the bag and Ryle leaned his head back in frustration. He could not live off bread and bread alone. His gaze wandered to the river and he wished for enough slack to wade in the water. Perhaps then he might catch a fish. But Edward had only allowed enough length for him to reach the edges of the river in order to drink or splash his face. He bit into one of the stale rolls and tried to be thankful as he walked back over to his rock. Sitting, he began rubbing the knot over the sharp point once more.

He had lived in the alcove of trees for several days now, and he did not know which side of the Lands he lived closest to. But he knew that should he free himself he would run to the nearest boundary line and cross back into the Realm immediately. He was done with these Lands. He was done with Lancer. And he most certainly was done with Edward. The Northern Prince grew more and more distant with every trip, and Ryle barely recognized Edward's gaze. Elizabeth and Edward had possessed the same crystal blue eyes as their father, but Edward's now shadowed. A shadow that did not disperse, and Ryle knew the darkness lingered closer to the surface than anyone anticipated. Edward could not be trusted. Not anymore. He wished he could send word to Samuel. Perhaps once he crossed back into the Realm and found his way back to the North, he could send word to Samuel about Edward's absolute untrustworthiness.

A small snagging sound brought his attention back to his ropes and he spotted one of the small threads had come free. He panted from the effort and felt a faint hint of victory at seeing the small thread blow in the wind. It would take time, but Ryle now had a means of escape. He raked his hands faster across the rock and prayed for freedom.

"Now what is the commotion about?" Elizabeth entered the Council Room and walked towards her seat as Isaac took his across from her. They were the last to arrive and Clifton gripped her hand under the table, her husband's nerves filtering through his touch.

"We received a letter from Katarina." Alayna began, her eyes wild with restrained fury.

"Does she not wish to align with us?" Melody asked curiously.

Alayna held the back of her hand to her lips, gathering her strength as she gripped the letter so tightly it began to crumble in her hand.

"Alayna?" Elizabeth asked, worry causing her to reach out and touch her sister's sleeve.

Alayna dropped her hand and turned to Isaac and Melody.

"She has your father."

Isaac immediately bolted from his seat. "What?!"

Alayna read Katarina's words and everyone sat with baffled expressions, minus Isaac, as he paced about the room punching the wall in various spouts of anger.

King Eamon inhaled a deep breath. "It would seem Abner outsmarted us all."

"We will go get him." Elizabeth stated adamantly. "It's as simple as that. Her offer is ludicrous. If she does not wish to align with us under peaceful terms, we will not be peaceful. We will fetch King Anthony with the full backing of the entire Realm. Her armies will not stand a chance against us."

"We cannot proclaim war on the Valleylands. We need them." Alayna stated.

"But her demands are preposterous." Elizabeth challenged.

"I agree. But we will meet them."

"What?!" Isaac turned and faced Alayna in horror. "You place my father's life in the hands of whether or not we find victory?! I will not stand by this decision." He looked to Clifton.

Clifton held up his hand for the letter and silently reread Katarina's words, as everyone around him continued to argue over what the next step should be.

"I believe I just found my next purpose." Elizabeth declared. "I will travel to the Valleylands and personally retrieve King Anthony."

"And how would you manage that, sister?" Alayna asked with slight annoyance.

"I will simply walk in and demand his return. Should she refuse, I will kill her." The dark thought surprising everyone at Elizabeth's boldness.

"You cannot just kill someone." Alayna pointed out.

"Yes, I can. She is withholding one of our kings, Alayna. Her action is a crime against the Realm. I understand we wish to have her help against Lancer, but we should not put King Anthony's life at such a risk. She should also know that such a request is unacceptable. I will demand she return him. And should she not, there will be consequences."

King Eamon sat silently as he listened to his daughter-in-law and the vengeful line of thinking she proposed. "Vengeance is never the answer, Elizabeth." He stated. "Vengefulness is what caused this mess to begin with. It is what constructed the Land of Unfading Beauty. It is what prompted Edward's crossing. It is what prompted our first attack. And it has caused nothing but more pain and turmoil. Katarina is seeking vengeance now; let her learn the consequences of such an action. We know the consequences, therefore we must rise above that line of thinking."

"Then what do you suggest? We cannot just leave King Anthony's life up to chance." Elizabeth leaned forward as she waited for King Eamon to speak.

"I say we agree to her terms." Eamon said and had Isaac falling into his seat in defeat. Eamon lightly patted the prince on the back as he continued. "We cannot achieve victory without the help of the Valleylands."

"But what if we don't?" Melody asked. "She will kill him."

"Should we not achieve victory, then we plan a rescue mission for Anthony. Let us try to maintain a peaceful alliance with Katarina while we need her. Should the time arise that the battle does not look to be in our favor, I will personally lead the fight against what little protection remains in the Valleylands and rescue Anthony. He is a dear friend; I will not let him die. But we must play our hand carefully to ensure our war with the Lands is successful. Let her think she possesses the upper hand. Meanwhile, we plan accordingly."

"Am I just to sit here and let my father be tortured?" Isaac asked.

"She said nothing of torture." Alayna pointed out.

"But how do we know?" He asked.

"I will send word back to her." Alayna explained. "That we will accept her terms but that should King Anthony be harmed in any way before the outcome of the war is decided, she risks war upon her own kingdom."

"I cannot believe we are agreeing to this." Elizabeth shook her head in dismay as Clifton squeezed her hand. "What do you think about this?"

Clifton shifted in his chair. "I like my father's plan. I realize we are asking much of Isaac and Melody in ways of trust, but again, we will not let her kill him. We will find a way to reach both endings that we desire. A victory in the Lands. And a rescue of Anthony. His fate is tied to the fate of us all. Should the Lands prevail again, we are all lost. So I say, we rally our forces and begin plans against Lancer immediately so that our loved ones will no longer be separated from us."

Clifton stared into Elizabeth's eyes and saw her disappointment, but she agreed by nodding. "Very well." She turned to Alayna. "What news from Samuel?"

Clifton pulled out the latest letter from Samuel and handed it to Alayna. Having briefed her earlier, Alayna did not take the time to read the note, but instead began retelling Samuel's proposals. "He feels his forces there in the Lands are as ready as we are."

"And our soldiers are ready to fight once again?" Alayna asked. Both Clifton and Isaac nodded in agreement.

"Very well. Samuel feels that we should take a different approach this time. He wishes to attack from all sides."

"Surround them." Isaac pointed out. "It's a good plan."

"One we have not done before." Clifton added. "It would take all armies. Though we have the Uniters on the inside, Lancer's army will not be able to withstand a full attack from all kingdoms plus the Valleylands. We would take over his loyal troops just by sheer number. Our biggest dilemma is how we reach Lancer himself. That boundary does not come down unless he does. And then there is the question of the darkness. Where does it go? And what of Edward? He possesses it to."

"They both must fall." Alayna pointed out, sadness in her words.

"Alayna, do you realize what you are saying?" Elizabeth asked.

"Yes, Lizzy, I do. Both Lancer and Edward need to be separated from the darkness. If we should find a way that does not involve death, we will try. But we must consider the possibility we may lose our brother in this fight."

Elizabeth's head dropped and she felt Clifton's reassuring touch to her fingers in her lap. She gripped his hand tightly in response.

"Can we be ready in a week?"

"I must travel to the West and send word to the East. We may need more time than that." King Eamon suggested.

"Two weeks time then." Alayna declared. Everyone silently nodded in agreement; the weight of their decision flooded the room and no one said a word.

Ryle felt the last of the rope threads snap and he leaned his head back in relief. The sun filtered through the tree branches and kissed his face as a fresh breeze ruffled the leaves. Sending up a prayer of thanks, he climbed to his feet and stepped out of the alcove. He did not recognize his whereabouts and decided to begin walking North. He figured Edward would more than likely take him as far from his desired location as possible. He stayed along the tree line; should he encounter any guards along the way, he wished to have the advantage of a hiding space.

He started jogging as fast as he could with the shackles clamped around his ankles, the heavy chain tiring him within minutes. He slowed his pace to a brisk walk and found it easier though frustratingly slow. He darted into the trees at the sound of hooves along the road and noticed several of Lancer's guards passing by. *He had to be near the castle,* he realized. He ducked back out to gauge his surroundings and spotted the veil not far from his location. Liberation in sight, he hurried as fast as he could move to reach the boundary.

The fog grew closer and Ryle felt his chest tighten with exertion as he wound his way over rocks and downed trees. The shackles around his ankles hooked on a stone as he tried to race over the pebbled terrain and he stumbled over his feet until he face planted on the ground. Grunting and rolling over to his back with a groan, he looked up and saw the sun shift behind the fluffy clouds in the brightest sky he had seen for months. Panting, he tried to erase from his mind the pain he felt in every inch of his body. Willing himself to keep moving, he shifted to his knees. "Get up, Ryle." He ordered himself. "Get up." He struggled pulling his weight to his feet, but he rose. Raising his head up towards the boundary line, he began moving again. One foot in front of the other until he cleared the tree line and the boundary line lingered before him.

Tunnel vision had always been a habit of his. When he focused upon a goal, he blocked everything out until he reached his desired outcome. His father had always called it pride. Ryle possessed too much pride in certain circumstances. His pride prevented him from seeking others' counsel when sometimes it was necessary. However, he felt his pride is what helped him from giving in to Lancer and Edward as well. Could it be that his stubborn pride was to be the one attribute that saved his life? He refused to stop and continued pushing forward. He was almost there. The veil beckoned him like a waterfall after days of thirst. As he jogged towards safety, he stumbled yet again and quickly gathered himself together and growled as he climbed to his knees and took a deep breath. His cheek marred by a bloody scratch from the ground. Taking one more deep breath he placed his right foot beneath him and began to rise.

He froze. The cold blade pressed into the side of his neck and he dared not breathe.

"What have we here?"

The voice sent chills up his spine and he felt the hairs on the back of his neck rise as Lancer circled around him with a smug smile; Lancer's blade, pressed against the Adam's apple, never left Ryle's neck.

"And here I thought you were dead." Lancer continued. He shook his head. "It would seem Edward did not quite have it in him to dispense of you. That's a shame."

"Do what you will." Ryle barked, his shoulders straightening as he knelt before the evil ruler.

Lancer laughed. "I had hoped Edward killed you, but his compassion is a black mark against him. I think I will take care of you myself. Though death will have to wait. I have other plans for you."

Lancer brought the hilt of his sword down hard against Ryle's temple, and the Prince of the East crumbled to the ground.

The Western armies arrived within days, followed by the Eastern Kingdom. Isaac and Clifton gathered all the forces together to explain their assault. The Southern Kingdom arrived next, led by Mosiah, King Granton's former Captain of the Guard. Clifton had never seen such a desire in the eyes of the South to save their king. Samuel was already loved by his kingdom, and for that, Clifton was thankful. They all had something to lose. Their freedom. Their kingdoms. Their lives. Everything was at risk and teetered on the edge of collapse, but he would not allow another failure. He felt positive they would restore the Realm and tear down Lancer's boundary. It was only a matter of time. And he felt the time was now. He looked up as Isaac galloped towards him. Pulling his reins, the Western prince grimaced. "Katarina's troops are here. They are headed this way. She rides with them in her caravan."

Clifton nodded in understanding. "I will see to it. Give these troops their orders." He slapped his reins and rode towards the front of the castle as Katarina emerged from her carriage. She smiled, a hint of malice in her expression. "Prince Clifton." She bowed.

He dismounted. "We were not expecting you to travel with your army, Katarina."

"You sound disappointed."

"Not disappointed." Clifton clarified. "Surprised. You will find a stiff welcome here, I'm afraid."

"I figured as much." She accepted the hand her attendant offered her as she climbed the steps to the castle. "I still maintain my agreement, but you can trust my word. My army will fight with you. We all must see the boundary line fall, I am not so blind to that fact. And if partnering with the Realm of Queen Alayna is how to accomplish the task, I will do it. But I still hold the King of the West until the end. Prince Isaac brought that upon himself."

"Very well." Clifton forced himself to remain polite as he walked into the castle with her and Elizabeth was making her way down the stairs. His wife froze, her blue eyes narrowing as she surveyed the Valleylands' newest queen.

"You are far from home, Katarina." She stated, as she finished her descent.

"Ah, Princess Elizabeth, good to see you again."

Elizabeth did not respond. Instead, she looked up at her husband. "I must get back." Clifton stated and brushed a kiss over her lips as he departed. Elizabeth watched him leave and turned to make her way to the conservatory, leaving Katarina standing in the doorway.

"Am I to receive the cold shoulder from you as well, Elizabeth?" Katarina asked. "I thought we were friends."

"We were never friends." Elizabeth turned to face her. "You are an acquaintance. You ruined all chance of being a friend when you captured one of our kings."

"I did not capture him, my father did." Katarina pointed out.

"Yet you keep him. Do not act so innocent, Katarina. It is unbecoming."

Katarina felt the verbal slap from across the room and smiled coyly. "I see. Well, we must learn to live amongst one another for the next few weeks. I hope you are able to handle my presence."

"Why would she need to?" Alayna walked into the room and nodded a greeting towards her sister and circled around Katarina as she took her seat on the edge of a chaise.

"Well we will be in the same castle, I hope we may learn to tolerate one another." Katarina smiled sweetly, her once quiet voice endearing, now reeked of poison, and Alayna found her off putting.

"You will not be staying inside the castle." Alayna clarified.

Katarina's false confidence wavered, as she stood dumbfounded. "What do you mean?"

"Your invitation to the North did not include a stay at our castle. Your army and your caravan will have access to camping within the Northern borders, but that does not give you an open invitation to grace the halls of the castle. Why, it doesn't even include access through the castle gates." Alayna waved for Tomas to step forward. "Please direct Queen Katarina back to her caravan and send the entry guards to guide her to their camp location."

Tomas bowed and waited as a shocked Katarina stammered a response. Not knowing what to say, Katarina turned in a huff and stalked out of the room.

Elizabeth's grin spread across her face as she slowly clapped her hands. "Bravo, sister."

Alayna smirked and smoothed a hand over her skirts. "You think I'm going to let that conniving queen lurk about our home and play on Isaac and Melody's feelings? Not in my castle."

Elizabeth chuckled as Melody entered with a panicked look on her face. "Was that Katarina? Is she staying here? Has Isaac seen her?"

Alayna held up her hand. "Slow down, Melody. Take a breath. No, Katarina is not staying here. She will be camped in the Northern kingdom with her troops, however, so we must attempt to be polite should we come across her. But she will not be within the castle."

Melody physically relaxed before them. "Thank you for that. Why, I do not know if I could even look at her at the moment without spewing words of distaste."

"You?" Elizabeth asked in amusement. "My goodness, it is bad if Melody cannot be nice." She and Alayna chuckled as Melody flushed and sat across from the two sisters. "Yes, well it is not me I worry about. Isaac would probably kill her, or at least entertain the thought."

"Prince Isaac has bigger issues on his plate at the moment. He and Clifton are gathering the armies and the next few days will be spent forming their strategies and rotations. Let's not worry him with the details of the Valleylands' queen. In fact, Elizabeth, I would like you to keep your eye on Katarina, if you don't mind?" Alayna asked.

Elizabeth, hungry for responsibility, accepted gladly. "It would be more than a pleasure, sister."

"Good. I do not want her out of sight. And should we need to delay her return to the Valleylands in order to rescue Anthony, I may need you to... distract her." Alayna continued.

"Again, it would be my pleasure." Elizabeth's lips curled into a smile that withheld her anger at Katarina, but told Alayna her sister would do whatever was necessary to prevent the Valleylands' queen from harming her friends or her kingdom.

Chapter 12

Samuel waved to Isaac across the line as he bent over to retrieve the letter the Western Prince tossed across the line. Samuel read the battle plans for the upcoming days. With a smile, Samuel nodded in agreement through the veil.

Isaac turned to leave but then spotted Edward riding up to the clearing on the other side. He watched as Samuel ducked into the trees unnoticed, and Edward pulled his reins to a stop. He noticed Isaac and he smiled as he dismounted. He offered a wave as Isaac stepped forward. Edward mimicked the writing motion with his hand and Isaac shook his head. He did not have any writing supplies with him. He had brought the letter from Samuel and that was it. Edward's brow furrowed in confusion. He hoped the Northern prince did not wonder too much about why Isaac would venture to the boundary line without writing supplies. Why else would he be here? Isaac looked around at the targets Elizabeth had once used as a training ground. That would be his excuse. Time away from the castle and a place to practice. Edward tossed a rock across the line, a small piece of parchment attached. Isaac bent to retrieve it.

Prince Isaac,

I must say I am surprised to see you. I have been patrolling the boundary for weeks waiting for word from the Realm, but no one has shown up until now. Any word on what my sister plans to do in the near future? I honestly thought the Realm would have acted by now.

"I'm sure you did." Isaac mumbled.

Please fill me in on upcoming plans. I cannot be of service to the Realm if I do not know the strategies going forward.

Isaac looked up at the expectant Edward, the Northern prince pacing back and forth awaiting a response from Isaac. Watching him, Isaac debated his response. Edward stopped walking and Isaac motioned over his shoulder and then flicked his wrist as if he were writing. He had nothing to write a response with, thankfully. Therefore, he signaled to Edward that he would have to leave and come back. Edward stepped close to the boundary and studied Isaac openly. His eyes narrowed, and Isaac stepped forward to study him in return. Edward's eyes were clouded and his mouth taut. Deciding Isaac told the truth, Edward nodded and turned to leave the clearing.

When Edward had ridden off, Samuel emerged once more and gave Isaac two thumbs up before scampering off into the trees once more. Shaking his head and rubbing a hand over his face, Isaac sighed. Their plans to not inform Edward were harder than he anticipated. The fact Edward would be awaiting a response from him worried him more, and he knew he had to talk with Clifton to see what information they decided to pass along. Meanwhile, Samuel had his own plans to execute within the Lands. A plan that he wished to allow a week's time to implement. A week. One week and the veil before him would be gone. Isaac flushed his hand into the fog and felt the tingling sensation course through him. He would cross in a week's time, and he prayed he would not be trapped on the other side. Victory was essential. He had assured Elizabeth that success was bound to happen. Now he just needed assurance for himself.

Edward pulled his reins to a stop and jumped from his saddle to the ground and walked through the trees to where Ryle would be waiting. He ducked under a low lying limb and his eyes adjusted to the shady alcove. He stopped. His breath leaving his lungs in one loud strangled cry of outrage. Ryle was gone. He searched through the alcove and came across the shredded rope and the rock in which Ryle used to escape. He flung the rock with all his might, the stone pelting against a tree and leaving a chip in the bark. Edward tried to calm himself, but his heart pounded. His ears drummed with every beat, and he felt his blood rush through his veins. He felt hot, his face flushed as he struggled to maintain his control. *How dare he escape?!* Edward sank to his knees as he wrestled with the anger rising up within him, the pounding in his chest causing his emotions to flare and his resolve to melt.

In a moment, Edward felt the last of his control slip away and an eerie calm washed over him. His breaths stabilized. His heart slowed to a normal rhythm. And when he stood to his feet, his legs felt stronger than ever. When he turned to survey the alcove one more time, a smirk tilted his lips. He hoped Lancer did not find out about Ryle's survival or his escape. However, Edward now felt a sense of peace in his purpose. *What did it matter if Ryle escaped back into the Realm? What did it matter that Edward had not received word from the Realm? All that mattered now was power.* And power was what he was after. Power is what he wanted, and power he would get.

With a new purpose, Edward set forth towards the castle. It was time Lancer recognized Edward's strength. It was time for Lancer and Edward to combine their powers together in the Reflection chamber. A slow, creeping, inner voice whispered to Edward, beckoning him to the chamber. Yes. He and Lancer would be strong in their fight against the Realm. Edward had lost his role in the Realm to his sister. His purpose relinquished to Alayna. But here, here in The Land of Unfading Beauty, Edward realized he had more than he could ever dream of. He had supremacy. Combining he and Lancer's power was the only way to ensure Prince Ryle and the rest of the Realm did not succeed in tearing down the boundary. Suddenly, the only thing that mattered was the boundary line.

Suddenly, all Edward desired was for his family to suffer the consequences of war. And suddenly, Edward was lost.

Samuel motioned towards the basket in front of Cecilia. "Are you not going to take it?"

Cecilia eyed him with suspicion. "Why are you releasing me?"

Shrugging, Samuel turned to leave.

"Wait!" Cecilia called to him. The young king, though lacking in age, possessed a domineering stance. *He was tall*, Cecilia realized. *And regal.* She had not noticed those traits until now as he patiently waited for her to speak.

"I don't understand." She said.

"I do not wish to hold you captive anymore. That is all you need to know. I am not like the other men in my realm. Malice is not in my nature. So I release you. Besides," he continued. "In a week's time the Unfading Lands will be defeated. The Realm will sneak upon him from the North and he will have no way of escaping the battle that is coming for him. So I do not care of your fate, Cecilia. Because in a week's time, theses Lands will be a memory."

Cecilia watched as he turned and walked away. *The Realm planned to attack from the Northern Kingdom?* She pondered the thought and quickly gathered the basket of food. She needed to find Lancer. She needed to inform him of the Realm's plans, and she needed to find Edward.

Samuel watched from behind a tree as Cecilia hurried away in the direction of the castle. His plan was in place. He knew she would run straight to Lancer for protection and to inform him of the Realm's plan to strike from the North. However, what Cecilia did not know was that Samuel had planted a false strategy in her mind. The Realm's intention was not to strike from the North at all. He smiled to himself. His purpose in the Land of Unfading Beauty had just been partially been fulfilled. Now all he needed to do was to make sure his Uniters were ready to fight one last time.

When he stepped back into the Uniters' camp he quickly ducked behind a tree once more as Edward stalked around the camp barking orders to the guards to gather their belongings. Listening closely, Samuel snagged a guard that attempted to flee the clearing. He covered the man's mouth as he pulled him behind the trees. "What is happening?" Samuel whispered.

"Prince Edward is forcing us to break camp and move back into the villages. He said there is no longer a need for our services. He plans to escort us back, with the help of Lancer's guards. We are surrounded." The man's panicked voice caused Samuel's heart to race.

"Keep calm." Samuel ordered him softly. "There must be a way to escape."

"They have us blocked on the other side. It will not be long until they come this way as well."

Samuel watched as horrified Uniters scrambled around the camp and gathered their belongings. Some sprinted into the trees disregarding their personal items. But others remained, panic stricken. Meanwhile, Edward rounded them up like sheep, herding them towards his guards. *What had made the prince fully turn against them?* He wondered.

"Hear me now," Samuel said to the guard next to him. "Run towards the river and navigate your way towards the Western Boundary line. And should you see anyone else, tell them the same. I will find you there."

The man nodded and darted away like a scared squirrel. Samuel climbed into the nearest tree and settled upon the branches as he watched events unfold before him. No one was killed, but he wondered if Edward were leading these people to their slaughter. Thankfully, Samuel had moved the weapons to another location a few days prior, so Edward would not be able to find their arsenal, another fact, he was sure would bother Edward. However, he watched as the prince overturned anything in sight hunting for weapons. Samuel noticed the hardened face held a shadow of panic as well. As if Edward needed to find their weapons. As though he needed to bring down the Uniters' camp himself.

The only thought in Samuel's mind was to save the fellow Uniters. What he did not know was how he was going to accomplish such a task without a full army supporting him. He needed to talk to Clifton immediately, but he did not know how he could notify the Eastern prince. As the camp cleared, Samuel slowly climbed down from his lofty position and travelled towards the Western Boundary praying he still had an army.

Days went by and a dreary mood had settled over the castle. Elizabeth wound her way through the halls and out to the gardens. Needing color, needing fresh air, and needing peace, she found her way towards Mary's stone. She lightly kissed the tips of her first two fingers and placed it upon the top before she sat at the bench across from the marker of her dearest friend.

"It is that time, Mary." Her words drifting through the wind. "We plan to attack the Unfading Lands in two days' time."

She reached for a pale yellow rose on the bush beside her. Plucking the small blossom she inhaled its familiar scent, a small comfort settling upon her heart as she rubbed a hand over her swollen stomach. Not much of a change yet, she knew, but her corset laces were slowly being loosened each passing day.

"You are seeking solace, and yet I find myself needing to speak with you."

She turned as Clifton walked towards her and sat.

"That is okay. You are the only one allowed to interrupt me." He smiled as she handed him the rose bud. "What is it you wish to tell me?"

Sighing, Clifton draped his arm over her shoulders as they sat. "Melody ventured to your clearing today to converse with Samuel."

"Yes, she has been doing that quite religiously." Elizabeth stated. "I think it quite cute."

Clifton's lips twitched into a partial smile before he continued. "Yes, well not today. She came back in a frenzy. Samuel had tossed a letter across the boundary but he was nowhere in sight."

"So he may not have been able to get away from the Uniters at the time. What is her concern?"

"His letter." Clifton continued. "He claimed Edward stormed the Uniters' camp and disbanded everyone sending them back to the villages."

Elizabeth gasped, her hand covering her lips. "No."

Clifton nodded. "I am afraid so. Samuel says he has a small group along the Western boundary lines, but that most of their number was escorted out of the camp by Lancer's guards. He wishes to execute a rescue mission, but Isaac and I feel we should wait until the actual battle. We do not wish to let on that we are coming any time soon. An escape mission so close to our plan to take down Lancer is too risky. We do not want him to be prepared for us."

"So what are you proposing?"

"That we continue with our plans to attack the Lands on schedule, and absorb the loyal Uniters as we condense towards the castle. They may join up along the way."

"What if Edward has them executed?"

"I do not think he will."

"Well he obviously has lost his mind if he betrayed them to Lancer already." Elizabeth's voice was pained. "He is lost, isn't he?

"No." Clifton replied, turning her chin towards him so he could gaze into her eyes. "He is confused. Edward is still in there somewhere. You must not give up on him. The darkness shades his judgment. That is all."

"Yet we have no idea how to rid him of it."

"Not yet. Other than wounding him like Alayna did Lancer, we have no idea. But we will think of something, Elizabeth. We will."

"Have you spoken to Alayna of these plans?"

"I have. Isaac as well. We are all in agreement. You are the last vote."

She searched Mary's grave with her gaze as if her friend held the answer. Tilting her head to read over the stone, she turned to her husband. "I agree with the rest of you. But I do believe a letter needs to be sent to Samuel. He needs to be informed."

"Yes, Isaac was headed there now."

"So you did not need my opinion after all?" Elizabeth asked, her voice intrigued that Clifton acted without first speaking to her.

"I knew you would agree." He tapped her nose and then stood. "I will leave you with Mary now. I must begin preparations. My armor needs fastenings replaced."

Elizabeth stood. "I should follow you inside. I am sure I am needed elsewhere."

He brushed his hand over her hair as she lightly kissed her fingers and bid farewell to Mary once more.

Clifton slid his arm around her waist as they walked back towards the castle.

"I would like to name the baby Mary, if it is a girl." Elizabeth stated.

Clifton looked down at her. "Are you so sure it is a girl?"

Elizabeth smiled. "No. I am just mentioning my requests."

Laughing, Clifton hugged her towards him as they continued walking. "I see. Well it is duly noted, and I will say that I find Mary to be a fine name." He kissed the top of her head as the guards opened the doors for them to enter into the castle.

Lancer stood before his fireplace, the licking of the flames over the blackened stones pulling him into a meditative stupor. He felt his strength returning day by day. And for some reason today he had felt a surge in his heart. He felt like his old self again. He was not sure what action initiated the process. Perhaps his stumbling upon the Eastern Prince, or quite possibly his trust in Edward. Edward had exceeded his expectations and Lancer could tell his friend now allowed the darkness to flow through him freely. *Why then did he release the Eastern prince instead of killing him like he ordered?* Lancer did not feel the normal anger that would flood him over such a direct act of disobedience. Instead, he would remain watchful of Edward. Yes, he was powerful and beneficial, but should a weakness for his former people weaken him to the point of acting against him, Lancer knew he would not hesitate in removing Edward from the Lands. He would kill him. And unlike Edward, Lancer did not pardon. He would kill him if need be and Edward would not escape his wrath. A knock sounded on his chamber door and he turned to find a guard standing in the doorway.

"You disturb me for a purpose?" He asked.

"There is someone here to speak with you, my Lord. She says it is urgent."

Lancer's brows rose in curiosity as he made his way to the door. "I'll meet her in the great hall."

The guard nodded and exited quickly. Lancer straightened his tunic and rolled his shoulders back. Inquisitive to who might wish to speak to him, he hurried down the hallway.

Cecilia stood with her back to him, but he recognized her immediately. His loyal Cecilia.

"You are brave coming to the castle, my dear." Lancer watched as she jumped in her skin before turning towards him. Her appearance dirty and unkempt.

"Are you ill?" He motioned towards her form.

She shook her head. "No, my Lord. I am fine. Well, not completely fine. I have grave news for you, my Lord."

"Is that so?"

She nodded. "News of the Realm, my Lord. They plan to attack again and soon."

"And how do you know of this?"

"I was kidnapped by King Samuel of the Southern Kingdom."

"King Samuel? You are able to cross the boundary freely?"

"No, my Lord. He is here... in the Lands. He has been living amongst a secret camp of Uniters against your kingship. Those loyal to the Realm of Queen Alayna wish to overthrow you. They live in secret so as to act as the guards for the Realm's causes within the Lands."

"You know this how? We killed all of these Uniters after the last battle for treason."

"No, my Lord. Some of them escaped your punishment."

"I see." Lancer's voice hardened.

"And what do you know of the Realm's upcoming attack? Edward has not mentioned anything to me about a possible attack."

"He does not know about it either. They do not trust him. King Samuel believes him to be lost to the darkness that you both possess and they withheld this information from him so he would not report their actions to you."

"And why did King Samuel expound upon these plans to you?"

"I do not think he meant to, my Lord. He is young and naïve. When he released me, he said he was not going to kill me because it was not in his nature. However, he said my punishment would come when the Realm invaded from the North in two days' time. That is how I know. The Realm will be attacking the Lands from the North." Cecilia nervously nudged her hair behind her ear, the smudges of dirt upon her face distinct against her pale skin.

Lancer smiled slowly and welcomed her with an outstretched arm. "Cecilia, welcome to my home." He motioned for two guards to step forward. "Make sure she receives the finest care." He nodded towards them as they escorted Cecilia to another wing of the castle. Her loyalty astounded him.

Edward's boots echoed through the great hall as he entered the castle. He slid to a stop when he saw Lancer bidding Cecilia farewell. Lancer turned and his smile widened. "Ah, Edward. We need to talk, my friend."

Edward's stomach dropped as Lancer walked towards him. "Now, my Lord?"

"Yes and it is imperative we talk in the Reflection chamber. Come." He waited for Edward to walk alongside him.

"What is Cecilia doing here?" Edward asked, trying to keep a calm tone in his voice.

"She brought great news. I have rewarded her with a stay in the castle. Though you are more than welcome to allow her to stay in your chambers. I did not think of that before. You two are still in a relationship, I presume?"

Edward did not know how to respond so he nodded. "Of sorts."

Laughing, Lancer patted his back as he bypassed him to enter the room first.

Closing the door behind them, Edward watched as Lancer walked to the center of the room with arms wide. "I feel incredible, Edward." His smile stretched across his face as he faced Edward. "I do not know why or how, but I feel stronger than ever."

Edward walked forward. "I have an idea why."

Lancer's right brow arched. "Oh?"

"Today I stumbled across a camp of Realm followers. I destroyed it."

Lancer threw his head back and laughed heartily. "That is the best news I've heard all day, Edward. Wonderful! You are brilliant. It is no wonder your family no longer trusts you."

"My Lord?"

"Cecilia." Lancer mentioned, pointing towards the door as he continued smiling and pulled a chair to the center of the room. "She came to deliver news of a surprise attack in a couple of days and I asked how you did not know this. She said they no longer trusted you enough to inform you."

"How would she know?"

"It appears we have a king hiding in our midst." Lancer acknowledged with a passing wave of his hand. "King Samuel of the South."

Edward thought back to the familiar face in the Uniters' camp and he nodded. "I see."

"Seems he held Cecilia captive for quite some time. The poor dear looked absolutely dreadful."

Her rescue, Edward realized, *was by King Samuel. That is why Ryle did not wish to tell him.* Something was amiss, Edward thought. A gnawing in his gut told him Cecilia's appearance was not by mere chance, but how did he explain this to Lancer without turning Lancer against him?

"Do you trust her words?" Edward asked.

"Of course I do. She informed us of the last attack and it was truthful. I do not doubt her now, that is for certain."

"What course of action do you wish to take, my Lord?"

"We will fight, of course. One thing about your sister's realm, Edward, is that they seem to forget who I am." He winked as he sat in the chair and sliced his palm. He tossed the knife to Edward for him to do the same. Satisfied, he allowed his hand to drip to the floor. "They forget that it is my blood that created the boundary and it is my blood that holds it. Should they present another attack, again they will be beaten. Those who cannot cross back will die. Same as last time. They will fail. I am surprised she continues to assault us."

"For Alayna to feel another attack necessary, they must be stronger than last time, my Lord. She is not unwise. She would not make such a sacrifice of her people if she did not feel she could win."

"That is where she is wrong, Edward. Your sister is rash. Look what she did to me in the clearing that day. She thought she could stab me and kill me." He laughed. "The look of horror on her face when you channeled the darkness back into me was priceless. She has no idea who she is dealing with. And it is our chance to show her. They will attack from the North in two days. I suggest you rally up the guard and be ready." Lancer closed his eyes and his breathing decreased to long, soothing breaths as he summoned the darkness that awaited their invitation. Edward mirrored Lancer's actions and before he could level his breaths, he felt the familiar climbing of the blackness crawling up his legs. Only this time, he welcomed it.

Two days. Alayna shook her head. When the days flew by quickly, she now faced herself in the mirror. Sitting at her vanity, she adjusted the crown upon her head. It was time for her to make her appearance to the armies of the realm and the Valleylands. Katarina would be present as well, but would not be given the opportunity to speak. Alayna slid another pin into her blonde curls to secure the crown to her head. Words of encouragement, words of support, and words of enthusiasm. Today was the day that all their lives would change. She stood and Jessa stepped forward to drape her emerald cape over her shoulders. The heavy fabric pulled behind her, and she waited for Jessa to lay the train of the cape across the floor. "You are ready, my Lady." Jessa bowed. "You look beautiful."

Alayna turned towards the door. "It's not about beauty today, Jessa, but thank you." She gathered the front of her skirts and made her way out of the room and down the grand staircase. King Eamon awaited her at the bottom and offered his escort to the front of the castle. "How do you feel, my dear?"

"A little nervous. I've never spoken to so large a crowd, especially a crowd I am asking to risk their lives."

"Leaders face such tasks not for others to envy, that is for certain. Such times and duties are a burden that we must bear. However, most times the risks are necessary in order to reach a positive outcome. These men know their risks, Alayna. They serve despite the risks, so do not feel you are personally responsible for all of their fates."

"Easier said than done, I'm afraid." Alayna stated as the doors opened and she stepped out onto the main landing of the castle. Troops spread as far as she could see, within the castle gates and beyond. She stood in awe at the sheer size of her army and turned a surprised glance towards Elizabeth. Her sister's brows rose in amusement and she smiled. Melody held Elizabeth's hand while Katarina stood towards the side with her chin held high as if the cheering throughout the crowd was for her.

Alayna placed her hand on her heart as she looked around. Knowing not everyone would hear her speech did not bother her, but she prayed those that did found her words encouraging.

"I am overwhelmed at the moment." She began looking at the faces of all the Captains that stood before her, Clifton, Isaac, and King Eamon within their ranks, as she studied the other leaders among them. "I feel unprepared as I stand before you. Unprepared to offer the words I know are expected of me. I had my words thoughtfully planned out until I stepped out onto these steps and saw you. All of you." She waved her hand over the crowd. "I am in complete awe at the sheer number of you willing to serve our Realm and your kingdoms. I am in complete awe at your sacrifices away from your families, from your homes, and from your comforts. We will be facing the worst war our realm has ever seen, and yet, here you stand. Willing and ready. I am honored to be your Queen. Truly honored. Our fight against The Land of Unfading Beauty ends now. The boundary line will fall and it will be credited to your bravery. I took a vow to serve this realm with my entire being, and I pledge to you now that my vow has not wavered. This war will ensure our realm's safety in the future. It will bring home loved ones. It will destroy an evil force like no other, and it will bring back our lands. To your safety, to your strength, and to your hearts." She raised her right hand as a trumpet sounded next to her. The leaders turned to face their troops and orders were shouted across the ranks. Feet began to stir as armies broke off into sections. Clifton, Isaac, and King Eamon walked up the steps. Isaac hugged Melody closely and whispered something in her ear as his sister cried. Elizabeth hugged King Eamon warmly and then lost herself in her husband's arms as Clifton struggled leaving his wife behind. Alayna accepted hugs from Eamon and Isaac, waiting for Clifton to release Elizabeth. His hand graced her small protruding stomach as he kissed her one more time and walked towards Alayna.

"Be careful, Isaac." Elizabeth stated, as the Western prince accepted the light hug she offered.

"I am always careful." He smirked as she looked at him in disbelief.

"I am being more than serious. Should anything happen to any of you, I will personally hunt you down myself."

Isaac placed his hand over his heart and all teasing vanished from his face as he spoke for only her ears. "I would never leave you, Elizabeth."

He turned leaving her in shock at his sincerity, and her husband quickly crossed towards her kissing her one more time before he vaulted into his saddle. Watching the three men leave left a slow gloom lingering in her heart. She watched as Clifton's blonde hair immersed within the guards and she tried to follow him with her gaze as long as possible in fear that she might never see him again. When she lost him in the crowd, she sought out King Eamon. He still sat perched upon his horse, regal and ready and the thought made her softly smile. Her gaze found Isaac upon his horse as well, ordering troops towards his section. Odd how they had become such friends over the last couple of years. His words did not sit well within her and she wondered why he dared say such things to her knowing she and Clifton were perfectly happy.

"He loves you, you know." Melody eased up beside her and followed Elizabeth's line of sight. Elizabeth jerked her gaze away from Isaac and continued perusing the rush of activity before her. "I do not think we should speak of such matters." Elizabeth whispered back.

Melody lightly rubbed her back. "It is not your fault, Elizabeth." She smiled sweetly as she continued. "My brother would never act upon it knowing you are married to Clifton. He respects the two of you too much. He told Clifton that for certain when you were unconscious all those days."

"He what?" Elizabeth's surprised blue eyes turned to Melody. "Why would he say such a thing to Clifton?"

"Because it was no secret how my brother felt about you and he wished to set the record straight. Isaac has not been the most honorable man in the past, but he has tried to become such, and he started then."

"It is not fair for him to love me." Elizabeth stated.

Melody shrugged. "It does not matter. He does. You're his best friend." She squeezed Elizabeth's hand. "And you are important to him. Clifton is important to him as well. He would never compromise your love for Clifton."

"Well he should move on and find a woman who has the ability to love him back. His affections will always be unrequited."

"I keep telling him that as well, but he is stubborn. I do not think he wishes for anyone else. Though he cannot have you, he still wishes to remain alone at the moment. In time, I think he will move on."

Elizabeth watched as Isaac glanced towards the castle steps once more, pausing as he caught her watching him. He then clicked his reins and rode away leaving Elizabeth unsettled and burdened with the current revelation.

Chapter 13

Isaac waited as he watched Clifton ride towards him and pull his horse to a stop alongside him. "Everyone is in position here. We ride to the Eastern border next. My father has led the Western and Southern forces to their locations. By the time we reach the Eastern borders he will have reached the South. I say you and I enter through the East since Lancer's attention should be focused upon the North."

"I agree." Isaac exhaled loudly. "Are we ready for this?"

Clifton sat silent for a moment as he surveyed his guards traveling across the fields towards the East. "We have to be. It is now or never. Listen, Isaac, if you are not comfortable crossing into the Lands, we could always use your presence on this side for leadership."

Isaac shook his head. "No, I am more than ready to visit these lands. I just pray we are successful, because I certainly do not wish to stay in there."

"May I ask something of you?" Clifton shifted in his saddle as if the upcoming topic were uncomfortable for him.

"Of course."

Clifton quieted while he readjusted his grip on his reins. "Should something happen to me in the Lands-"

Isaac held up his hand. "Cliff, stop. No."

"Let me finish." Clifton growled.

"Nothing is going to happen to you." Isaac assured him.

"We do not know that. Now listen to me." Clifton's voice held a desperation Isaac had never heard before.

"Okay, I am all ears." Isaac replied begrudgingly.

"Should anything happen to me in the Lands, I ask that you please," he trailed off to gather himself. "Please see to Elizabeth for me? And the baby? I know it is much to ask-"

Isaac's head spun and he felt the weight of Clifton's question and knew it was hard for his friend to ask such a thing. "You have my word."

"Thank you." Clifton forced a smile as he cleared his throat.

"But for the record-"

Groaning, Clifton turned to him in amusement. "Enough Isaac. You know how hard it was for me to ask that? Let's move on now. I cannot keep thinking along those lines. I need to ready myself for what's ahead."

"Hey, I was just going to say that for the record, nothing is going to happen to you." He smirked as Clifton slapped him on the back.

"Right. Well, let us hope not. Now we focus upon our mission. We are to handle Lancer and Edward."

"Are you prepared to face off against your wife's brother?" Isaac asked. "Because it may come to that."

"I know, and I am."

"Very well."

"We ride." Clifton nudged his horse forward to merge into the group of guards heading towards the East, Isaac not far behind him.

"Troops are at the ready, my Lord." Edward walked into the Reflection Chamber and Lancer turned.

"Good."

"I will be heading out now." Edward stated.

"Actually, no, Edward, I wish for you to remain here."

"Here?"

"Yes."

"May I ask why?"

"Because I have already placed you in command along the lines. I am there as well." Lancer stated.

"What do you mean?"

Lancer grinned and stretched out his arms. "It feels so wonderful having my full strength back."

"My Lord?" Edward asked impatiently.

"Oh calm down, Edward." Lancer waved him off as he sat in the lone chair in the center of the room. "I simply made several guards look like us in order to throw off the chase. They will never think to come here, they will be too blindsided by the multiple Lancers and Edwards roaming about."

"Like you did with the servant girl that day?"

"Yes." Lancer replied. "Clever, hm?"

Edward rubbed a hand over his face. "Indeed. So you wish for me to stay here instead of commanding our troops?"

"Yes. On the off chance they discover our plan, I need you here. I have a plan. A brilliant plan."

"You wish to share with me?"

"No. Not yet. I will need you to act surprised at the moment and I do not wish for you to fake your shock."

"You have me worried, my Lord."

Laughing, Lancer stood and walked about the room. "Relax Edward. Today we will find another victory. Thanks to Cecilia's information we are ready."

"Should we find it necessary my Lord, should we cross into the Realm?"

Lancer's brow furrowed. "Why on Earth would we cross into the Realm, Edward? I have no desire to go there. And just because we may have the ability to do so, does not mean we should. You must be wise with your powers, Edward. You cannot go brandishing them about carelessly."

A guard knocked and rushed into the room, interrupting their conversation. Lancer looked at him in annoyance. "The Realm has been sighted my Lord."

"And what are you doing in here?" Lancer asked in irritation.

The guard's eyes widened like saucers. "Because they do not come from the North, my Lord."

Lancer stood straighter and Edward took a step forward in urgency as well. "Where are they coming from?" Lancer asked.

"Everywhere." The guards word a whisper of fear.

"I must go." Edward began to walk forward but Lancer placed a restraining hand on his arm. "Leave us." He ordered the guard.

"My Lord, I must go. We must divide the guard and cover all sides."

"Leave them be."

"But we do not have the forces to cover such a breach. If all the Realm's armies enter the Lands, we will fall."

"We do not know if they will enter the Lands. All we know is that the Lands are surrounded." Lancer clarified.

"Are you not worried?" Edward asked, his brain clouding with fear. Fear of death. Fear of the unknown. Fear of failure.

"No. We both know that boundary does not fall until I do. And we have the darkness on our side. The darkness will not let me fall. It needs me." Lancer's voice darkened. The Realm can kill every soldier out there, but none of it will matter. The only person that matters- is me."

Edward shook his head and paced about the room. "We cannot hide in this room while our army is slaughtered. That is cowardice."

Lancer's eyes flashed as he quickly appeared next to Edward. "Never call me a coward, Edward." He gripped Edward's elbow in a tight grip and Edward jerked his arm free. "We cannot stay here like sitting ducks."

"Remember Edward, I have a plan."

"We move." Clifton nodded to Samuel on the other side of the veil and the Southern King shouted to his remaining Uniters as Clifton's horse breached the boundary. Isaac inhaled deeply and followed, the buzzing through his body settling after a few moments. His lungs expanded and the location of his previous wound hummed as if the last remaining soreness was being pulled from it like poison. He felt incredible. The weary bones from riding all day suddenly felt refreshed and the throbbing in his head had subsided. The Unfading Lands healed unceremoniously and he found it remarkable. Terrifying, but remarkable. He caught Clifton's amused gaze. "I am done gawking, Cliff. Let us move."

Chuckling, Clifton and Isaac turned the lead over to Samuel and they ventured further into the Lands.

"The castle is at the center?" Isaac asked.

"Yes."

Clifton held up his fist for Isaac to pause as they waited for several Unfading Lands guards to pass by. "What the-" Isaac's voice trailed off as they watched four Edwards ride by and two Lancers.

"And now the game has started." Clifton whispered.

"How is that possible?"

"Clearly Edward is more powerful than we thought, and clearly he is in alliance with Lancer." Clifton pointed for them to move forward again.

"So how do we know if we kill the real one? This was a bad idea." Isaac gripped his reins in frustration.

"No. It is just a diversion. They are meant to confuse us. We continue towards the castle." Clifton slid from his saddle and tied his horse to a tree limb, Isaac doing the same. Comfortable in giving Clifton the lead, Isaac followed him stealthily through the trees.

"Once we reach the castle, Samuel said there is an entrance to the East that leads straight to the hall where the prison chamber resides. I say we rescue Ryle first, and then move towards the center of the castle."

Isaac nodded in agreement as Clifton shoved a tree limb from his path and released it as he passed, the limb slapping Isaac in the face. He grunted as Clifton turned to him. Isaac forced a thumb up as his nose throbbed. However, the power of the Lands quickly caused the pain to subside.

As they neared the castle, the area was quiet. Deserted. No one mingled in the streets, all was still. Creepily still. Clifton ducked behind merchant's cart as one guard patrolled the front of the castle. "Does this seem odd to you?" Isaac asked. "Something is not right."

"I agree. Makes me wonder what is happening inside those walls." Clifton waited until the guard turned before running towards him with silent steps and hitting the man with the hilt of his sword. "We must tie him up. He will not be out long."

Isaac grabbed a rope from a nearby cart and they tied the man to one of the stone pillars before moving towards the Eastern side of the castle.

When they reached the door, Isaac stood on one side while Clifton flanked the other. Isaac reached for the handle and pulled it open quickly, both princes ducking away from the opening as if expecting someone to rush out and attack. But no one came. Isaac peered over the side of the wall and looked inside. "It's clear."

Clifton then stepped inside the castle, his boots barely audible on the smooth floor.

"It looks like glass." Isaac whispered. "What stone is this?"

"I do not know. I've never seen it before."

They worked their way to a door on their right and Clifton lifted the heavy iron clasp. The door creaked, and both men froze. No one investigated the noise and they slipped inside. The steep steps leading down towards the prison cells, Clifton groaned when they reached the bottom. Empty.

"He's not here."

"You thinking what I'm thinking?" Isaac asked.

"Unfortunately yes. He's gone."

Isaac shook his head. "No, that was definitely not what I was thinking."

"It wasn't?" Clifton looked confused.

"Reflection chamber." Isaac stated. "If Ryle is still alive, he's being held in there with Lancer and Edward."

"You think that is where they will be?"

"I feel positive that is where we will find them all."

"I do not know where that room is." Clifton explained. "Samuel did not know either."

"Then we check them all. I am not leaving until Lancer is dead. I will not be trapped in these God forsaken Lands." Isaac hurried back up the steps and neither man cared of the noise they made now. They opened doors, searched rooms, and found nothing.

A gasp sounded down the hall and both men spotted Cecilia. She nervously darted her gaze for a hiding place, but instead she sprinted towards a door further up the hall and to the right. A door they had yet to open. Isaac and Clifton sprinted down the hall towards the room she entered.

Samuel felt the rush as he merged with the Eastern troops. Their presence in the Lands would be felt. He knew the Realm had completely surrounded Lancer's army, and though he spotted Edward and Lancer moving throughout their troops, he felt victorious already. He prayed victory would come. Edward's horse rotated, bringing him face to face with Samuel. Samuel charged towards him, the prince's gaze never wavered as the two of them clashed blades. Samuel sliced the straps of Edward's saddle and sent the prince to the ground. Quickly maneuvering his horse back towards Edward, he galloped forward and cut his sword through the air, the prince falling to the ground clutching his arm. Samuel dismounted and rushed towards the prince, but the man held up his hand in retreat as his face contorted and faded into the fear stricken eyes of a man Samuel had never met. This was not Edward. He looked up as another Edward rode passed and shook his head. Blinking his eyes he looked at the bleeding man before him. "Where is he?"

The man shuddered as King Eamon swiped his blade from behind and beheaded the man before Samuel.

"You must not hesitate, Samuel."

"My Lord," Samuel gripped King Eamon's shoulders, rocking the older man back on his heels. "He was Edward."

"No. He was not. Look at him, Samuel. He was not Edward. Calm down, son."

"No, I mean," Samuel reached for his horse's reins as he tried to explain what was happening to the Eastern King.

"He held the face of Edward until I injured him. Another Edward has ridden passed us already."

Believing the young prince was not ready for the sights he was seeing, King Eamon ushered him towards him. "Wait in the clearing, Samuel. We are pushing their forces back towards the castle. You will be safe in the clearing."

"No!" Samuel shrugged away from the fatherly touch. "You have to listen to me! I am fine. I-" He paused as King Eamon looked up to see two Edward's and one Lancer riding by and battling against some of the Northern troops.

"Oh my…" Eamon trailed off and then looked to Samuel.

"Apologies later, my Lord. For now, I believe we have bigger issues." Samuel spun and blocked the blow of an Unfading guard as King Eamon vaulted into his saddle to charge the remaining forces that refused to retreat back towards the castle. How were they to defeat the darkness if they did not know which target possessed it?

Lancer groaned in annoyance as the door to the reflection chamber clattered behind him once more. Thinking it was the guard he turned with his hand outstretched. Cecilia froze, her feet stuck to the floor and her voice gone. Seeing it was her, Lancer released his hold and she fell to her knees. Neither man went to help her.

"What brings you inside this room, Cecilia?" Lancer asked, his gaze wandering to Edward.

Edward, never leaving his current position, eyed her suspiciously. "The princes are here, my Lord. In the castle." She rushed towards Lancer and he held up a restraining hand. "Princes?"

"From the Realm." They are coming up the hall this very moment.

Edward cringed. *Had Ryle come to exact his revenge upon him? Would Clifton kill him knowing how he had treated his brother?*

Lancer glanced at Edward and grinned. "Looks like I was right, Edward. My plan will unfold exactly how I imagined. Brace yourself, I hear them coming."

Isaac flung open the door to the reflection chamber and felt the air leave his lungs as he was tossed from the entry and back out into the hall. He hit the opposite wall with a thud, his body crumbling to the floor. He groaned and looked up at Clifton. "I know, I should have been smarter." He slowly rose to his feet as Clifton slowly approached the doorway.

"Come in. Come in." Lancer beckoned from within. "That first shot was just a warning."

Clifton looked back at Isaac before entering, his sword at the ready.

"Ah, Prince Clifton of the Eastern Kingdom and Prince Isaac of the West, it's a pleasure." Lancer bowed. "I must say, nephew, I had hoped to meet you under other circumstances."

Clifton gazed upon his uncle. What little Clifton remembered of his mother was shown in Lancer's eyes. He had the same blue eyes as his mother, and the sentimental thought had Clifton shaking his head to clear it.

Lancer waved his hand and the door slammed closed behind them. "Edward." He summoned Edward forward and he nodded. Edward unsheathed his sword and immediately darted towards Isaac, while Lancer circled around Clifton like a wolf on its prey. "My, you are a spitting image of your father when he was your age. Did you know that? It's a shame really," he brought his blade forward. "Because I truly hate your father." He lunged and Clifton blocked the blow easily, but the force sent both men into a parry that Clifton felt himself losing. His strength was no match to the power Lancer possessed.

Edward accepted the blade to the shoulder without flinching and Isaac stumbled backwards as he released it from the Northern prince's muscle. "How?" He growled as he lunged for Edward again. Their blades crossed and brought them face to face, the gleaming blades between them. Isaac's gaze drifted down to the shoulder wound, a black inkiness began to seep out of Edward.

"Injure him!" He yelled at Clifton. "He will lose some of the darkness if you injure him, Cliff!" He pushed Edward back with all his might and their blades untangled. A new energy arose in Isaac as he tried to maim Edward with every strike.

Lancer laughed as he continued to parry with Clifton, what small cuts he had received inhibited him little. A darkness began to shadow the room. A heat began to rise, and a female moan filtered through the air. Cecilia shrunk into a corner, terrified of what was before her. Lancer spun out of the hold Clifton had on him and swiftly reversed his approach taking the Eastern prince by surprise. Clifton felt the sharp stab as it entered his chest and his strangled cry had Isaac hesitating long enough that Edward disarmed him. Edward nodded his head towards Clifton and Isaac slowly walked towards his friend as he lay bleeding on the floor.

The walls seemed to close in around them. The flames of the sconces shot into the air. Lancer smiled. "You see, Prince Isaac, this is what you are up against. It is not Edward or me you parry blades with, but this power. The ultimate power that sustains these Lands. You cannot defeat us." He nudged his boot at Clifton's knee as Clifton's breathing became steadier and steadier as his wound began to heal. "See it heals you now." Lancer winked. "Quite handy considering the current circumstances. However," he flourished his hand and Cecilia was forced to her feet. "There is one way to die in these Lands, and I believe we all know what it is. The door, Cecilia, open it."

The horrified Cecilia slowly opened the door and stepped back. "Allow me to demonstrate for you." He snapped his fingers and Prince Ryle stood in the doorway, free of shackles and free of ropes. Edward's chest tightened. *Could it be?*

Clifton bit his bottom lip to remain quiet and calm. The sight of his brother a welcome relief. He was alive. Before he could rejoice, Ryle entered the room and another Ryle appeared in the doorway. One after the other, eight Princes Ryle emerged.

Alayna peeked her head into the conservatory and spotted Elizabeth and Melody standing at the window facing the boundary line.

"You ladies ought to come away from the window. It will only happen slower if you keep staring."

Elizabeth slowly eased into a chair, but her gaze never left the countryside. "I will not stop watching. I wish to see it fall."

"I thought you were to keep watch on Katarina." Alayna reminded her.

"I am. She is on the parapet."

"You allowed her in the castle gates?" Alayna asked in surprise.

"Yes. It is the best view of the Land of Unfading Beauty. I felt it only fair now that her army has crossed the boundary. Though she is still not allowed inside the walls of the castle." Elizabeth explained, her back still towards Alayna.

Melody sat, her hands twisting in her lap. "Do you think we will know when it happens?"

"Yes. The veil will fall."

"No, I mean when something happens to them. Prince Clifton, King Samuel, King Eamon, and Isaac?"

"Nothing is going to happen." Elizabeth's voice held a hard edge.

"But-"

"There are no buts, Melody. Nothing is going to happen. Nothing has happened to them. I would feel it. I would know."

Melody shrank back into her chair and eyed Alayna. Pitying the Western princess for receiving a lashing from her sister, she walked forward. "Elizabeth, perhaps you should go and rest for a bit."

"No. I am staying right here. Leave me be."

Alayna eased onto a chaise as she respected her sister's wish, but remained watchful of both princesses at the window. She worried too. She shuddered at the thought of one of the men, or all of the men, not returning. It was hard enough not having Ryle with them any longer, but to lose Clifton would devastate her sister. To carry a child of the man she loved and him not be a part of their life seemed too ghastly to imagine. So she wouldn't. She forced her mind to more positive thoughts and prayed their armies achieved success.

The formation of Ryles kneeling before Lancer made Clifton's blood run cold. Lancer walked behind them, his blade tapping each of them on the shoulder. Every man flinched, but one. The fourth Ryle appeared calmer than the rest. Clifton tried to make eye contact with all of them to see if he could find his brother amongst them. But other than the one Ryle that did not flinch, nothing set them apart.

"You see," Lancer slashed his blade and the first Ryle's head fell to the ground, his body afterwards. Clifton struggled against the hold Edward had on his arms as he tried to rush forward. "Losing one's head will cause death." He snickered. "I mean that figuratively and literally. Funny how that works, isn't it. Prince Ryle was a prisoner here in the castle for quite some time. Edward took the liberty of torturing him every day, and I watched in approval. It was when your prince refused my final offer of sanctuary that I ordered Edward to kill him." Another Ryle crumbled to the floor, the others fidgeting against the invisible hold Lancer held on them as they waited their turn for execution.

"Edward disobeyed me." Lancer shook his head and tsked his tongue. "Not that I blame him. I know Edward only wished to save him for a future purpose. And now here we are. Only, I discovered Prince Ryle as he tried to escape the bondage Edward had set him in. And I changed my plans accordingly. So here he is before you. Well, multiple Princes Ryle." Lancer smiled, pleased with himself. "His purpose fulfilled. His purpose to weaken you." He pointed his blade at Clifton.

Edward's hold on Isaac loosened as he focused his attention on restraining Clifton. Isaac felt the decrease in force and slowly crept his hand towards his sword beside him on the floor. Lancer continued parading around the Prince Ryle line up as Edward used all his might to contain Clifton. Isaac's fingers slowly and gently slipped around the hilt of his sword. He inhaled a deep breath as he watched Lancer approach the fourth Ryle. Clifton jolted and tossed and twisted his body to escape Edward and Isaac knew his moment was now.

Haste and stealth were his practice and he thanked his hours of training as he quickly snatched his sword from the ground and plunged the blade upward over his right shoulder to an unsuspecting

Edward. The sword lodged straight in his heart and the Northern Prince stumbled backwards, his hold dropping from Clifton's shoulders. Clifton darted to his feet and sprinted across the room, diving towards Lancer before the man could even turn around. Tackling him to the floor, Clifton landed blows to the man's face as he tried to disarm the blade from Lancer's grip. Lancer laughed between punches as he kicked Clifton back.

Edward lay on the floor, Isaac standing over him watching as blackness poured from the Northern prince's chest and onto the floor. It circled around Isaac's feet and climbed his legs. The teasing thrill of power drifted over him like a woman's touch, tempting him to savor it. His vision clouded as he watched Clifton struggle to overcome Lancer. *He should help him, he knew that, but suddenly not having Clifton in his life seemed the better option. He could finally have Elizabeth to himself, that thought more tempting than the power being offered.* He looked down at Edward again, the prince heaving as he rolled to his knees and allowed the darkness to spill out of him and drip to the floor. Isaac was now blinded by the black smoke that now circled around him.

Clifton glanced over his shoulder. "No!" He shoved Lancer away from him as he darted back towards Isaac. He would not lose his friend to the enemy even if it cost him his life.

Isaac felt the grip on his arm and he shook his head to clear his thoughts. Reflection chamber. Fighting. War. Clifton. Lancer. Edward. As he came back to his normal self, the darkness slowly drifted away from him and hovered around Clifton's ankles. The Eastern prince watched as it moved quickly towards Lancer.

The Ryle guards collapsed to their faces, their gazes glazed as Lancer swiped his hand out before him. Not one of them survived the blow as he reached out to the darkness and accepted the power it offered him.

Edward's breathing labored as his wound slowly began to heal. His strength gone. His body weak. His lungs compressed as he struggled to take a breath. *What just happened?* He watched as Isaac and Clifton approached Lancer as the darkness swirled around him,

Lancer blind to anything and anyone as he consumed the rest of the darkness. Edward's power was gone and it now moved over the only vessel willing to accept it.

Edward tried to rise to his feet as the two princes approached the evil before them, their swords held with clenched fists and fierce determination.

The flames from the sconces extinguished instantly, the room shrouded in darkness, and the only sound Edward could hear were blades falling to the ground.

One Year Later...

Chapter 14

Cecilia brought her hands down the ribbed board in front of her and hissed as she brought her knuckle up to her mouth. The raw skin peeled back to reveal a small wound of wear. A blister that caused her to seethe. She looked up as her mother exited their small cottage and placed another basket full of linens next to Cecilia's feet. "You'd best get a move on, girl. There's only more where these came from."

Cecilia straightened her shoulders and raised her chin. "I am done for today, Mother." She stretched her back and plopped the sheet she had been cleaning back into the water trough before her. The steaming water flushed her face and made her sweat. "You will be finished when I say you are finished." Her mother barked. "Now get back to work. You have years to make up for."

Cecilia cringed and balled her hands into fists as she turned to look at what used to be The Land of Unfading Beauty. There was no boundary line now. No means of escape from the dreadful life she had once left behind. Her life with Edward was over now that the boundary had fallen. She had loved him. He had promised her a life of luxury here in the Realm, but that was before she had betrayed him. Now here she stood, her old life of washing the village's laundry with her mother, her old and new reality. Bitterness laced her heart, and she longed for the Unfading Lands. Her time there seemed as if it were a dream. A long dream she wished for every single day. Edward's promises and the life she had were but a bittersweet dream.

"Graham!" Elizabeth's voice drifted through the halls as her sprightly toddler walked as fast as his little legs could carry him across the stone floor. Stumbling to his bottom, the child teetered on his hands and knees as he attempted to stand once more. When he regained his footing, he set out again away from his mother. She smiled as his blonde curls bounced and he turned to flash her a grin that was the spitting image of Clifton. Isaac stepped into the hall and intercepted the child with gusto, tossing him up into the air and causing a stream of giggles to erupt. He set Graham back to his feet and surveyed Elizabeth. "Good morning."

"Morning. You look well for a day such as today." She lightly patted him on the back as he shook his head and laughed. "You should see my father."

Elizabeth mustered a look of sympathy and grinned.

"Has everyone arrived yet?" Isaac asked, his hand brushing through his dark hair as he nervously tapped his foot. Graham grabbed his hand and pulled, wishing for more air time. The sweet face of innocence looking up at him did not take long to convince Isaac and he picked up the young prince once more; Graham petting the wolf pelt that draped over Isaac's shoulders. "Oft." His little voice called out making the grown ups chuckle.

"Right you are, little man, it is rather soft." Isaac tapped Graham's nose as Alayna exited the Council Room and smiled in greeting. "Why, Isaac, you look handsome."

"You seem surprised?" He winked and accepted the light shove to his shoulder from Elizabeth.

"Your father?" Alayna asked.

"Pacing in his chambers. I imagine we will not see him until the last second."

Everyone turned as the door to their right opened slowly and Samuel stepped out dressed in his finest. The Southern King's royal robes, dashing on his young frame, swayed behind him as he stepped into the hall.

"And there he is!" Elizabeth embraced the young king in a hearty hug. "You ready?"

Samuel bit back a nervous smile and nodded. "I am."

Isaac slapped him on the back. "Relax. The ceremony will pass by quickly."

"Thanks, though I must say I feel as if my heart may beat out of my chest."

"All normal feelings." Elizabeth's face split into a wide smile as her husband walked up and slid his hand to the small of her back. Clifton lightly kissed her on the lips before a squirming Graham pulled away from Isaac's shoulders and reached for his father. Clifton accepted the joyful toddler with glee, burrowing his face in the child's curls and kissing the top of his head. "It would seem we are all ready." Clifton turned towards Alayna and she nodded.

"Tomas, please fetch King Anthony and tell him it is time. We will go to the great hall and take our places."

Tomas bowed and hurried off to the opposite wing of the castle.

"Here we go." Elizabeth rubbed her hands together and squeezed Samuel's hand in encouragement before walking away with her husband and son.

"You two find your places." Alayna ordered Samuel and Isaac. "I do not wish for things to be interrupted by men scurrying about at the last minute."

Chuckling, Isaac bowed. "Yes, my Queen."

Alayna rolled her eyes and watched them leave. She smiled and sent a silent prayer of peace for Samuel as she watched him walk down the stairs. She heard the trumpets sound below and the murmuring voices cease, as she knew her family and friends took their places. It was her turn now. She sighed thinking of the last time she walked down the center aisle for her coronation, Prince Ryle by her side. Heavy hearted, she shook away the thought. Today was about Samuel, and thoughts of Ryle, though they haunted her every night, were not welcome on such a joyous day as this.

They had defeated the Land of Unfading Beauty. The boundary line had fallen, but Ryle's whereabouts remained a mystery. Lancer could not remember where he had held Ryle prisoner, the Valleylands' king deeply remorseful for the unfortunate incident. It had taken the last year to embrace the changes in their realm and the Valleylands. Katarina and Lancer had joined forces in an effort to display a united front between their two families. So far, the Valleylands had prospered, Lancer finding true salvation from the darkness. Clifton still bore the mark on his hand, the scar from the burn his dagger etched when coming in contact with Lancer's flesh. Clifton and Isaac had dived straight into the darkness to overcome Lancer in his reflection chamber. The way Isaac described the situation still left Alayna breathless. The darkness had drained from Edward and swarmed around Lancer ready for the taking, but the impact of Clifton and Isaac's assault had stalled the consumption. Though Lancer's strength disarmed them in the midst, Clifton had fought with what little strength that remained and had forced his dagger into Lancer's heart. That was all it took. As the leader of the Land of Unfading Beauty fell to the floor, his blood seeping out, the darkness left with it. In its place was a new Lancer, a man whose memory had but vague recollections of his life in the Unfading Lands. No trace of darkness remained in him, and after a long recovery in the North, he finally took his rightful place as King of the Valleylands, with Katarina as his Queen. Her father, King Granton, was right. The darkness had always been their true enemy. Lancer now was an entirely different man than the one who had controlled the boundary line, and from what King Eamon believed, a different man than he was before the Unfading Lands came to be. The two men continued to work on their interaction, as Lancer adjusted to life outside of the Lands, mending relationships and creating a new life in his father's stead.

Alayna watched as King Anthony emerged at the top of the stairs, the elaborately carved cane at his side the only reminder of his captivity within the Valleylands. He looked regal. *And completely anxious*, she realized. She lightly squeezed his arm as she passed him and began walking down the stairs. King Eamon awaited her at the bottom, her escort for her journey down the aisle to her throne. When she reached him, he offered his arm. "You look lovely, my Queen."

"Thank you." She slipped her arm through his. "Shall we do this?" She grinned as he joyfully walked her into the great hall to an awaiting crowd.

Edward pulled at his collar as he shifted from one foot to the next, his emerald uniform fitted to him perfectly. Elizabeth squeezed his hand as they watched King Eamon escort Alayna to their father's throne. It still felt odd that he and Elizabeth appeared to be the same age now. When the boundary line fell, he still remained the age he was when he had first crossed. Now, his younger sister was not his younger sister in technical terms. And surprisingly, he felt no envy of Alayna now that she sat as Queen of the Realm. His position as future king was relinquished the moment he crossed the boundary line into the Land of Unfading Beauty. Now he stood as Captain of the Royal Guard, a position he felt both honored and regretful for accepting. Prince Ryle had once held the position, and he still felt the blame and responsibility for the lack of Ryle's presence now in the Realm. He'd been searching for the prince for the last year. In the reflection chamber, as Lancer's power drained, the faces of the Ryle imitators faded back to their real owners, not one of which was the real Prince Ryle. And as the darkness escaped into the void, with it went Lancer's memory. Though the man had regained most of his former recollections, there were still some things hazy or lost. Lancer's recovery and turn around took the Realm by surprise, and though many had trouble trusting his change of heart, it was not long for everyone to see he was a changed man. The darkness had changed them both. Edward felt more himself now than ever, and he thanked Isaac continually for stabbing him in the reflection chamber that day. Had he not, Edward might have been lost and missed out on the life with his family back in the Realm. A life he had longed for and fought for all those years in the Lands.

He hoped his father would be proud of the man he had become, and the way he and his sisters ruled the Realm. In his heart, he felt King Granton would be immensely proud. Elizabeth had held her promise to the Western prince and princess and demanded King Anthony's release from Katarina as soon as the boundary fell. The Valleyland's Queen, lost in the awe of the momentous occasion, eagerly agreed. And her attitude towards the Realm had quickly changed back to her original appreciation. Everyone celebrated in unity. Clifton and Isaac had rescued Edward and Lancer and brought them to the North immediately. Seeing to their care was Arnos, the Eastern healer whom everyone seemed to love and trust. He also had no objections treating Lancer's wound. A hated man by many, it took the people of the Realm over a year to learn to trust the Queen's judgment and forgive the man, but Arnos did not seem bothered by Lancer's reputation and he tended to Lancer diligently.

Alayna took her position and stood in front of the throne, and lifted her hand towards the back of the room. Everyone turned as King Anthony and Princess Melody began their march down the aisle. Melody dressed in a white and silver gown encompassing her new role as the Queen of the South. Though she and Samuel were young in age, everyone felt their match a solid arrangement. It was also no surprise considering the two royals grew considerably closer throughout the previous two years. Melody's letters with Samuel across the boundary line were not only beneficial to the Realm, but also to the budding relationship between Samuel and herself. Edward saw the nervous smile that spread over Samuel's face as he stood in awe of the beautiful princess.

Elizabeth nudged Isaac's elbow as his eyes were riveted on his younger sister as she accepted Samuel's hand and King Anthony stepped to the side. Isaac visibly relaxed, but he stood firm, his gaze never wavering as he soaked in the love surrounding his sister. Melody would be queen, the thought bringing a small smile to his face. She had never hoped to be queen, and now here she stood accepting the position with a happy heart. Funny how love could change a person's mind. He felt a slimy hand touch the back of his neck and he jolted, turning to see Graham leaning out of Elizabeth's arms and reaching towards him. She grimaced and tried to pull her son's hand down to his side so as not to interrupt. Isaac reached for the boy, the young prince quickly becoming a part of everyone's family and he bounced towards Isaac with enthusiasm. The young prince remained in Isaac's arms the remainder of the ceremony as they all watched Melody and Samuel exchange their vows and oaths to the Southern Kingdom. Isaac watched as Samuel kissed Melody, a shyness to the young royals' actions making everyone smile as the young king proudly escorted his new wife down the center aisle and out onto the front castle steps. Isaac fell in line with his father and friends as they exited to the sound of a cheering public. Roses and tokens tossed to the steps as well wishes for the union. Melody embraced Elizabeth, the two women exchanging tears of joy as his sister then embraced Alayna. Melody would be missed around the West and the North. Isaac already dreaded living in the Western Kingdom without her. Though the Council made regular trips to the North for meetings, everyone missed the days of all living within the Northern castle. Yet responsibilities remained in their separate kingdoms, responsibilities that were now the focus since the Unfading Lands were no longer a threat. Isaac watched as Lancer and Katarina bowed to the new King and Queen of the South. The two made a perfect match for the Valleylands. Katarina caught his eye and smiled shyly, the queen now more like her old self. Isaac flashed a polite smile before accepting the large embrace from Samuel. "We shall see you soon, brother." He grinned, making Isaac laugh at his enthusiasm.

"That you will," he paused for dramatic affect. "Brother." The endearing term lighting up Samuel's face as he hugged Isaac once more before moving on towards Clifton. The young king was everyone's brother now, having shed the shadows of his past and united with them during the Realm's toughest times. The alliance with the South and the West would forever be a strong one now that Samuel ruled the kingdom. Isaac watched as they climbed into the Southern carriages and the caravan began drifting through the castle gates. A heavy sigh escaped him and he turned to find Elizabeth's amused eyes.

"What?" He asked.

"Nothing."

"Obviously something, you have your look about you."

"My look?" Elizabeth asked innocently, as she accepted her son from Isaac's arms, the little boy eager to see his mother. "Did you receive lots of hugs?" She asked the boy with enthusiasm. The little prince nodded vigorously and she kissed his cheek. "I just see the older brother look of sentimentality weighing upon you. You watch her go off into the sunset with her prince charming and you feel that your role as protector of Melody is over."

"Is that how I feel?" He asked curiously.

Elizabeth nodded confidently. "I've seen it before."

"Oh really?"

She laughed. "Both Alayna and Ryle had that same look when they watched Clifton and me ride off."

Isaac shrugged his shoulders. "It's in our nature as older siblings, I guess. Speaking of Ryle," he nodded towards Alayna's departing figure. "Any word from Edward on that front?"

Elizabeth shook her head. "No, but we plan to speak with Lancer before he and Katarina depart. We wish to probe his memory a bit more. He has to remember something eventually."

"At least he remembers not killing the real Ryle. His line up in the reflection chamber was just meant to torture Clifton and me into thinking we failed. So that's a start. He has to be somewhere in the Realm."

"But don't you think he would have turned up by now?" Elizabeth dropped her voice as King Eamon walked by them to head back into the castle, Clifton walking towards her to escort her inside. "I see you two conspiring. What is it you two have up your sleeves?"

"Nothing." They both answered innocently.

Clifton looked doubtful. "Right. Well your teamwork is admirable, but your believability is lacking."

Elizabeth feigned innocence as her husband laughed. "Tell me."

"We were discussing Ryle." Elizabeth replied truthfully, and watched as her husband's good humor immediately vanished.

"I thought we agreed to let that go?" He asked, looking from one to the other.

"You did, yes." Elizabeth began. "But we feel there is still hope."

Clifton shook his head. "I wish you two would let the matter drop. Ryle would be here if he were able. The only other possibility is that he did not survive the fall of the boundary line. And since he is not here, well… I think we can figure out the rest."

"We must not give up, Clifton." Elizabeth squeezed her husband's hand and he shook his head reaching for his son.

"It is best left alone, love. Come." He tilted his head towards the castle and Elizabeth cast Isaac a defeated glance as she followed.

Cecilia plunged her hands into the scorching water once more and rinsed the shirt that she quickly sent through the ringer, rotating the wheels to flatten the garment before hanging it on the line. The labor was intense, and she remembered with each passing second why she loathed it. When the boundary line fell, Cecilia had waited for Lancer to come to her aid. Realizing what had happened in the reflection chamber moments later, she knew she had to flee before Edward discovered her lingering in the shadows. She quickly made her escape and hid amongst the loyal Lands' followers until the last wave were brought out of the Lands and back into the Realm. Most people went back to the kingdoms they originated from or those that married within the Lands chose where they wished to settle. Cecilia did not have the luxury of a partnership due to Edward's rejection, and now she found herself swamped in the drudgery of her old life. She finished her last garment and began the process of draining the tubs.

She had but a few moments of rest before her mother sought her out to help with supper, and Cecilia quickly put away her supplies and gathered the basket she kept hidden within their single horse stable. "Where are you going?" Her mother crossed her arms as she watched Cecilia pull her cloak on and cover her head. "For a walk, Mother. I shall return shortly."

"Best be shortly; you have potatoes to peel. Supper does not make itself."

Without a retort, Cecilia slinked out of the stables and walked towards the Rollings River. She followed the curve of the river bank as it neared an enclave of trees that projected so high in the sky she would need to lie on her back to see their tops. She pushed aside several branches and stepped over a rocky steppe. Finally, she spotted him. She laid the bucket down on the rocks. "Your food." She announced.

The man glanced up and nodded in acknowledgement before setting about stacking firewood. She sighed and huffed her way towards him, grabbing the ropes that bound his hands and inspected them. "This is frayed." She held up his wrist and tossed it aside in anger. Reaching in her apron pocket she began replacing the frayed rope with a crisp strand. "All my wages are going towards these ropes. Stop fraying them."

"You could untie them."

"No."

"Why not? What is the purpose of all this?"

Cecilia looked up into Prince Ryle's agitated expression and a smirk tilted her lips. "Why should I be the only one who suffers?"

"Is that really your only reasoning, Cecilia? I helped you. I had Samuel rescue you from the prison chamber. Why do you not release me and do the same? The boundary line has been gone for a while now."

"A year." She clarified, knowing he possessed a skewed sense of time passing since his capture.

"A year." He repeated. "A year… and yet you still think there is a chance the Land of Unfading Beauty will return? And what of me? Are you hoping to hurt Edward by keeping me in restraints? I can tell you right now Edward does not care of my fate."

"I do not care about Edward." Cecilia barked. "Queen Alayna must suffer."

"And what makes you think the Queen would care for my wellbeing after all this time?"

"Edward spoke of her feelings for you."

Ryle's brows rose. "Did he?"

"You cannot fool me, Prince Ryle. You are more than her Captain. And she must suffer. Because of Queen Alayna, my life is completely ruined. Edward and I loved each other. He loved me! And now that the Lands are gone, I have nothing." Her words hissed like a venomous snake. "She must feel the same punishment."

Ryle shook his head and sat on the ground. He tapped his finger against the iron chains bound around his ankles. He had lived in chains for more than a year now. But despite his escape from Edward in the Lands, Lancer had kidnapped him and placed him within his personal chambers until he needed him. From what Cecilia had informed Ryle that day, Lancer had been killed by Isaac and Clifton. The boundary line had fallen, and she was escaping. Only, she would be taking him with her. Out of his three captors, Cecilia was by far the most diligent. She inspected his constraints daily. Any sign of wear or slack, she replaced them. She brought him food and allowed him to drink from the river. He had constructed his shelter for weeks out of fallen limbs and logs he could scavenge within his rope's radius. Though not a comfortable life, he felt grateful to now have a roof over his head to protect him from the elements. He sent up a silent prayer. He did not have the patience for this captivity anymore. He did not have the patience for this life, and he prayed someone would find him or that Cecilia would have a change of heart.

Elizabeth slid from her saddle and stepped through the trees, her familiar clearing coming into view and a sense of peace filling her soul. The familiar sound of the Rollings River rushed by, the leaves rustled in the trees, and the sweet scent of green and earth filled her nostrils. She had not ventured to the clearing since her injury, and sitting on her familiar boulder looking towards where the boundary line once existed, she felt a sense of home. For five years, she had sought solitude in this small oasis to converse with Edward in secret. Five years of letters and moments of sibling communication she cherished.

It was odd that day, sitting in the conservatory. She and Melody watched the horizon, watched the shimmer of the veil that separated them from the men they loved as the battle waged. No sound ventured from the Lands, but an eerie quiet had settled across the kingdom as if everyone knew that even the slightest breath could send a ripple of disruption in their plans. So all was quiet. Elizabeth remembered the feeling of relief as she saw a bolt of light erupt within the Lands and slowly the veil began shimmering down. It appeared to melt, but no puddles remained. Then, after what seemed like ages, Clifton came back to the castle. With him came Isaac, Edward, and an extremely wounded Lancer. Alayna's hope that Ryle would walk in next dissipated with time, and her sister's acceptance to treat Lancer's wounds slowly came around. Elizabeth witnessed

Alayna reading over her letter from their father. A constant reminder she was doing the right thing despite her hurting heart. *The evidence and actions of a true queen*, Elizabeth thought proudly.

She watched as the patch of thistles to her left began to move and Thatcher, her furry companion emerged, the small rabbit causing tears to burn her eyes. She scooped him up and began nuzzling his fur. The poor rabbit had been through much and most in part due to her. As she stroked his fur, her blue eyes travelled around the clearing, most of her targets still hanging from the trees. Smiling, she set Thatcher to his feet and walked towards her horse. She always carried her sword and now she also carried a bow. She withdrew her bow and readjusted several of her targets.

While she had a moment's peace to herself, she would take advantage of it. She stepped back and took her stance, the strings of her bow taut and ready. She released and the arrow shot forward barely missing the bullseye. Grunting, she loaded another arrow and adjusted her stance. Inhaling a deep breath, she released, the arrow landing right in the middle. "Aha!" She cheered as she looked over to Thatcher and smiled. "I've still got it, Thatcher." She reached down and scooped up the small rabbit. "Why don't you come and live with me? We may have to discuss rules with Graham, but I should think you would find the Eastern Kingdom quite lovely. I would see to you, and you may live in the gardens. They're lovely." She kissed his head and tucked him into her robes as she swung herself into her saddle.

She reached the top of the hill and looked out over her sister's kingdom. Their father's legacy. A beautiful land of rolling hills and sweet meadows. She missed the Northern markets. She used to walk them weekly, and now living in the East, she did not have the luxury as often as she'd like. She slowed her horse to a steady gait and entered the castle gates, hooves clacking against stone as she spotted King Eamon shaking King Anthony's hand as the Western King began his preparations for departure.

"I did not know the West planned to leave so soon?" Elizabeth asked, as she pulled her reins to a halt and slid from her saddle.

King Anthony smiled. "My dear," he bowed. "I return today. Isaac will remain for a few more days and then follow. He wished to spend time with Prince Clifton in regards to trade talks between the two kingdoms."

"I see." Elizabeth stepped forward and hugged the older man. "You will be missed."

Anthony smiled and lightly tapped her nose. "So much like your mother, is she not Eamon?"

"Very much so." Eamon agreed.

"I will see you at the next Council meeting, my dear."

"Of course." She watched as he climbed into his carrier. "Please tell the Queen I say hello."

Anthony nodded and tapped the top of the carrier with his cane and the caravan began to move.

"I always hate seeing everyone separate." Elizabeth turned to her father-in-law. "We should just all rule from the same location."

Eamon laughed. "Now that would be a chaotic mess wouldn't you agree? Alayna and Isaac in such close proximities?"

"And having to work together?" Elizabeth grimaced playfully and had the king chuckling.

"We all have our responsibilities in our own kingdoms for a reason." He sobered and lightly nudged her towards the castle, Elizabeth handing her reins to her attendant. "Everything in the North seems to be doing well. I am pleased to see your sister and brother working cohesively."

"Me too."

"But now that everyone seems to have found their places, it is time for us to travel back to the Eastern Kingdom. We have our own work cut out for us."

"I know." Elizabeth sighed. "When did you plan to leave?"

"I imagine we will leave when Prince Isaac heads back to the West."

"I see. Well, I will make sure Clifton and I are ready."

Eamon nodded as they walked inside the castle and Edward shook a letter at his younger sister. "Alayna, you are not listening! Do you read what this says? He has been spotted!"

"It is a false statement." Alayna countered. "Do not get your hopes up, Edward. But if you feel you must pursue it, then go ahead."

"I do. This is the first sighting we have had in months. I would think you would be excited."

"False hopes are never exciting."

"What if it is Ryle? What if we do not go and rescue him? We are condemning him to a life he should not have, and robbing him of a life he was destined to have." Edward turned as Elizabeth and Eamon entered the room. "Do you agree, Elizabeth?"

Alayna looked to the two Eastern royals.

"If it sounds like a solid lead, then I suggest we look into it." Elizabeth reached for the letter in Edward's hand and read it then passed it to her father-in-law. King Eamon's jaw tightened, and Elizabeth lightly rested her hand on his arm. "It is worth a try." Without speaking, Eamon nodded and handed the letter back to Edward. He cleared his throat and smiled. "You have worked diligently in searching for Ryle, Edward. I thank you."

"Of course, my Lord." Edward grabbed Elizabeth's hand and tugged her towards the side hall towards the back of the castle. "Where are we going?"

"To follow this lead."

"But I just got back. Clifton will wonder where I am." She quickly retrieved Thatcher from her riding cape's pocket and handed the small creature to her father-in-law. "Don't lose him." She called over her shoulder as Edward pulled her away.

"Don't you see, Elizabeth, this is the closest I have come to news in months. It has to be him."

"We do not know that, Edward. We must be prepared for disappointment."

"Disappointment?" Lancer's voice drifted towards them as he stepped out of his chambers heading towards his exit caravan.

"We have a lead on Prince Ryle." Edward explained. "We are leaving to search for him."

Lancer turned towards Katarina and handed her his travel cape. "I will go too."

Elizabeth's eyes widened in surprise as Lancer joined them in their quest. She hurried to match her pace to her brother's as he dragged her towards the stables. "Your horse has yet to be undressed." Edward pointed and waved his hand at the stable boy. "Princess Elizabeth needs her horse, and I will need mine."

"Yes, my Lord." The young man scurried off.

Lancer darted down the hill after them and reached Elizabeth's horse as she pulled herself into her saddle. He disappeared into the stables and began saddling a horse as Edward climbed into his own saddle. When Lancer joined them, Edward set the pace.

Chapter 15

"And you let her leave with them?" Clifton's voice bellowed down the hall as his father attempted to keep stride next to his son. "Edward insisted she join them, Cliff. I did not see the harm."

"Edward and Lancer- and you did not see the harm?"

"They no longer have the darkness, Son, you must let that go."

Clifton bit back a quick retort and took a deep breath. Isaac appeared at the landing of the stairwell. "Where were you? You did not wish to go?"

"I was not invited." Isaac quipped.

"You could have invited yourself."

Isaac shrugged. "I did not feel like riding. Besides, three is more than plenty. I would have just been in the way."

"And you feel she is safe with them?"

Isaac's brow furrowed. "Of course I do. I would not have watched her leave if I didn't. Do you still question their integrity?"

Clifton ran a hand through his blonde hair.

"Or is it perhaps that you fear for her safety for an entirely different reason?" Isaac asked with a wink.

King Eamon looked confused at the turn in the conversation and watched as his son's shoulders relaxed. "Yes."

"Aha! I knew it!" Isaac clapped his hands and laughed, sending a friendly pound on Clifton's back. "I thought she looked a bit pinky lately."

"Wait," King Eamon interrupted. "Am I to have another grandchild?"

"Yes, Father." Clifton grinned and accepted the excited embrace from King Eamon. "But not everyone has been told as of yet, so may we please keep the news quiet. And right now I wish to be concerned over her wellbeing."

Isaac laughed and mocked him. "Lighten up, Clifton. Elizabeth could take down both of those men with one arrow if she needed to."

"It's not just Edward and Lancer I still worry about. Who was this anonymous tip from? That is what worries me. They could be riding right into a trap."

Isaac shook his head. "How about you and I go keep Alayna company during this? Perhaps that will take your mind off of Elizabeth."

"Doubtful."

"Or perhaps I can leave you here and let you sulk?"

Clifton stopped in his tracks and looked to his friend, insulted. "I am not sulking."

"Actually, you are."

Stammering, not knowing how to respond, Isaac laughed at Clifton's dumbfounded expression. "Oh she will be the death of you one day, Clifton. You worry too much."

"You would worry too if your wife was with child and riding off to engage in a hostage negotiation."

"The letter did not speak of hostage negotiations. It was a sighting. They are investigating. Nothing more. Now come, let's check on our Queen. I imagine she is as wound up as you." Isaac opened the Council Room doors to an anxious Alayna and he pointed to Clifton's disturbed expression.

"Misery loves company, I believe." Clifton mumbled, as he stepped inside and Isaac closed the doors.

Edward read over the letter's description and stopped. Elizabeth and Lancer saddled up on either side of him. "It says this is the spot, but I do not see anything."

Elizabeth listened quietly. "Someone is there." She whispered. "I heard a twig snap."

"So they are watching us." Lancer shifted in his saddle and looked around. "I do not like being watched."

Elizabeth sent him an amused glance and he rolled his eyes. "Not anymore." He waved his hand as if having to explain. She chuckled softly as she turned her attention back to their quest. "I'll go." She said.

"No." Edward placed a restraining hand on her arm. "I will. I will enter first, then Lancer, then you. Should we need someone hidden, you are the smallest and quickest."

"Plus she has better aim than either of us." Lancer finished for him.

"Exactly." Edward whispered.

"Flattered." Elizabeth nodded in approval at their acknowledgement of her skill. "Now get going. If he's in there, we must retrieve him." As she finished her sentence a figure appeared at the edge of the trees. Elizabeth quickly grasped her bow and had an arrow at the ready before Edward and Lancer had found their swords.

"Cecilia?" Edward's voice betrayed his shock.

"I see you received my letter." She grinned as she disappeared into the clearing. Edward slid to his feet.

"Brother," Elizabeth warned softly.

"I know." He looked up at Elizabeth and then nodded to Lancer.

Lancer dismounted as well and both men began their way through the trees.

"Welcome." Cecilia lifted her hands in greeting as the two men appeared in the enclave. Ryle stood quickly to his feet in surprise.

Edward watched as hope filled the prince's eyes and then hardened as they landed upon Lancer.

"What are you doing with him, Cecilia?" Edward asked.

"I've been holding him as prisoner."

"All this time?" Lancer asked.

"Yes." She giggled as she clutched her hands in front of her. "Quite brilliant, don't you think?"

"But why?" Edward asked, stepping closer.

"Ah, ah, ah, Edward. Stay where you are. We have terms to discuss."

Edward growled under his breath. "Speak your terms then."

"You ruined my life, Edward. I hope you know that."

"Me? I do recall you are the one steeped in betrayal."

"And yet, there you are." She pointed towards him and Lancer. "Standing by the very man you claim I betrayed you to?"

"Lancer is different now." Edward explained.

Cecilia laughed. "I'm sure." Doubt laced her voice as she pulled on Ryle's ropes. He walked forward. "Kneel."

Ryle remained standing, and Cecilia kicked out the back of his knee, sending him to the ground.

"You do not have to do this, Cecilia." Edward explained. "I am sure we can come to some sort of understanding."

"Yes, Edward, I believe we can." She produced a dagger. Gripping Ryle's hair she pulled his head back exposing his neck and placed the blade just below his Adam's apple. "You will give me the life you promised me. Then you may have your prince."

Lancer turned to see Edward's reaction, the steel eyes and firm jaw more telling than his words. "State your claims."

"You promised me a life of luxury." Cecilia pointed out, her eyes wild as her dagger glinted in the sunlight. "You promised I would never want for anything, and yet you left me. You tossed me aside when all I wanted was to be with you!"

"You betrayed my Realm." Edward clarified. "You betrayed my family."

"How can you not forgive me for that when you can forgive him for everything?" She pointed towards Lancer.

"Lancer was bewitched by the darkness. He is a new man now." Edward explained. "We both are."

Cecilia laughed. "I saw the darkness leave your body, Edward. It went straight to Lancer."

"And then you ran away." Edward barked. "There is more to the story you are missing. The old Lancer died that day. He shed the darkness to become a new man."

"And where did that darkness go, Edward?" She asked, her voice meek. "All that power? Did you not love it too?" She lowered her dagger and shoved Ryle's head forward before moving to a small box she had placed on a boulder near her. She opened the lid and grinned wickedly. "It had to go somewhere." She began. She looked into the box and giggled wildly. "I could not let all that power go to waste."

Lancer looked to Edward in confusion.

"There is nothing in the box, Cecilia." Edward pointed out, curious as to what she believed she saw.

"Yes there is!" She squealed. "I have held onto it for this very day. When you grant me my requests, I will then possess the life I've always wanted and I will have the power to keep anyone from taking it from me."

"You're mad." Edward stated. "There is nothing in the blasted box!" he turned towards Lancer. "Is this how it started for you?"

Lancer shook his head. "No, the darkness is a very real, tangible being. She is conjuring her own delusions."

"Cecilia," Edward's voice softened. "I will give you your request. Now let Prince Ryle go and set the box down. You may come with us."

"No. That is not part of the deal. You give me my life now! I leave. I do not want to be a part of this realm any longer. Should you detain me, I will kill the prince. Queen Alayna deserves the heartache anyway."

Ryle eased to a crouching position as if he was about to stand, and Cecilia brought her dagger back to his neck. "Not so fast, Prince."

Cecilia sat the box on the ground and opened the lid. She spread her arms out wide.

Nothing emerged from the box and everyone stared as she summoned the darkness. Nothing happened. She opened her eyes, the hate shooting barbs towards Edward. "What did you do? Why is it not coming?"

Lancer took a step forward, his hands relaxed as he held them in front of him to calm her. "It is not coming, Cecilia. The darkness is not coming. Now put away the blade."

She spit into the ground at Lancer's feet and pulled Ryle's head back again. "Not another step. You have robbed me of my life and you have robbed me of my power." Hot tears began running down her cheeks as she released a wail of desperate anger. She grimaced as she yanked Ryle's hair even harder, murder in her eyes.

Before Cecilia could slide her blade across Ryle's throat an arrow pierced her heart and she stumbled backwards. Shock marred her once beautiful face, and her hands shook as she yanked the arrow from her body. Elizabeth stepped into the clearing, her bow by her side as she watched Cecilia crumble to the ground. Edward rushed forward and caught her in his arms as he eased her to the forest floor. She gasped for breath as she stared up at him. He gently brushed his knuckles over her face. "I am sorry, Cecilia. Truly." He whispered and he watched as her eyes clouded and her body went limp.

Leaving Edward to Cecilia, Elizabeth rushed forward and dove towards Ryle, embracing him in a tight hug. She kissed his cheek and then stuck out her tongue in disgust. Laughing, he pulled her towards him again and she hugged him. "It is good to see your face, Elizabeth."

She smiled back her tears as she looked to Lancer. "Dagger?" Lancer walked forwards and Ryle took a step back.

Elizabeth placed a hand on his arms. "It's alright. He is-" she paused, looking Lancer in the eye before turning back to Ryle. "He is a good man, Ryle. He has overcome the darkness. So has Edward."

Ryle eyed Lancer suspiciously as his uncle cut the ropes binding his hands. When his hands were free, he rubbed his raw wrists before turning a wide smile onto Elizabeth. "I cannot believe this day has come."

"I cannot believe we almost gave up on you." She watched as Lancer began picking the locks on the shackles at Ryle's ankles. "Everyone will be so happy to see you. Well, minus Samuel and Melody."

His brow furrowed and Elizabeth realized her blunder. "Oh no, yes, they will be excited to hear about your rescue. I meant they will not be here to see you. They left for the Southern Kingdom already... as man and wife." She added with a grin.

Ryle placed his hand over his heart and a slow smile spread over his face. "And what of my father? What of Clifton? Did they survive?"

She nodded. "Yes. Much has happened while you have been away." She linked her arm in his. "Perhaps you should come back to the castle. Bathe. And then we can fill you in."

Ryle laughed, the feeling foreign to his weakened body. But the physical exertion of joy brought new life to his legs as he stepped forward and shook Lancer's hand. "It is nice to meet you, Uncle."

Elizabeth bit back a wide smile as emotions swam in Lancer's eyes at the familial act and he pulled Ryle towards his horse. He helped his nephew into the saddle as Lancer pulled Elizabeth behind him on her horse.

They waited several moments before Edward emerged. When he did, Elizabeth placed a reassuring hand on his arm. "I am sorry, Edward."

"No." He replied softly. "You did what you had to do. I am the one who should be sorry to her." He clicked his reins and they all made their way back to the castle.

Elizabeth had found the act exhausting. The remainder of the day Ryle's rescue had remained a secret between Edward, Lancer, and herself. Waiting for the perfect time to present the prince to his family and friends had caused her to avoid her husband most of the day, much to his concern. Lancer and Katarina had chosen to prolong their stay one more night so as not to miss out on the festivities that Elizabeth had been planning with the kitchen staff all day for this very moment.

Alayna walked into the dining hall and stood behind her chair, everyone waiting for the queen to take her seat before following suit. "Good evening, all." Alayna greeted. She waited as Tomas pulled back her chair, but before she sat, Elizabeth held up her hand. "Wait." Her hurried response catching her sister by surprise.

"Is there something in my chair?" Alayna twisted and Elizabeth laughed. "No, sister, nothing like that. I have an announcement."

Clifton, not realizing they planned to announce their second child just yet, looked to his wife in surprise. She shook her head. "Today was a momentous day. I journeyed with Edward and Lancer in response to a lead on the whereabouts of Prince Ryle."

"We know." Alayna stated. "Now may we be seated?"

"I just wanted to say that the trip was quite… refreshing."

"Yes, we all love having both Edward and Lancer as peaceful relations and friends." Alayna's reply stoic as she began to ease to her chair.

"No." Elizabeth stopped her again and stepped towards Alayna. She grabbed Alayna's hand and small tears escaped as she rubbed her sister's hand. "Alayna-"

"You're scaring me, Elizabeth, what is it?"

Elizabeth turned towards the entryway as everyone followed her line of sight. Alayna's gaze collided with Ryle's and she gasped, her other hand flying to cover her mouth. Everyone began gasping and whispering. Ryle stepped into the room, his strong frame much thinner than his old self, but his face still as handsome as before. His face split into a wide smile as his father rushed towards him and enveloped him in a tight hug, murmurs of "My boy, my boy, my boy," fumbling from the king's mouth as he reached for Clifton to step forward as well. The three men embraced for a long moment, everyone else watching. Alayna looked at Elizabeth, her eyes glassy as Elizabeth smiled. "We found him." She whispered.

"I-I can't believe it." Alayna's words were muffled against Elizabeth's shoulder as she hugged her sister. "Thank you, Lizzy."

"Now go." Elizabeth released her and nudged her towards Ryle. When Ryle spotted Alayna walking towards him, he eased out of his father's embrace and accepted the pat on the back from Clifton as encouragement.

Alayna studied him a moment, soaking in his appearance. *His hair was longer,* she realized. The once shaggy mass of black hair graced just above his shoulders, and his new emerald tunic moved with more room than in the past, but it was Ryle, and that thought made her want to burst into tears.

"Alayna."

Her name on his lips sent her flying towards him and jumping into his arms. He accepted the hug and swung her around as she brushed back his hair and roamed her hands over his face in disbelief. "I can't believe it." Tears poured down her cheeks as he held her close.

"It is me." Ryle pulled her towards him again in a firm embrace. He felt her sobs of joy against his chest as he hugged her, and he looked up to see the smiling faces of his family before him. Joy filled his heart. Grateful, he nodded his thanks towards Edward, Lancer, and Elizabeth before swooping his head down to capture Alayna's lips in his.

Cheers erupted in the dining hall as everyone celebrated Ryle's return. A flurry of movement darted passed Elizabeth as she watched her son hurry towards Ryle and Alayna. He fell to his bottom right before reaching them and whined up at her sister. Ryle pulled his lips away from Alayna's and looked down. The happy toddler smiling up at him. Ryle chuckled as he knelt down and swooped the happy child into his arms. "I do not even have to ask who you belong to, dear one." He buried his face in the child's neck and accepted the happy slaps to his face as Graham enjoyed being held and snuggled. Ryle slipped his hand around Alayna's waist and slid Graham to his other arm as he walked further into the room. Seeing Lancer seated at the dinner table, it surprised him yet again that he was so readily accepted. Elizabeth moved to a seat across the table. "Please, sit here." She pointed to her vacated seat next to Alayna and Ryle nodded his thanks. Alayna sat in her chair, a blissful smile upon her face as the food began being served.

"You will have to fill us in on the last year." King Eamon stated with a joyous smile at seeing his son.

"I will, Father." Ryle replied, turning towards the rest of the table. "It appears I have missed much as well." He looked towards Lancer, who was not paying attention, and Isaac slapped the king on the back in a friendly gesture, the king fumbling his goblet as he turned.

"Yes, your uncle is quite a different man." Eamon continued. "We are all different now that the boundary line is gone."

"And it seems my old position has been filled." He smiled at Edward, the Northern Prince sitting proudly with his family.

Elizabeth squeezed her brother's hand. "I am sure we can think of another position for you, Prince Ryle." She winked at him and tilted her head towards her sister.

Laughing, Ryle took the hint and nodded. "Maybe so. That is, if Alayna would have me?"

Alayna's head popped up from her plate. "What?"

Ryle reached for her hand. "If you will have me," he repeated. "Spending the last year and more not having you in my life has shown me you are the one thing I wish to have. Always. In whatever capacity that you will have me, I am yours." He kissed the top of her hand and Alayna blushed from the attention of the table and Ryle's confession.

"Well?" Isaac asked, waving his hand. "I swear, you people take forever when coming to decisions."

"You do not have to answer right now, Alayna." Ryle squeezed her hand. "But I would like you to think-"

"Yes." Alayna stated quickly. "Yes, I wish to marry you."

Ryle's face split into a handsome smile as he leaned forward and kissed her.

Clapping his hands, King Eamon stood. "A new Realm, indeed. A king and queen will now grace the thrones of the Realm, and I know Granton would be so happy. May you prosper. To our new king and queen." He raised his glass as everyone followed suit and toasted to the new beginnings that promised love and hope.

****

My Dearest Alayna,

If you are reading this, then Prince Clifton must have found this letter upon my death and given it to you. I am glad he did. I know you are probably still wondering why I chose the boundary line as my deathbed, but I had to see Edward. I needed your brother to know I loved him. I know you and Elizabeth are saddened by my passing, but please do not dwell upon things lost. But look to things that are to come. Your sister's marriage to Prince Clifton will be a joyous occasion and she will need you to calm her nerves. Elizabeth may seem strong, but beneath her bravado is the tender heart of your younger sister. She will need you, Alayna. Not as queen, but as a sister.

I feel most confident in our merger with the East. I also feel confident in the change in guard. Prince Ryle will serve the Realm well, and he will guard you with his life. Together, I know you two will discover a path to defeat the Unfading Lands and Lancer. Utilize your friends of the East and West. Do not underestimate Prince Samuel of the South and his contribution either. Be open to change and suggestions. Most importantly, always choose the path your heart feels is right. Sometimes the hardest course is the one that must be taken. Know your enemy. The true enemy. Lancer, though potentially evil, is not the enemy. The darkness that consumes him is the enemy. Remember that, my dear. Should there be a way to spare his life, I beg of you to consider it. Even the most lost of people can potentially be saved. Think like a Queen in regards to the protection of your people, but think with your heart through the process.

The Realm is in good hands with you, Alayna. You will be a wonderful queen. My hope for you is to one day find a love like your sister and share the burden of leadership. For it is a blessing, but sometimes a burden. It helps to have a confidant and supporter by your side. I cherish the times I had with your mother, and I wish for you to have the same. Keep your chin up, my dear. Keep your eyes on the boundary and the enemy. But keep your heart focused on hope and the goodness of our people. I love you dearly.

Your father

Catch up on the entire series:

The Unfading Lands
Darkness Divided
Redemption Rising

Where will YOUR allegiance lie?

All titles by Katharine E. Hamilton
Available on Amazon and Amazon Kindle

Adult Fiction:
The Unfading Lands
Darkness Divided, Part Two in The Unfading Lands Series
Redemption Rising, Part Three in The Unfading Lands
Series

Children's Literature:
The Adventurous Life of Laura Bell
Susie At Your Service
Sissy and Kat

Short Stories:
If the Shoe Fits

Find out more about Katharine and her works at:
www.katharinehamilton.com

Social Media is a great way to connect with Katharine.
Check her out on the following:
Facebook: Katharine E. Hamilton
Twitter: @AuthorKatharine
Instagram: katharineh
Contact Katharine: khamiltonauthor@gmail.com

ABOUT THE AUTHOR

Katharine E. Hamilton started her writing career nearly a decade ago by creating fun-filled stories that have taken children on imaginative adventures all around the world. By using her talents of imagery and suspense to illustrate the deep, underlying issue of good and evil within us all, Katharine extends the invitation for adventure to adults everywhere. She finds herself drawn time and again by the people behind her adventures and wishes to bring them to life in her stories.

She was born and raised in the state of Texas, where she currently resides on a ranch in the heart of brush country with her husband, Brad, and their son, Everett, and their two furry friends, Tulip and Cash. She is a graduate of Texas A&M University, where she received a Bachelor's degree in History. She finds most of her stories share the love of the past combined with a twist of imagination.

She is thankful to her readers for allowing her the privilege to turn her dreams into a new adventure for us all.

www.ingramcontent.com/pod-product-compliance
Lightning Source LLC
Chambersburg PA
CBHW031946240626
47153CB00003B/883